DEADLY TO THE SIGHT

EDWARD SKLEPOWICH

DEADLY TO THE SIGHT

THOMAS DUNNE BOOKS / ST. MARTIN'S MINOTAUR
NEW YORK

THOMAS DUNNE BOOKS.
An imprint of St. Martin's Press.

www.minotaurbooks.com

Design by Lorelle Graffeo

ISBN 0-312-26955-2

First Edition: February 2002

10 9 8 7 6 5 4 3 2 1

For my Tunisian and Moroccan friends, colleagues, and students, especially Anwar Amara, Henda Ammar, Sihem Arfaoui, Asma Ben Yahia, Riadh Boujnah, and Amel Guizani, and with particularly warm *shukrans* and *mercis* for Monia Bayar and Nessim Effassi

This is the city of mazes. You may set off from the same place to the same place every day and never go by the same route. If you do so, it will be by mistake. Your bloodhound nose will not serve you here.

—JEANETTE WINTERSON, *The Passion*

DEADLY TO THE SIGHT

PROLOGUE
Return to Florian's

The best time at Caffè Florian's is five o'clock on a winter afternoon. The best room is the Chinese salon. And the best company, as far as Urbino Macintyre was concerned, was his good friend, Barbara, the Contessa da Capo-Zendrini.

Out in the Piazza San Marco, the chill January air schemed with a sudden burst of rain to send the blessedly few tourists scurrying for shelter. But all was warmth in the intimate room, with its dark wood and old-fashioned radiators, Urbino's sherry, and the Contessa's first-flush jasmine tea and, most of all, their long-looked-for and too-long-delayed reunion.

Together again, Urbino said to himself, taking in the sight of the Contessa as she leaned gracefully back against the maroon banquette. What more could he ask for? The Contessa and Florian's, the magical, winter-haunted city beyond the glass, and everything else that had recently come his way.

He was falling in love all over again.

These were his comfortable and somewhat sentimental thoughts as he bathed the Contessa in a look that could express only a part of what he felt for her and all the rest.

"I like to think of this as the still point of our wheel," she said, abandoning in mid-flow her account of mutual friends to show how in tune they were. "Not only at this time of the year, *caro*, but even in the midst of high season. It's our own special place."

"Ours, yes, but only because it's first of all yours."

His words were nothing less than the truth, for the Contessa possessed the scene like a gem in its proper setting.

Around her, mirrors reflected her attractiveness, which hadn't diminished over the years, at least in his eyes. Bronze *amorino* lamps on the walls enhanced the tender glow of her skin.

How much art? How much nature? It was something that still kept him wondering after all these years.

She seemed to have stepped down from one of the elegant portraits, framed in dark wood and sheathed in glass, that graced the walls. The intricately patterned ceiling and the burnished parquet floor were, for the moment, the only imaginable canopy and anchor for her charms.

The reigning quiet at this serene time of the year, both within the Chinese salon and beyond its windows, seemed an extension of her soft, well-modulated voice. On this afternoon, and during the past weeks he had heard it, recounting some of the thousand and one details of what had transpired since he had left Venice for Morocco almost two years ago. Her letters and phone calls, and one golden weeklong cruise of the Mediterranean on *La Barbara* had communicated only a small portion of them.

Urbino momentarily shifted his glance out into the Piazza San Marco where the rain had temporarily abated. He marveled all over again at how the square's gleaming stones and strutting pigeons, its colorful clock tower and brightly-restored Basilica, its graceful arcades and crimson-and-gold banners—how, in fact, everything conspired to let him pass back into the picture so comfortably.

Even mundane details took their necessary places: a short, fat woman in a knit cap pushing a souvenir cart out of the arcade, the wooden planks providing dry passage over deep puddles in front of the Basilica, and an unmuzzled dog dashing ahead of its master toward the pigeons.

And then came the church bells to wash the square with their liquid tones. The sounds of Venice were dear to him, whether they were the cooing of pigeons and the plaint of cats, the lapping of water and the shouting of boatmen, the groan of mooring rope and the mourn of foghorns, or the cries in the Rialto market. But the sound of its church bells was one of the dearest. They now brought not only music but also, somehow, splashes of color to the scene that a few moments before had been pearly gray and reminiscent of Sargent's palette for *Venice par temps gris*.

His attention returned to the Contessa. She was an attractive woman approaching sixty, as best he could figure out, if she hadn't already passed it. She looked at least ten years younger. Stylish in a subdued manner, she wore this afternoon her multicolored Fortuny dress that had belonged to the actress Eleonora Duse. Her choice of the dress vaguely disturbed him, however. It was a sign that she was either especially weary or depressed, since she believed there was some talismanic quality in the garment that dispersed clouds and lifted fatigue.

She selected a petit four—a slim oblong of yellow with lime-green icing—and examined it as if she were admiring its perfection of color and shape. She prepared to take a bite.

"And it seems, *caro*," she said, "as if Oriana and Filippo are finally, after all they've gone through and put *me* through, ringing down the curtain on their strange and long-playing performance."

What she meant by her theatrical metaphor was the marriage of her friends, the Borellis. For as long as Urbino had known them, they had been in the midst of domestic disputes and extramarital intrigues that had not so much brought them to the brink of divorce as saved them from that ultimate step. But now Filippo had moved out of the Ca' Borelli on the Giudecca and taken an apartment in the Castello quarter.

"Dreary, dreary rooms, Urbino. Scarcely any better than the ducal dungeons and literally a few paces away. The whole situation depresses me. What if they never get back together?"

Where Oriana and Filippo thrived on the ups and downs of their opera buffa marriage, the Contessa despised change. Her decision not to go back to her native England after her husband's death was in large part because she felt sheltered from it here among the slow rhythms of the city, its self-contained, monastic air, and its immutable face that seemed to defy and outwit the passing years.

In truth, the Contessa's rather complicated, even perverse love for Venice was not much different from Urbino's. They were both willing victims.

He smiled at the thought.

"I'm afraid I don't find it as amusing as you do," the Contessa said. He had no chance to explain before she went on: "I'm appealing to you. Perhaps you can help Oriana and Filippo."

"I don't see what I can do."

She finished off the petit four and seemed about to reach for another. He had seen her demolish an entire plate in no time at all if she happened to be in an agitated mood.

"You're a friend of fifteen years, but you're not emotionally involved. You can get inside a person's head and skin and—and understand him, can't you?" What she meant by this somewhat startling image was that he was a biographer. "And there's something else you can offer those two poor souls, the most important thing of all."

She gave a longish pause, which had the effect of drawing his attention to her gray eyes. They had a peculiar, discomfiting sheen of purpose.

"What's that?" he prompted.

"Your own experience with these matters. You *were* married, you know, or have you managed to forget it?"

Exasperation sharpened her voice.

Not for the first time since his return did he hear a discordant note that seemed to indicate that not all was perfect with their reunion.

"And divorced shortly afterwards," he pointed out.

"Precisely."

The Contessa paused again, this time to survey him with a tender, almost commiserating look. He was put on his guard.

"Don't you see, Urbino dear," she went on in a softer tone, "that advice from you would be precious? That is, coming from

someone who once was in their position and—who knows?—
might regret having divorced? It would mean much more than
whatever I can offer. Alvise and I had an ideal marriage."

There were so many ways to respond that he required a few
moments of reflective silence. The Contessa spent the time eye-
ing the plate of petit fours.

"I don't regret divorcing Evangeline," he began. "I regret
having married the poor girl." Then he added, "As you well
know—or did, before I went off."

"Ah, yes, before you went off."

"And also," Urbino said, ignoring the sigh that had followed
her words, "happy marriages are all alike, as Tolstoy said, but
an unhappy marriage is unhappy in its own particular way."

"I believe he said *families* and not *marriages*."

"Whatever limited and very particular experience I had with
marriage—and divorce—couldn't be of much help to Oriana and
Filippo. And they have to want my help."

Knowing the couple as well as he did, he realized there was,
fortunately, little chance of this. He had no intention of getting
involved.

The Contessa touched the sleeve of his tweed jacket.

"How much you want to be wanted and needed! It's one of
your most appealing qualities—and dare I say American as
well? Just don't get carried away by it."

A confused look came over her face as she realized that this
last piece of advice was, on the surface, very much at odds with
what she was trying to persuade him to do. But she refrained
from making any clarification, knowing that he was more than
capable of unraveling the various strands of what she said and
what she meant.

His only response was to peer out into the Piazza.

"Are you expecting someone?" the Contessa asked.

She too looked into the large, open space as if searching for
a familiar face or figure. She was about to return her attention
to the Chinese salon and their discussion, when her eyes opened
wider.

"Oh, my," she said, with unmistakable distress. "Could she be coming here?"

Urbino followed the direction of her gaze.

He saw a small, old woman with a shock of white hair and thick glasses a few feet away from the window. He had never seen her before. Dressed in a long, black shawl, she stood against one of the columns in front of the Chinese salon. She wore black fingerless gloves, and she held her shoes. Her feet were wrapped in black trash bags to make easier passage through the *acqua alta* that had seeped and washed into the city during the night.

She was piercing the Contessa with eyes magnified behind the lenses of her glasses.

"Who is she?"

"Nina Crivelli. A lace maker from Burano. She may be here to see me."

"Why?"

"She—she wants something from me," the Contessa said.

Urbino was intrigued. He didn't feel encouraged, however, to ask anything more about the woman, who was now shuffling past the windows. The Contessa followed her slow progress.

"I'll tell you about it later, *caro*, not now," she said. "I know your detective instincts have been aroused."

She gave him a strained smile.

"Dare I confess something?" she said, trying for a light air. "I've been afraid that you'd find me changed, physically, I mean."

She bowed her head as if shy of his scrutiny.

"Fishing for compliments? You're *toujours jeune*. You haven't changed the slightest."

"The same old Barbara, you mean? Well, I suppose I am. You've changed a wee bit yourself though. Oh, not for the worse! The desert sun didn't burn away your Bloomsbury and Brideshead look any more than the years have since we first met. But you look both older and somehow younger. Will it all fade with your bronzage and those sun streaks? We'll have to wait and see."

She finally yielded to another petit four, this one with mauve-colored frosting that matched one of the colors in her dress.

"I can go on and on about you, you see! It's because I've missed you so much. I've become rather ridiculous even to myself. For example, the changes at the Ca' da Capo," she said with a slightly deprecatory air that wasn't matched by the appreciation with which she took a bite. "You'd think it was a matter of each and every stone pulled out and put in a different place. Oh, I knew that Mauro was getting on and couldn't be with me much longer, and Giorgio is as good as Milo, or will be, when he knows the canals better. He cuts a much better figure, according to Oriana! But it hasn't been easy getting used to the changes, not with you being away. And as for Silvia, the girl leaves a lot to be desired, even without comparing her with dear, lost Lucia."

This lament referred to Mauro, her former majordomo, now replaced by a younger man, and to Giorgio, her handsome new boatman, obviously the object of Oriana's roving eye, and to Silvia, her troublesome personal maid.

"I just know that my ball is going to be a complete failure this year with all of these changes, and I so want it to be the best ever!"

The Contessa was planning a *ballo in maschera* at the Ca' da Capo-Zendrini on Shrove Tuesday to celebrate the end of Carnevale. Inspired by Urbino's recent stay in Morocco, the theme was to be *The Arabian Nights*.

"Mauro knew how to help make things run smoothly. And Lucia could see a problem brewing long before I could. As for Silvia, the poor girl—"

The Contessa broke off nervously as someone approached the entrance of the salon. It was an attractive, middle-aged woman in a long black coat.

"Listen to me!" she continued with evident relief. "Here I am going on about my silly ball and the Ca' da Capo when you have more serious problems at the Palazzo Uccello. I cry every time I think of the Bronzino! And that poor chandelier!"

The Palazzo Uccello was the grandiose name for Urbino's

humble building in the Cannaregio quarter. He had returned from Morocco to find a great deal of damage done to the interior and to some of his most prized possessions, by an American couple engaged to look after the place. The Contessa had managed to have them vacate and to replace them with a German woman, who had turned out to be an ideal tenant.

"Pignatti examined the chandelier." Carlo Pignatti was a glass maestro from Murano. "He shouldn't have much trouble matching the broken pieces. It will never be the same," he added, "but what can I do? I'm more concerned about the Bronzino."

The Bronzino, a gift of the Contessa, was a portrait of a pearl-and-brocaded Florentine lady. The American couple had removed it from the wall of the parlor and leaned it beside an open window, where it had been saturated during a storm.

"Someone's coming from Florence to assess the damage. It's beyond anything I can do for it."

Urbino had taken courses in art restoration in Venice and Florence to prepare for a biography he had been writing on the Minolfis, a Venetian family of restorers.

"You did an excellent job on the Bartolomeo Veneto."

"A competent job." The engagement portrait of a young lady, also a gift of the generous Contessa, had only suffered from yellow varnish and grime. "The Bronzino needs the attentions of a professional. And so do the manuscripts, but I can manage with the confessional, perhaps with the mirror, as well."

He watched the Contessa out of the tail of his eye as he added, "Habib will be a lot of help." Habib was a promising Moroccan painter pursuing his art in Venice with Urbino's financial help and encouragement. "He's a real handyman."

The Contessa showed no reaction unless it was a barely perceptible inclination toward the plate of petit fours.

"I'm pleased to hear that," she said, with nothing in her voice to indicate that she wasn't. "Sebastian would have been of no use. He can't hang up a curtain rod." Sebastian Neville, her second cousin, had been Urbino's traveling companion in

Morocco until their falling out. "It makes it convenient for Habib—or should I say for you?—that he's staying right in the midst of the things that need his attention. But I hope you're letting the poor boy out of the house. Perhaps you've been so intent on scanning the Piazza to see if he's escaped from his duties?"

Almost against his will, he glanced into the Piazza again. A few people had reclaimed the open space. None of them was Habib.

"He has language classes this afternoon."

"If his Italian ends up being even half as good as his English, he'll be able to charm the rest of Italy."

"And Spain and France as well," Urbino observed.

"A veritable Tower of Babel!" the Contessa enthused. "And at such a young age. Twenty-two, isn't he?"

"Twenty-four."

Urbino had done all the computations before. He was about to point out that the difference between Habib's age and his own wasn't much more than what separated the Contessa and himself, but he held his tongue. His silence was a signal that any further pursuit of the topic would be an assault on her part.

The Contessa, who knew the script of their special friendship well, since she had fashioned much of it herself, let the matter drop. As if to make up for her surrender, she captured another petit four, this one chocolate with a sliver of almond.

"For the rest of our time here today, *caro*, why don't we forget about the Ca' da Capo and the Palazzo Uccello." Her eye strayed to the entrance again as someone came in. "Let's enjoy our still point. Because, you see, I'm blissfully glad you're back, as blissful as—as one of the angels of the Basilica dome! The rest will take care of itself."

Having delivered these last encouraging words with all the aplomb of a well-rehearsed actress, she then showed how well she could take care of her third petit four.

Urbino sipped his sherry and looked at the plate of cakes. A colorful, dainty phalanx remained. He was sure, however, that she would polish it off in good order with all the energy and appetite of her frustrated aggression.

Yes, he said to himself, casting an eye out into the Piazza and then back at his self-indulgent Contessa. He was most definitely back.

PART ONE
THE LACE HANDKERCHIEF

1

It had begun from their first moments together in Venice three weeks earlier.

The train had just pulled in from Rome. Urbino and his young companion, Habib Laroussi, stepped down from their carriage. Habib was of medium height, with close-cropped black hair and dark olive skin. But his most striking feature was his expressive dark eyes, which had been hungrily devouring everything since they had arrived from Morocco.

"Go out to the steps and see," Urbino said.

"But our bags," the young man halfheartedly protested.

"I'll find someone. Go."

Ten minutes later Urbino, followed by a porter and their extravagance of bags, joined Habib. The young man was standing motionless, looking at the scene. Urbino hadn't seen it for eighteen months. He drank it in himself: the bridges and domes, the sparkling water and the dancing light, the boats of various kinds and even the dampness that in winter, against all logic, somehow registered not only as a smell but also as the color gray.

"It's beautiful," Habib said. "It's better than you said."

"I was afraid you'd be disappointed."

Habib gave a radiant smile.

"You are a foolish man! And now we must take one of those old-style boats."

Habib pointed toward a moored gondola, rocking in the Grand Canal from the wake of the water traffic.

"My friend said she'd have her own boat waiting."

"*La comtesse*? She has an old-style boat?"

"A new-style one," Urbino said with a smile. "That's it."

He indicated the Contessa's sleek *motoscafo* a short distance away. An unfamiliar man, dressed in a white cap and dark blue suit and tie, descended from the boat and walked toward them. He limped slightly on his left leg.

"But please, *sidi*!" Habib said, using the term of respect with playful urgency. "Let us ride in an old-style one."

The man in the white cap approached them.

"Signor Macintyre? I am Giorgio, the Contessa da Capo-Zendrini's boatman," he said in Italian. He was much younger and seemed more fit than Milo.

"We've decided to take a gondola."

"A gondola, signore? As you wish. And your baggage?"

"You can take it to the Palazzo Uccello. Do you know where it is?"

"Yes." He hesitated for a brief moment. "The Contessa is expecting you."

"Please tell her we'll see her in an hour. No," he corrected himself, "an hour and a half."

Several minutes later Urbino and Habib glided out into the Grand Canal. At first the young man was silent as they passed beneath the stone bridge of the Scalzi and made their way between the palaces and churches on either side of the waterway.

And then the questions began, coming as thick and fast as those of a child. What is that tower? Those striped poles? Is that a mosque, *sidi*? And why are there Moorish windows? What is that porch made of wood on the top of the palace? Look! There's another! Why do the chimneys have funny shapes?

"There's plenty of time to ask all the questions you want. Just lie back and look."

Slowly, silently, first down the Grand Canal, then through a maze of small canals and beneath narrow stony spans, they were floated toward the Palazzo Uccello. Habib's dark glance moved in all directions as he fed his artist's eye with images. "It is like *The Arabian Nights!*" he had cried out on that first day as they approached the landing of the Palazzo Uccello. "And this is our magic carpet!"

2

Urbino threw open the library shutters and looked straight into the silent night.

A short while before, as the church bells were ringing the second hour, he had awakened from a peculiar dream that still had him in its grip.

Actually, it had been less a dream than a persistent feeling that had wound itself through his thoughts that, even in sleep, seldom were completely still.

The Ca' da Capo-Zendrini was in danger.

It would have been more appropriate, given the damage done to the Palazzo Uccello, if he had been awakened by the urgency of its own, all-too-real problems.

Perhaps, he thought, this mild panic—for that was what it felt like—was simply a matter of displacement, for he had, in fact, been worrying about the Palazzo Uccello before dropping off to sleep.

And yet it was vivid, this sense that the Contessa's own home was threatened in some way. He remembered her uneasiness at Florian's the other afternoon.

He pulled on his clothes and threw his Austrian cape over his shoulders. He would take a walk. He would go to the Ca' da Capo-Zendrini.

He scribbled a brief note for Habib in case he awoke to find him gone, and then slipped out into the night.

Wisps of fog were brushing the bridge and drifting into the alley. He had a quick, sharp inward vision of the snowy domes of the Church of the Salute and the oriental cupolas of the Basilica floating above the mist as it performed its conjuring tricks of levitation and disappearance.

He breathed the air in gratefully. A realization, as strong as the concern that had set him in motion, struck him.

He would be turning his back to the Palazzo Uccello just as he was now, even if he hadn't been seized by this notion about the Ca' da Capo-Zendrini.

For Urbino's preference for the night had only increased since his return. While in the hot sun of Morocco, he had yearned for the damp, fog-filled nights of Venice when he could wander through the watery city as if he were its only occupant—or at least its only privileged one.

Nights in Morocco had been vibrant and spice-scented, filled with flutes and keening songs, and almost always crowded with people who had the gift of turning the most routine of experiences into an occasion for celebration.

To be alone the way he wanted to be, he had sought out the most remote spots beyond the cities, or, on two or three occasions, had sat musing on one of the flat medina roofs until the morning prayer. The desert had brought him solitude, and a restorative kind of peace that healed some wounds he didn't even know he had, but it was a solitude that was—paradoxically perhaps—too absolute. There had been no place in it for the Urbino who both loved and hated sociability.

His commitment to Venice, made almost twenty years ago upon inheriting the rundown building in the Cannaregio, had been largely because he could be splendidly alone, and alone on his own terms. Behind the walls of the Palazzo Uccello, which was like some stationary, elaborately appointed ark, he was far from the crowds and the distracting beauties of the museum city, and yet also in their midst.

He was well aware that he was considered an eccentric by many of the Venetians, and in fact by many of his own friends both here and back home. And there was no doubt that he struck an eccentric pose, but not intentionally so, during these late-night walks in his cape, negotiating the familiar city with an air of aimless purpose.

As he kept to his elastic stride in the direction of the Grand Canal through twisting alleys and across secluded squares, moving more slowly up and down the slick, slippery steps of bridges, he didn't meet another living soul. All he heard, other than his own echoing footsteps, was the slap of water against stone steps and wood hulls, and disembodied voices that sometimes rose up from the black waters and other times floated over the rooftops. It was like wandering through someone else's meticulously detailed dream of an impossible city where gravity was in abeyance, and reflections—even during the night hours— might be mistaken for the real thing if you stared too long.

But tonight Urbino didn't linger on bridges as he usually did, peering down into the dark mirrors of the canals over which wisps of mist were curling. He was soon on the small, graceful bridge that provided the only land access to the Ca' da Capo-Zendrini, whose large iron door was still, at this hour, illuminated by its ornately embossed lamps.

Like all the palazzi on the Grand Canal, the Ca' da Capo-Zendrini turned its aristocratic back on the plebeian activity of the alleys, squares, and bridges, and risked courting envy by presenting all its restrained beauty only on the side of the broad waterway. With its classical facade in Istrian stone and an elaborate attic frieze of lions set off by gentle pilasters, projecting balconies, small oval windows, blue-and-white mooring poles, and trim landing stage, the imposing building was a marriage of austerity with grace, of a simple formality with playfulness.

When the Contessa had married the Conte Alvise, the building had been denuded of its many decorations and severely damaged by the war and industrial pollution from the mainland. She had dedicated herself—in an obsessive way, said some jealous Venetians—to return it to its former glory. Before Urbino had met her, he had heard unkind stories about her hard line with architects and restorers, her search throughout Italy and Europe to find pieces to fill in the gaps in its furnishings, her physical and emotional exhaustion afterward, and her extended stay in a Swiss sanatorium.

Rather than forming a negative impression of her, as many of the gossips intended, he had become fascinated, recognizing in her passion for her adopted city an image of his own, although her passion had considerably more money to keep it afloat. When they had met seventeen years ago at a Biennale reception, they had formed an instant rapport. Ever since, they had been close friends and confidants, and, somehow, more than this.

Light glowed behind shuttered windows on the second story. The windows belonged to the Contessa's bedroom. If it had been the windows of her *salotto blu*, it would have been almost definite proof that she was waiting for someone. Instead the Contessa, who usually retired before eleven, had turned on her lights because she couldn't sleep, as was her custom.

Should he ring the bell and speak with her? As soon as he formulated this question, however, he moved backward slightly, to conceal himself in a mass of shadows cast by the building behind him. He didn't want her to see him if she happened to look out of the window. This was the indirect, but clear answer to his question. He wouldn't disturb her, for he knew his friend well. Whatever distress she might be feeling would only be increased by this sudden descent on her privacy. When she was ready to confide in him, he would be there to help. Until then, he would keep his distance.

As he turned away from the Contessa's palazzo, he felt the presentiment again that something was not quite right behind its walls. Exactly what, he didn't know, but he was certain that it must have something to do with the old woman who had been staring so solemnly at her outside of Florian's.

3

Since that first day in Venice when Urbino and Habib had floated in style to the Palazzo Uccello, Urbino had played the indulgent *cicerone*, answering the younger man's constant flow of questions and showing him around the city that he himself was discovering again. It wasn't just that absence, like some fine gold dust, had restored value to all the familiar scenes, but that in the deep pool of Habib's enthusiasm he saw a distant reflection of his own original feelings.

It would be wrong to assume, however, that everything was a delight to Habib. He was critical, usually of smells, and impatient of all the walking.

On more than one occasion, he would come to an abrupt halt on the parapet of a bridge or at the foot of a palace's staircase or in a long museum corridor, and loudly lament, "*Sidi*, my uncles!" Urbino would good-humoredly correct him—"*ankles*, not uncles"—and, with just as much good humor, wait for him to regain his strength so that they could cross off another sight from Urbino's impossibly long list.

The Contessa had been making things a bit easier for the both of them lately by putting her motorboat at their disposal when she didn't need it herself.

One of the things Urbino could count on during these outings—other than Habib's malapropisms and theatrical displays of fatigue—was his painter's eye for details. Whether it was a question of a bossage of gargoyles and *putti* on the facade of a palazzo, or a lion's head door knocker, or a shrine in an out-of-the-way corner, Habib saw it and pointed it out to Urbino. He then drew it in his sketchbook, which he always had with him.

At one-thirty in the afternoon, two weeks after Urbino's conversation with the Contessa at Florian's, Urbino went to join Habib in the Corte Seconda del Milion. Habib was completing some sketches of the boyhood home of Marco Polo and one of the nearby covered passageways. He showed them to Urbino.

"Very good, Habib."

"I want to come back and capture this same spot with my paints. The light in Venice is very tricky."

"And it's not the only thing that is! You've done enough for today. You've more than earned a good lunch."

"I could eat a horse!" Habib enthused, for whom idioms and clichés were mint-new.

"Good, but I have something different in mind. But not here. On Burano."

4

The Contessa's *motoscafo* cut across the shallow waters to Burano. As the sun broke momentarily through the layer of clouds, the lagoon, with its marshes and mud banks, shimmered ahead of them.

Giorgio commanded the craft lightly and with a touch of elegance, as if in compensation for the limp that hampered him on land. He answered Habib's questions about the sunken islands with their ruined buildings along their route. Although his information wasn't always accurate, it was given in good spirit. It wasn't difficult to see how the handsome man had captured Oriana's perpetually straying eye.

Burano, with its campanile leaning at a precarious and picturesque angle, soon came into view. Urbino gave a little shiver as they approached the quay. He attributed it to the characteristically damp chill of the island, which he always felt more keenly here than in Venice. It seemed to penetrate the closed, heated cabin, and made him feel vaguely unwell.

The last time he had been to Burano had been in summer several years before, when its notoriously filthy canals were being drained. The odor had been terrible, but then—as now—with a chill spreading over his skin, the sight of the improbably bright colors of the small houses had almost made up for the unpleasant assault on the other senses.

Gallons and gallons of red, purple, blue, green, and yellow had been mercilessly spilled to adorn the huddled buildings with an abandon that was both crazed and childlike. The stunning effect was itself responsible for the squeezing and mixing of further gallons of oils and watercolors by artists, and the scrolling of innumerable miles of film by photographers.

Yet, charming though it could be, Burano wasn't a place where Urbino would have been happy to live. It was too relentlessly cheerful in its brightness and with its jaunty strings of washing hung between the houses and across the squares. Its bridges, canals, and houses were too small to suit him. And worst of all, life here was almost a blueprint of conventionality, with the women at their lace and the men at their nets. Or so it had always seemed to Urbino, who during his visits had frequently screamed silently for something more subversive.

Surely Burano must have its dark secrets, now as it had in the past. And perhaps the primary colors of its houses were a trap of delight for the eye, distracting it from contemplating the inevitable cost of the island's perpetual performance of normality. Yet even the colors couldn't deceive the eye for long, at least not an eye like Urbino's, which inevitably—and almost gratefully—noted the way these colors spilled and bled into the invasive waters of the lagoon.

He didn't give Habib the benefit of these impressions, however, for he knew too well the melancholy burden of never seeing things as they actually appeared, a burden all the more melancholy when the appearances were as lovely as those of Burano.

"It's beautiful," cried Habib.

"Yes, it is," Urbino responded.

Stretching ahead of them when they got out of the motorboat was a gauntlet of stalls and shops, presided over by what seemed to be interchangeable, middle-aged women. Urbino would soon have negotiated the danger with barely a slackened pace. He hadn't counted on Habib, however.

"I must buy something for my mother on this beautiful island!" he cried out when he saw the first stall dripping with lace. "We can send it to her. Yes?"

"A marvelous idea. I should have thought of it myself."

Habib had already collected enough gloves, perfume, shoes, belts, towels, and other items to furnish not just his mother but their whole extended family. He had bought hardly anything for himself, however, which to Urbino indicated an innate generosity that made him, in his own turn, generous and all the more happy to be footing the bill.

Habib began to diligently examine doilies, antimacassars, handkerchiefs, napkins, curtains, bedcovers, blouses, vests, shawls, scarves, umbrellas, and designs of cats, gondolas, and flowers in thin wooden frames. He passed from stall to stall and shop to shop, holding items up to the light, turning them over, feeling and even sniffing them, as if he were looking for an immediate position as a quality inspector. The more things he looked at and the more time he spent, the more difficulty he had in deciding.

Every suggestion Urbino made was rejected, albeit pleasantly, because of some personal or maternal or cultural or religious inappropriateness that Urbino didn't understand. After a while, Urbino left him to his own devices, stepping in only when the women's English or Habib's Italian was inadequate.

Finally, to Urbino's relief, Habib settled on a particular tablecloth because the shop owner with her head scarf, he whispered to Urbino, reminded him "too much" of his mother. But when Urbino translated the amount into dollars, Habib reached out to hold back his hand.

"It is a fortune! I will choose something else."

He began to search through some smaller items.

The price was indeed high. Urbino, not a good judge of the quality of lacework, found the tablecloth attractive and without any obvious flaws. He wished the Contessa was with them, but knowing her, she would have scorned all these shops and insisted on going to Jesurum behind the Basilica, which was much more expensive. And then Habib would have missed the pleasure of buying something on "the island made of lace," as he kept calling Burano, and from this particular woman with whom, despite the language barrier, he had developed a rapport.

"We'll buy it," Urbino insisted, and handed the woman the

money. He also asked her to wrap up six butterfly adornments that Habib had been admiring. He could give one to each of his sisters.

They wandered over the island for half an hour, down narrow quaysides beneath wrought-iron balconies, over a wooden bridge, and past row after row of the painted houses, some with geometrical designs. Even the boats were brightly painted.

Urbino conducted Habib to one of the more whimsical houses. It was decorated in a kaleidoscope of different-colored squares, rectangles, circles, diamonds, and stripes. Every year or two the owner arranged the shapes in entirely different combinations as if in harmony with some ever shifting, mysterious celestial pattern.

"Maybe it is to push away the evil spirits," Habib suggested.

"Possibly."

"You should have warned me!"

"Of what?"

"Of all these colors. I should have brought my paints!"

"Some other time. Look at the doors along here. Each is a different color from the house, and from each other."

"And all of them are framed in white! The windows too! You like doors, I know," Habib said with a smile. "You always looked at them in the medina."

Urbino then brought Habib to the quarter where the Contessa owned two adjoining buildings. One was bright green, the other a deep purple. The German writer who had been staying at the Palazzo Uccello now occupied the green house. But it wasn't to pay her a visit that they had come. At any rate, they'd be going to a reception at Frieda Hensel's in a few days. But because the reception would be in the evening, Habib wouldn't be able to appreciate the color of her house.

As usual, Habib was full of questions. He wanted to know whether neighbors agreed on what colors they would paint their houses, and why some of the houses had different colors for different stories, and what the geometrical designs meant. And did the women who made lace also make the fishnets, which were drying in the sun? Why were all the lace curtains in the

windows white? And why weren't there any big palaces anywhere, and instead so many small buildings, even smaller than
the one in the Fez medina where his family lived?

He opened his sketchbook and started to capture some of
his impressions, lamenting again that all he had were his pen-
cils.

While Habib sketched near a covered wellhead, accompanied by two young boys and a little girl amused by his Italian,
Urbino sat on the water steps of the little square, surrounded
by fish traps, and took in the scene. A plump matron threw hot
water against her steps. Steamy vapor drifted toward a woman
in a wool cap speaking to her from a nearby window. She held
a *tombolo*, a round cushion used in lace making. A swarthy man
repaired a fishnet and joked with a companion applying caulk
to his boat. A striped cat, its body low against the ground,
started to move toward a sea bird perched on the wellhead. Urbino followed its movement until his eye returned to Habib. The
rich darkness of his skin was a sharp contrast to the Venetian
fairness of the children.

Habib laughed and waved to the little girl, who was now
being led away by her father. The man scowled and kept throwing glances back at Habib as he gripped his daughter's hand
tightly.

Anxiety coursed through Urbino as a rushed voice within
him spoke of Moors and open natures and mistaken trust.

He got to his feet. He tried to dispel his mood by reminding
himself of the pleasant surprise he was about to give Habib.

5

Ten minutes later, however, a sign with CHIUSO written on it in large black letters greeted them on the door of the Trattoria Da Romano in the Via Galuppi. Urbino couldn't restrain an expression of irritation.

"Don't be a foolish man, *sidi*. We won't starve to death! There are many restaurants to choke a horse!" Habib said, showing today a preference for idioms associated with that particular animal.

But the Trattoria Da Romano wasn't only a restaurant, and one of the best on Burano. Like the Montin in the Dorsoduro quarter, it was an art gallery as well, with paintings by Gino Rossi and other members of the Burano school, whose vivid colors and rough surfaces were similar to Habib's work. Urbino's little surprise would have to wait for another day.

A short distance down the street was Il Piccolo Nettuno. The Contessa had recommended it, but Urbino had never eaten there.

"Il Piccolo Nettuno, the Little Neptune," Urbino translated automatically. "Neptune was the god of the sea."

He sometimes felt like a nineteenth-century tutor engaged to accompany a young man on his grand tour or, more to the point, some ambiguous avuncular benefactor in the same role.

As they entered the restaurant, it appeared that they were in for another disappointment. Most of the chairs had been taken from the floor and turned upside down, their seats resting on the tabletops. The room had all modern appointments, from its tables, chairs, light fixtures, and a brightly tiled floor, to a multitude of mirrors that adorned the walls and even the pillar in the center. Urbino lamented all the old dark wood that must have been stripped away in a misguided desire to improve.

A bespectacled woman with white hair was sweeping the floor. She was dressed in a wrinkled gray dress that had a large stain on one arm and was ripped at the hem. Urbino immediately recognized her as the woman outside Florian's.

She looked up and pierced them with her gaze.

"You are closed?" Urbino asked in Italian.

"But no, signore. Not for you and your young friend. *Avanti!*" She leaned her broom against the wall. "Salvatore!" she called out in a strong voice.

A man in his early fifties, wearing a soiled red apron, emerged from the kitchen. He walked unsteadily.

"We are closed," he said.

He showed the vestiges of a former handsomeness. Dark circles underscored his eyes and burst veins crept across his face.

"No! Do not be so unfriendly!" she said in a nasty tone. "We are always open for the Contessa da Capo-Zendrini and her friends." Her voice now dripped with solicitude. "The cook has gone home, signore, but I can cook even better! The Contessa is with you?"

"Unfortunately not."

"I thought I saw her *motorboat*. But my eyes . . ."

"We did come in her boat. She made it available to us."

"Ah, so kind and generous of her. I know you are called Signor Urbino, yes?"

Her smile revealed large gaps and decayed teeth. Her foul breath struck Urbino's nostrils.

She raised her hand. With one finger extended she traced a pattern of some kind through the air, and then started to speak slowly in heavily accented English.

"I can speak a little of the English, but I must to write my finger before I speak. Me, I am called Nina Crivelli, and he is my son, Salvatore." Then, addressing her son, she rasped out in

Italian, "Don't stand there like a useless cucumber! Put down some chairs!"

Dutifully, silently, Salvatore started to remove chairs from one of the front tables. His mother went to a cupboard against the wall.

"We shouldn't eat here, *sidi*," Habib said in a low voice, cradling the package of family gifts. "It is not clean."

His head was down as if he were concentrating on one of the floor tiles.

This wasn't the first time he had shown fastidiousness in circumstances that Urbino, discriminating enough himself, had no complaint about. The restaurant looked and smelled clean, if a little damp. Urbino pointed this out. Nina riveted her eyes on them, eyes grossly magnified by her thick glasses.

"But the chairs on the table, *sidi*! People sit on the chairs, yes? And the chairs were kissing the table. We eat where people sit! Let's go somewhere else, please!"

Urbino detected an underlying note of fear. He was often puzzled by Habib's reactions, and sometimes by his lack of them. He ascribed it to the cultural gulf between them that could never be breached. It was, in fact, greater than the one created by their ages.

To try to josh Habib from his peculiar mood, Urbino said in a low voice, "the niece of your father's brother!"

It was a little game they enjoyed playing. Urbino had realized early in their friendship that Habib, like most Moroccans, had a keen sense of kinship. Urbino had got into the habit of throwing out complicated family relationships as a mental and verbal exercise for Habib, who sometimes became confused about the English words for these connections.

"My father's brother is my uncle, and his niece—his niece is my sister!"

He gave Urbino a strained smile.

"Good. That's one possibility."

Nina took a lace tablecloth out of the cupboard. Salvatore finished arranging the chairs.

"Now wipe off the table!"

Nina's voice grated harshly. Salvatore shuffled off, not quite steadily.

He came back a few moments later with two cloths. He gave the tabletop several hard swipes, first with the wet cloth, then with the dry one.

Nina arranged the tablecloth. Even Urbino's untrained eye identified it as of superior quality to the one Habib had bought.

"Salvatore will bring you the menu. I can cook many things that are not on it."

"Let's sit down," Urbino said as the mother and son went into the kitchen.

"But, *sidi*, I feel something bad here. It is not a place to make a happy meal."

"You'll see you're wrong."

"I hope so."

During the meal that followed—a delicious one of grilled shrimp and *coda di rospo*—Habib hardly said a word. He tried to be his usual open self, but he seemed under a shadow of some kind. He picked at his food in desultory fashion and kept his head down.

Urbino looked into one of the mirrors. He caught sight of the old lace maker, sitting in a corner with her eyes screwed in their direction. He could be mistaken, but he had the impression that Habib was avoiding her glance as if it were poisoned.

6

Half an hour later, their meal finished, Urbino and Habib were about to strike out down the Via Galuppi to return to the motorboat, when Nina emerged from the restaurant. She was dressed in her black shawl and fingerless gloves.

"If you are returning to Venice," she said, "perhaps you could take me? If it isn't too much to ask you to do for a poor woman."

"With pleasure, signora. We'll drop you wherever you wish."

Habib fell in a few steps behind Urbino and the lace maker as they walked toward the boat landing.

They had gone only a short distance, however, when an attractive, slightly overweight woman of about thirty-five came striding toward them. She was stylishly dressed in a voluminous woolen cape of muted colors and shining leather boots. A bag from a San Marco shop weighed her down on one side. When she reached them, she took a cigarette out of her mouth and ground it beneath her boot.

"Everything is done?" she asked Nina.

"Salvatore will finish."

The younger woman consulted her gold bracelet watch.

"But my friends will be here in an hour!"

"Do not worry, signorina. Nella will be returning soon."

The signorina was about to say something but she checked herself. She gave Urbino a bland and slightly quizzical smile.

"This is Signor Macintyre," Nina explained. "He is the friend of the Contessa da Capo-Zendrini."

"My best client! I'm Regina Bella. Il Piccolo Nettuno is my restaurant."

Nina made a little snorting sound that the younger woman ignored.

"We had an excellent lunch," Urbino said, "and excellent service. The Contessa recommended your place."

"We owe her much of our success."

Urbino introduced Habib as his Moroccan friend. Habib was giving his attention to an edge of the tablecloth that was sticking out of his package.

"I love your country," she said to him in Italian. "Does he understand Italian?" she asked Urbino, when she got no response.

"If you speak slowly."

"Yes, well, I love your country," she said again. "I've been there twice. You have very colorful customs. And delicious food. I should be a good judge of that, shouldn't I? It's my profession!" She laughed. "I hope you enjoy your visit."

"I am not a tourist," Habib said, pronouncing the words slowly and clearly.

"All the better for you. Have you immigrated here?"

She seemed to scrutinize Habib more closely.

"I am an artist."

"But surely artists can be immigrants, and immigrants can be artists!"

This was too much for Habib to absorb. Urbino stepped in to clarify.

"He's a painter. I'm sponsoring him. He's studying Italian and getting a firsthand look at the art. We hope he'll show his work."

"Marvelous! I'm sure that Signor Macintyre will be of great help to you, and the Contessa da Capo-Zendrini also. But excuse me. I must see if everything is in order."

Her eyes flickered quickly over Nina's face before she picked up her shopping bag and continued up the Via Galuppi.

During the trip across the lagoon, Habib stayed outside with Giorgio despite the chill. In the cabin, Urbino praised Nina's cooking and tried to explain why Habib had left so much food on his plate. He laid the blame on his unfamiliarity with a different cuisine and not on his reluctance to eat at the restaurant at all. The old woman didn't seem particularly interested.

"Forgive me, Signor Urbino, but I feel I know you. The Contessa da Capo-Zendrini speaks well of you, as do others. Natalia Vinci, for example."

Natalia was his housekeeper.

"You know Natalia?"

"Si, signore. Though it was her mother, may God rest her soul, who I knew best." She peered at him sharply. "You are a man who respects mothers. You were a good son to your mother. She had Italian blood. She is dead."

She rattled off these simple truths as if she had gained her knowledge from some source other than Natalia or the Contessa, neither of whom in any case had ever known his mother. There was nothing for him to say.

"That is why I know you will help me."

"Help you, signora? In what way?"

"By speaking in the name of Nina Crivelli to the Contessa da Capo-Zendrini. She is not a mother but she has the heart of one. And the heart of a good mother is open to the world and all its pain, and all its needs."

The old woman spoke in a somewhat fawning manner. The closed cabin had an unpleasant odor from her decaying teeth and unwashed garments.

"What is it that you want of the Contessa?"

She took a white lace handkerchief from beneath her shawl. It was tied at the corners.

"It is something she can give easily. Something she has given before. I do not want to name it. She knows. But she hesitates. Nina Crivelli has never asked for such a thing in my long, long life. The Contessa's name is Barbara. Santa Barbara appeared to me when I fell asleep in the Oratorio di Santa Barbara." The oratorio was on Burano. "Holy Santa Barbara"—she crossed herself, with the handkerchief still in her hand—"told me that I could help the Contessa Barbara and the Contessa Barbara could help me."

There was something unmistakably false and calculating in her words.

"What help does the Contessa need?"

The old woman shrugged.

"It is not my business, signore." She gave him a sidewise glance, and then looked through the window at the front of the boat, where Giorgio was explaining something to Habib. "But all rich people need help, even more than the poor. You are not rich," she added. "Not as rich as the Contessa. You understand what I am saying."

Urbino was far from sure that he did.

"You will speak in the name of Nina Crivelli?"

"I'll tell the Contessa about our conversation," was all that he promised.

But it appeared to be enough for the lace maker.

"You are a good man, signore," she said, patting his hand.

She then withdrew completely into herself and stared out the window. Her gaze kept straying away from the lagoon, however, and fixing on Giorgio and Habib. The young Moroccan was now crouched down next to Giorgio to keep out of the wind.

Not until they had passed Murano and were approaching the cemetery island of San Michele did Nina break her silence.

"It is not a good thing for a young man to like cemeteries."

Urbino was startled. San Michele was one of his favorite spots, for reasons that he didn't think were morbid. He wanted to show Habib some of its well-known graves, but he had so far made no inroads against the Moroccan's superstition of cemeteries.

He looked at Nina. She was peering out the window at the brick-walled island with its cypresses, which was slowly sliding by in the dusk on their left. A grim expression darkened her worn face.

"Please tell Signor Giorgio to leave me on the Fondamenta Nuove."

He opened the door and told Giorgio.

A few minutes later as Urbino was helping Nina out of the boat, she turned to Habib.

"That tablecloth, young man. It is bad work. Every stitch will bring a tear of sadness."

Habib, uncomprehending, nonetheless drew back. Nina gave an unpleasant laugh.

As Giorgio pulled the boat away from the quayside, where the old lace maker stood gazing after them, Habib asked Urbino what Nina had said. Urbino reluctantly translated it.

"That lady is a witch, *sidi*! She has the evil eye! I must not give such a gift to my dear mother! It is bad luck!"

"You are being superstitious."

"Forgive me for saying it, *sidi*, but you are wrong! She is a bad woman. You will have a spell put on you and you will be deceived!"

He added something in his native tongue. Fear, naked and vivid, glittered in his dark eyes.

7

The next afternoon Urbino stepped out of the Palazzo Uccello into a rain that was being driven against the city by a wind from the lagoon.

The Contessa expected him at the Ca' da Capo-Zendrini in an hour. He needed to do some thinking first, and he preferred to do it in motion and on foot. He often joked that if he had been a Greek, and one of a much more distant time, he would have been a philosopher of the peripatetic school. The magical connection between walking and reflecting had been his secret resource since his solitary years as an only child.

Since settling in Venice the old habit, or call it the ever-new compulsion, had been intensified by the geography of the labyrinthine city. Despite his familiarity with it after all these years, it could still give him, if only momentarily, the sense that he was lost. This suited the usually meandering rhythm of his own thoughts, especially when he was trying to puzzle out a problem in one of his biographies or investigations.

And the rain only made things better, not least of all because it encouraged his peculiar little fantasy that the city was closer to being his alone.

For on days like these, he could imagine himself a prince of some rain-country making the circuit of his small, but sumptuous realm where his subjects kept themselves at a respectful—though not fearful—distance. Rainy days in January were best, for then that scarce breed of tourist who came in winter sought out cozy spots to protect their Baedekers and enthusiasm. Even Venetians understood the good sense of keeping their feet dry in their apartments or neighborhood café.

This latter thought inevitably reminded him of what had provoked his wanderings this afternoon. Nina Crivelli, with her plastic trash bags on her feet.

And, according to Habib, with her evil eye.

The incongruity of these two images might have been humorous in other circumstances but not this afternoon. In spite of his attempt to soothe Habib yesterday, he did sense something vaguely sinister and threatening in the old lace maker.

He turned his umbrella to the rain gusting along the Fondamenta della Misericordia. Small moored boats, most of them covered with plastic or tarpaulin beaded and pooled with water, rocked in the canal. The buildings on the embankment seemed closed in on themselves.

He soon was in the narrow Campo dei Mori where he cast a familiar glance at the statue of Sior Antonio Rioba, the damaged nose protected by a metal guard. Habib had made sketches of the statue along with several impressions of the facade of the nearby Palazzo Mastelli, with its bas-relief of a turbaned man leading a camel.

Urbino stopped his pace to take in, as best he could pummeled as he was by wind and rain, the dilapidated Gothic building where Tintoretto had lived and died. It seemed slightly menacing in the gray light, as if painted with Tintoretto's dark palette.

His interest in the building was because of his new project, a biography of women associated with Venice. Marietta Robusti, the daughter of Tintoretto, had lived there. She might not be one of the most famous of the women of Venice—in that category she was easily eclipsed by Desdemona, George Sand, or Peggy Guggenheim—but she was certainly among the most interesting. She was one of his and the Contessa's favorites, because of the unfortunate circumstances of her life. An excellent painter, who probably had contributed to her father's canvases, she had been confined by her husband to vanity portraits of his friends and associates.

"The poor Marietta ghost," the Contessa had once said with a sigh, "roaming around the building and wondering what she might have been."

As he resumed his walk in the direction of the Rialto Bridge, avoiding the Strada Nuova in a preference for the smaller passageways, he considered how the Contessa might react if she were to confront the ghost of the person she would have been without her own particular advantages. He was fairly certain that she wouldn't have been frightened—or have, in her turn, frightened the ghost—but she would have felt more than a little melancholy. At any rate, the ghost, even without her privileges, would never have taken anything resembling the form of Nina Crivelli.

In fact, the Contessa's almost legendary benevolence was related to his realization of this indisputable truth. There were fates in store for one, and fates avoided, but none of these encompassed, for the Contessa, the kind endured by Nina Crivelli and poor women like her.

Was this, then, the simple answer to the question of what the lace maker wanted of her? Urbino asked himself as he skirted a large puddle in the middle of a *calle*. Did Nina want her to bestow some of her largesse on her, as she was accustomed to doing, usually on women?

This solution to the little mystery was comforting, although it didn't account for the Contessa's uneasiness at Florian's.

He went over in his mind how she had reacted and what she had said on that occasion, and recalled his own encounter with the lace maker yesterday, as well as Habib's all-too-obvious aversion to her.

He had become so absorbed in these thoughts that he reached the foot of the Rialto Bridge before he realized that it was no longer raining. The Rialto, usually one of the busiest areas of Venice, and in centuries past its commercial heart, on this afternoon was almost deserted.

He shut his umbrella and walked up the steps of the bridge to the middle of the broad stone parapet. He looked out at the marble wall of Gothic and Renaissance palazzi on both sides of the Grand Canal. The three-branched iron lampposts were not yet lit, but some illumination from private residences, shops, and hotels spilled out into the scene.

His only companions were an elderly French couple and a woman swaddled in furs, with a muzzled cocker spaniel on a fashionable leash. They soon moved off, leaving him alone with the familiar but never stale perspective. He cast his eyes farther down the Grand Canal. From this side of the bridge, the Grand Canal was a long, straight sweep down to the Ca' Foscari, where there was a bend in the waterway. The impression of a flooded city, with the water lapping at the building foundations only a short distance from the lighted windows, was nowhere stronger than from his present position.

The palazzo was where the Doge Francesco Foscari had died of a broken heart. It was now the center of the University of Venice, but its associations with Verdi's opera were most vivid in Urbino's mind. He restrained himself from taking advantage of the solitude and breaking out in his weak, uneven tenor with some lines from "Ah, si, ch'io sento ancora." This melancholy greeting to Venice by the exiled son of the Doge had long been one of his favorite arias. It was even more so now, with its words and sentiment eerily approximating his own situation after his long absence from the city.

Since his return, he had been reclaiming, day by day, what he had felt slipping away from him in distant Morocco. The resumption of his special relationship with the Contessa, despite some understandable strains, was having its tonic effect. To be with her was not only to be with someone he loved, but also with someone who shared his passion for Venice and even embodied part of its mysterious essence.

But, he thought to himself, he needed two more things before he could sink back into full possession. One was to become immersed in working on a new addition to his *Venetian Lives*. His plans for *Women of Venice* were helping to take care of that.

The other was a direct appeal to his enthusiasm for detection. The feeling was so attuned to the Venetian scene that it didn't function quite properly without it. And it appeared that he was provided with this stimulus in the figure of Nina Crivelli and her relationship to the Contessa. He had already formulated a tentative explanation. He hoped the Contessa would shed the necessary light this afternoon.

As he walked down the outer steps of the bridge, he almost came to an abrupt halt as a realization flashed over him. He would be disappointed if the mystery surrounding Nina Crivelli turned out to be just a banal story, easily explained away.

The implications of this troubled him as he made his way into the San Polo quarter in the direction of the *traghetto* that would ferry him back across the Grand Canal.

8

Usually Urbino enjoyed a *traghetto* ride across the Grand Canal. This afternoon, however, he found it a disquieting experience, especially because of the thick fog that had been creeping into the city since the rain had stopped.

Ferries, placed at strategic points along the Grand Canal, provided not only a convenient way to make the trip but an inexpensive, if all too short, gondola ride. Usually it was only Venetians who used them, standing up in no-nonsense fashion.

He had forgotten, however, that this particular *traghetto* between the Fondaco dei Turchi and San Marcuola stopped at two in the afternoon. It was only by chance that two men were there, and that one of them had a gondola. It had taken a great deal of convincing for them to agree to ferry him across at even ten times the usual rate, since they refused to believe he wasn't a tourist who wanted a cheap gondola ride.

He considered the money well spent. He would have given them even more, for he was already late for his rendezvous with the Contessa, and couldn't wait twenty minutes for the next *vaporetto* from either of the two nearby stops.

He was the only passenger. The oarsmen, muffled in scarves and speaking gruffly to each other in dialect, kept throwing him surly glances. To his susceptible mind, they evoked twin ghoulish Charons as they deftly maneuvered the boat through the fog and fading light and miraculously avoided a delivery boat loaded with crates of mineral water.

Midway, he became slightly dizzy, and sat down. Ever since his trip to Burano, he had been feeling a bit under the weather. The oarsmen looked down at him with an amused, disdainful air. In their eyes, he had been caught in a lie, for only a tourist or an elderly or infirm person would sit down during the crossing.

He was relieved when the boat nudged against the almost invisible landing. Here was something substantial. He got out with too much haste and had to be steadied, with unnecessary roughness, by one of the oarsmen. He felt chilled and walked briskly through the *campo* in front of San Marcuola.

Within a few minutes he reached the small bridge of the Ca' da Capo-Zendrini. As he was going up the steps, the iron door of the palazzo opened. Through it came a figure swathed in fur that the next moment, benefiting from the illumination from the intricately patterned globes on either side of the door, he recognized as Oriana.

"So you're finally here!" she called out in the English she preferred to use whenever she spoke with him. "No, no, stay right where you are. The two of us standing on the bridge will make a pretty picture if Barbara's watching from the window, which I'm sure she is. I could tell she wants to be alone with you," she said when she had joined him. She gave him two quick kisses on each cheek. "She's getting very impatient."

Oriana was an attractive middle-aged woman who always dressed in the extreme of fashion and sported apparently limitless pairs of oversized eyeglasses.

"If I didn't know you better—and I mean the *both* of you, Urbino dear—then I would begin to wonder! Ha, ha! But I have no such suspicions, and never had from the moment I saw you and Barbara together." Her voice was perpetually throaty from all the cigarettes she smoked in her flamboyant holders. "I have my radar. No sense in going after unavailable men. Speaking of which, how is that good-looking young specimen you smuggled out of Morocco in your trunk, hmmm?" she rattled on.

In the air was not only the scent of her expensive perfume and gin, her preferred drink in all seasons, but also something very much like nervousness, almost desperation. Was it possible that she wasn't weathering her latest marital problem with her usual combination of nonchalance and arrogance?

"Habib is fine. Don't you have your boat?"

As soon as he asked the question, he regretted it. Perhaps she had lost the use of the boat as a consequence of her separation from Filippo. Oriana laughed.

"Not a subtle way to change the subject. My boat? I'm afraid you've caught me in a little deception, my dear. You see, I thought Barbara would have gorgeous Giorgio take me back to the Giudecca by the longest route, but she's overly protective of the boy. As if I'd do him any harm! Well, I must be off, Urbino dear. I hope you and your charming young friend are still planning to go to Frieda Hensel's. See you then."

She stepped away after pecking him again on each cheek. But then she hurried back and, leaning closer to him as if someone might be lurking beneath the bridge to hear her confidence, added, "Oh, by the by, please don't get involved in Filippo and my little—how shall I call it?—tangle, our imbroglio! I know what Barbara's cooking up. I wouldn't want someone as sweet and considerate as you to get caught in the cross fire! There are much better things to do with your valuable time. We'll work it out ourselves, or kill each other first. Ciao, *bello!*"

9

I 've been going mad waiting for you," the Contessa said when Urbino entered the *salotto blu*.

"I'm not that late," he said, dropping into one of the Louis Quinze chairs by the fireplace. His accustomed spot, it stood next to a small table holding the Contessa's collection of eighteenth-century ceramics. The fireplace, with a Veronese above it, crackled in homey fashion from wood brought down from Asolo, near the Contessa's villa. "In any event, Oriana must have been more than a little diversion."

"So you saw her. *Diversion*, do you say? It was like being in a cage with a tigress! I don't think she sat down once."

"She was a bit hyper, but then she's never been a mellow type. Nonetheless," he said, "it doesn't seem as if she broke anything as she stalked the room."

His eyes surveyed the familiar surroundings. If the Contessa's *salotto blu* had been cluttered when Urbino had first seen it, it was even more so these days. It wasn't that the room was small—in fact, it was a good size—but that the Contessa had furnished it with most of her favorite things.

"If the house ever starts breaking apart and floating off," she had said several years ago, "I'll run to the *salotto blu* and hope to reach a desert island somewhere."

Urbino contemplated one of the recent additions to the room. It was a portrait of the Contessa, showing to fine, but not flattering advantage her generous cheekbones, slanted gray eyes, and patrician air. This portrait dated from the time of the devastating storm shortly before Urbino's departure for Morocco. Murder and intrigue at the Ca' da Capo-Zendrini had surrounded the portrait. Although someone had viciously slashed it during that nightmarish weekend, it had been so skillfully repaired that you would have found it difficult to detect the damage easily. Originally planned to hang in the family portrait gallery, the Contessa had decided to keep it before her as a reminder of a difficult time.

Those jealous of the Contessa, however, might have said that she kept it in her favorite room out of vanity. If they had seen her now, reclining on her sofa and looking careworn and abstracted, they might have had a private thrill of satisfaction that it might not be too long before her portrait outshone her.

A small table near the sofa was set out for tea. Urbino regretted not having stopped somewhere on his walk for a bit of what Oriana had been having. His eyes flicked in the direction of the bar.

"Ah, here is Silvia. I'm sure you're just dying for a cup of tea on an afternoon like this," the Contessa said with a slight note of appeal.

Urbino understood. Tea was always soothing for the Contessa, but never more soothing than when shared, and this afternoon she gave every sign of needing the benefits of more than one mutual cup.

The maid, of whom the Contessa had so many complaints, carried in the steaming kettle to the small table a bit unsteadily and placed it above the silver lamp. She gave Urbino a quick glance as she was leaving. If youth and prettiness made up for everything else, Urbino thought, then Silvia could be allowed many errors. During his visits to the Ca' da Capo-Zendrini since returning, however, he had more and more missed the assured, mature presence of Lucia, as well as that of the now retired Mauro.

"You know, Barbara, I'm beginning to agree with what you said at Florian's the other day. No, not about Oriana and Filippo," he forestalled her as she began to say something. "I'll get to them in a moment. No, I mean about the changes here. There've been quite a few, but not necessarily for the worse," he tried to assure her. "Vitale, Silvia, and Giorgio, there's no question they're splendid physical improvements over their predecessors, and Vitale seems to live up to his name—"

"Doesn't he!" the Contessa wailed as she proceeded to make the tea. "I've told him time after time that he needn't announce you of all people, but he does it just the same. He doesn't know what to do with his energy."

"Oriana could give him a few suggestions—him and Giorgio."

"You'd think that woman would mend her ways considering she's facing divorce. She didn't fool me by not coming in her boat!"

Urbino repressed a smile, not wanting to give Oriana away any more than she did herself. In a more serious tone, he said, "You also mentioned at Florian's that you were counting on me to 'save' Oriana and Filippo, and in the process also save you—and myself as well, I suppose—from suffering further changes—"

"Why do I detect a *but* in your voice?"

"Oriana just told me quite plainly that she doesn't want or need my help." He explained what Oriana had said to him. "I'm not going to blunder around, make a fool of myself, and probably cause more harm than good."

"My, my haven't you grown humble! You still take only one lump? Here!" She handed him his cup. "I won't press you on the point. Reluctant peacemakers can do too much damage. Besides, *caro*, I may need your efforts in a different area, something more personal. I know there's your new book, and helping me plan the ball, and your readjustments to being back, not to mention the repairs at the Palazzo Uccello, and—and Habib, of course, but . . ."

She trailed off.

"What is it, Barbara? It's Nina Crivelli, isn't it?"

She poured out her own cup and added sugar before responding.

"I suppose it was a little obvious, the way she was stalking me outside Florian's."

"Is that how you describe it? Maybe it's more serious than I thought. What's this all about?" It would be best to wait to hear what she had to say before telling her about his own encounter with Crivelli.

She took a sip of tea to fortify her.

"It's all rather embarrassing," she began. "Or that's all it was at first. I suppose that was why I didn't say anything all this time. But things have changed since then. I guess the best place to begin is the day I showed Frieda the Casa Verde. I wanted to help get her established before I left for London since you'd be returning shortly after I got back. I didn't think that Burano would suit her, especially after she had stayed at the Palazzo Uccello, but—" She broke off abruptly. "Just listen to me! I'm getting off the point already. I used to be such a good storyteller."

"Calm down. You're all wound up, like Oriana. Maybe you should have something other than tea?"

"Maybe you mean *you* should have. But it will just sap your strength. You haven't been looking all that well since you got back, you know."

"My body hasn't readjusted to the weather."

"Is that it? Go right ahead, then. Suit yourself."

He was tempted, but he showed his solidarity by raising his cup and taking another sip.

"Go on," he urged.

She took a deep breath and continued at a slower pace. Urbino settled himself in his chair, determined to keep to tea drinking for the moment, and not to interrupt her as she relived what he soon realized had been a distressing series of events.

On the morning the Contessa took Frieda Hensel to Burano it was clear and bright, but it started to darken for her as soon as Giorgio was maneuvering the *motoscafo* to the landing.

An old woman was standing alone on the quay staring at the boat. The Contessa recognized her as a lace maker from Burano. She had become acquainted with her when she had tried to set up a lace making scholarship there several years before. The woman had been given a large amount of money in anticipation of giving lace making lessons, but, according to the Contessa's agent, she had given only two afternoons of instruction and then refused to give any of the money back. The Contessa had not pressed the matter.

She now gave a little shiver. The Contessa had seldom felt so assaulted by a gaze as she was by the woman's. Her eyes, magnified behind thick glasses, seemed to invade the very privacy of her thoughts and leave behind a chill.

Frieda gave a full-hearted laugh. She was a tall, attractive woman in her late forties with slightly protruding eyes. She wore, as was her custom, a large colorful scarf tied around her head and draped over one shoulder.

"You are cold, Barbara?" she said. She had a strong accent, but spoke excellent English. "But today, for November, it is so warm. It is not like the winter at all. You have become Italian after all these years!"

On their walk to the bright green house on a small canal,

and all the time the Contessa was showing it to Frieda as if she were an estate agent, she couldn't shake her chill despite the sunshine and the German woman's enthusiasm. She realized that it was the chill of a premonition. She had felt them before. Although they usually turned out to be nothing, whenever one touched her, she expected the worst.

All during their meal at Il Piccolo Nettuno, a small restaurant on the Via Galuppi where she often ate when she was on the island, she was abstracted and apprehensive. Frieda joked with her, perhaps perceiving that the Contessa was disturbed about something. She assured the Contessa that the little Casa Verde was delightful, and that she'd take good care of it, and that she was completely prepared—in fact, she insisted—that the Contessa accept at least a token amount from her in the way of rent.

The Contessa responded to her exuberance with a wan smile that she saw reflected from odd, unaccustomed angles in one or another of the restaurant's unavoidable mirrors. She attributed these ill-considered new additions to the vanity of the woman who owned the restaurant and who kept throwing glances into them as she moved from table to table.

The Contessa noticed that the waiter, who had worked at the restaurant for as long as she had been coming, was reeling more than usual as he carried plates. She had always suspected him of frequent nips from a bottle in the kitchen. Obviously the mirrors only added to his disorientation and lack of surefootedness these days.

The Contessa was beginning to feel more at ease by the time they were lingering over coffee, Frieda's having been "corrected" by a generous dose of anisette. Regina Bella, the *padrona*, joined them to chat, speaking in English and only now and again breaking into Italian.

"Everyone here on Burano is grateful for your attempts to help its delicate art, Contessa," she said in a voice made hoarse from all the cigarettes she smoked. "We Buranelli are one big family. We hope you will try again to establish a scholarship. The time wasn't right before."

The Contessa's immediate response was to give a perceptible start and an equally perceptible gasp. She stared into one of
the mirrors.

In it, the face of the old woman from the boat landing peered
at her with her grotesquely magnified eyes. She pressed a lace
handkerchief against her mouth and then drank from a glass of
water, all the while staring at the Contessa.

This sudden appearance of the old woman in the restaurant
would have been enough in itself to startle the Contessa. Her
distress was heightened, however, by the way that Bella's comment had seemed to invoke the face of the very person who had
been largely responsible for the failure of her benevolence. It
suggested to the Contessa the old adage, Speak of the devil and
he will appear.

Bella followed the Contessa's gaze. She gave a nervous
laugh.

"That's Nina Crivelli," she said.

"Yes," the Contessa said, "I recognized her."

"People always remember Nina! Those eyes! They stab right
into you! She used to be one of the best of the lace makers in
her day, before her sight started to go. It was all the lace making
that did it. She can hardly see beyond her nose, even with the
glasses. I think that's why her eyes seem like knives, from the
strain. But she manages to see quite a bit, don't you worry about
that. She's become very attached to the restaurant recently," she
added in a lighter tone.

"Almost blind?" Frieda said with exaggerated sympathy.
"How sad, and from making beautiful lace. There is a story to
be found, yes, don't you think?"

"A story?" Bella repeated.

"I am a writer, my dear. Be careful. Some of us have been
known to steal a person's life before they know it!"

Bella, who seemed to follow the spirit of this if not quite all
the sense, retreated behind a confused smile.

"Steal? I never said that Nina would steal even a button!"
She lit a cigarette and glanced uneasily in the direction of the
kitchen. "The waiter, Salvatore, is her son. She comes to check

up on him every day. She's a very attentive mother, even after so many years. She does some of his cleaning up to get him home earlier. Sometimes she cooks meals when Nella isn't here. You must excuse me."

Bella threw her lamb's wool coat over her shoulders and dashed into the street, turning toward the main square.

The Contessa paid Salvatore, and indicated he could keep the rather generous amount left over. She wanted to get out of the restaurant, and back to the Ca' da Capo-Zendrini as soon as possible. She had a vague sense of insecurity as long as she stayed on Burano.

Frieda stopped at one of the lace shops on the way to the boat landing.

"If it's good Burano lace you're looking for," the Contessa told her, "you won't find it in one of these places."

"Unfortunately, Barbara, I don't have your large purse. Nor your good taste, I am sure. Please indulge me. I need a special piece of lace for my costume for your ball. I will be Scheherazade, and wear a lovely lace veil instead of a mask, yes!"

While the Contessa waited impatiently as Frieda started to look through the lace items, she felt a tug at her coat sleeve. Turning around, she was face to face with Nina Crivelli. It would have been almost comical to the Contessa, the way the old lace maker seemed to be popping up out of thin air—comical, that is, if she didn't find it more than a little alarming. And in a few minutes she had even more reason to be dismayed.

"You are kind and generous, Contessa," Crivelli said in Italian without any preliminary.

A foul odor emanated from the old woman, a smell of decay and death. She lifted a gnarled hand in the air, with one finger pointing toward the Contessa. The Contessa drew back. The woman gave her a mocking smile as her finger moved slowly through the air between them. Crivelli nodded and put her hand down.

"Is poor woman, Nina Crivelli," the lace maker said in English. "Money."

She rubbed the fingers of one hand together, still with her mocking smile.

The Contessa made no response except to open her purse and take out three ten-thousand-lira notes, feeling a sense of desperation as she did it. If this was all she needed to get rid of the woman for good, she thought, she would give her double or triple that amount. She was, in fact, about to extract another ten thousand lire, when she noticed Crivelli's reaction.

She was staring at the money in the Contessa's hand with her alarming eyes. Whether this was because she was offended at being offered such a relatively small amount or any money at all, despite her plea, it was impossible to determine.

"Later!" Crivelli said in Italian. She slipped behind the neighboring lace kiosk. The Contessa waited for her to come back, but she appeared to have vanished.

Frieda didn't seem to have observed the encounter, but all the way back to Venice she kept asking the Contessa if she was feeling all right. The Contessa's halfhearted assurances that she was fine didn't seem to satisfy the German woman, who was reluctant to part with her new friend.

Five days later, after making the necessary arrangements for the changes at the little house on Burano and Frieda's smooth move there from the Palazzo Uccello, the Contessa took the train to London. She was caught up in visits, shopping, theaters, and museums. Only at odd moments did she think about her encounters with Nina Crivelli. When she did, however, she felt the same sense of premonition as she had that day on Burano, a premonition that neither distance nor time had weakened.

As a consequence, it wasn't a total surprise when one of the first things Vitale told her on her return was about the "strange old woman" who had been loitering outside the Ca' da Capo-Zendrini and who, on one occasion, had rung the bell and asked for her. Vitale had been cautious enough to inform the woman only that the Contessa was not at home and to ask for a message.

There had been none.

11

If the Contessa had no doubts that her path would cross with Nina Crivelli's again, it wasn't because of the nature of Venice, whose waterways and alleys and profusion of squares made privacy impossible as soon as you stepped out of your door. Nor was it because she was obliged to visit Frieda and thus was treading the even more public spaces of Burano where the old woman lived.

Her certainty came from the echo in her mind of the lace maker's urgent "later!," which, now that she was back in Venice, sounded with a particularly disturbing loudness. Anxious to get the next inevitable encounter with Crivelli over with, she was restless at the Ca' da Capo-Zendrini, and found excuses to be out and about, and especially to go to Burano. But yet she was shy of seeking Crivelli out more directly by going to Il Piccolo Nettuno, which she avoided. She realized that she was a bundle of inconsistencies.

When a week passed with no sight of the lace maker, the Contessa's nerves were at the breaking point. It was with the hope of soothing them that, one morning, after visiting a friend who lived above a shop on the Calle del Paradiso, she walked the short distance to the Church of Santa Maria Formosa.

The Contessa had special places scattered throughout Venice where she sought out repose. She thought of them as way stations on a long journey. Like the Chinese salon at Florian's, they were public spaces, but because of association and familiarity, she had made them her own.

The Church of Santa Maria Formosa fell into this small but special category because of one of its paintings. It was by Palma Il Vecchio, and it portrayed the Contessa's namesake, Santa Barbara. The Oratorio on Burano, because it had its own portrait of the same saint, was another of the Contessa's refuges, but on this particular day and with her particular problems, Burano was out of the question for any kind of restorative reflection.

Leaving behind the lively square with its palaces, market, and cafés, she slipped into the Renaissance church, drawing her silk scarf around her head. When she touched her forehead with the water from the stoup, it felt so unusually cold that she realized she might be slightly feverish.

She was pleased to see that her accustomed chair, with its view of the great painting, was not only unoccupied, but that there was no one else in the church except two art students making studies of the Vivarini triptych. She seated herself and looked at the Palma Il Vecchio.

This sixteenth-century portrait of the patron saint of bombardiers, who was blond, buxom, and graced with a small cannon at her feet, somehow had the ability to comfort her despite its martial associations. She liked to think that if she shared anything with the portrait—other than her blondness—it was the painted woman's air of calmness and faith in the presence of the inevitable. In Santa Barbara's case, this inevitability was her own immediate death.

Sitting there in the late-morning quiet, the Contessa contemplated the saint's serene face beneath its crown and the delicacy of colors blending together so smoothly. For a few moments she closed her eyes, and started to recite a brief prayer to St. Barbara that she had learned from the nuns at St. Brigid's-by-the-Sea.

"Sudden death, Contessa," said a voice in Italian. "Lightning. Bombs."

The Contessa's eyes flew open. Standing in the aisle beside her was Nina Crivelli. In her hand, sheathed in a black fingerless glove, was a large plastic bag. It bore the name of one of the fashionable shops on the Calle Large XXII Marzo.

Somehow the Contessa found her voice.

"Are you following me, Signora Crivelli?"

She looked up at the woman, forcing herself to stare directly into her magnified brown eyes. Surely it was a pose worthy of Santa Barbara, thought the Contessa, who could indulge, despite her distress, in this bit of self-importance—unless, of course, it was something more like bravado.

"Perhaps, Contessa, it is you who are following Nina Crivelli!"

There was no answer to this. Crivelli might have been in the church when she came in, concealed by the shadows or even sitting inside one of the confessionals. This thought, however, was even more disturbing. It seemed to compromise her sense of freedom even more if the place she had chosen to escape from the lace maker was the one where the woman already was, waiting for her.

"You are a busy woman," the lace maker continued. "Even your prayers must be scheduled, yes?"

This only confused the Contessa more. She showed her state of mind by saying, more loudly than she intended, "What is it that you want with me, signora!"

The two art students paused in their work to look at her. What did they see, she wondered? Probably a haughty woman disdaining the pleas of one of the city's poor. The thought that she could be so misunderstood would, in other circumstances, have made her more concerned about appearances, but today was different.

As a response to her question, Crivelli seated herself in the chair behind the Contessa, obliging the Contessa to twist her body slightly to look at her. The lace maker then leaned toward her, fixing her with her eyes. Once again, as there had been in front of the lace shop, there was the odor of something foul in the air.

"I need money," she said as quietly as the Contessa had almost shouted. "Much more than thirty thousand lire. If you cannot find it in your heart to give it to me, Contessa, I am prepared to sell you something. I would give it to you free, but I have to consider my needs. I am a desperate woman."

Indeed, at that moment, because of the shadows that conspired to darken all her face except for the thick glasses and the magnified, invasive eyes behind them, the lace maker did look desperate enough for anything.

The Contessa's gaze involuntarily flickered in the direction of Crivelli's plastic bag, now lying on the stone pavement. An absurd hope that the woman wanted an exorbitant price for a handmade lace tablecloth stuffed inside the bag flashed through her mind. It was quickly quashed, however, as her eyes returned to Crivelli's.

"What is it that you have to sell, signora?" she asked in as firm a tone as she could muster.

The answer came quickly and in the same low, urgent voice. "Information, Contessa."

Hesitant footsteps sounded at the entrance. The lace maker, who had a more direct view of the door, peered in its direction nervously. The Contessa shifted herself to get a view.

A man stood motionless by the entrance. The dimness of the church made it impossible to see his face. With her poor eyesight, the lace maker could surely see even far less than Barbara could. The Contessa returned her full attention to the woman. She perceived a wariness in her that hadn't been there before.

"Information, signora? Information about what?"

The Contessa sensed the gradual approach of the person who had just entered the church. He appeared to be moving slowly from place to place as if examining the architecture and art. The lace maker kept peering in his direction, with a frown of concentration.

Crivelli, who had been so eager to speak before, now fell into silence. She appeared to be thinking. Then, she brought out with effort and much more loudly than before, "I—I speak of someone dead. Yes! Someone who is dead, Contessa." She looked over the Contessa's shoulder, presumably in the direction of the approaching man or perhaps someone else. "He is long dead. He was—he *is*," she corrected herself, "close to your heart."

She grabbed her bag and stood up. She leaned toward the Contessa.

"Money, Contessa! Money for information about someone dead! Think carefully, but make the right decision! Good-bye!"

"But you can't go!" the Contessa cried out, once again drawing the attention of the art students and the man who was now beside her. To her surprise it was Giorgio.

Nina Crivelli said nothing more. She didn't even acknowledge Giorgio's presence. She made a wide angle around him and scurried across the stones of the church out into the square more quickly than the Contessa would have thought she could have moved.

"Giorgio!" the Contessa cried out, feeling embarrassed and agitated at same moment. "Whatever are you doing here?"

"Are you all right, Contessa?"

As she started to get up, he put out a hand as if to steady her. She fell back into the chair. She was trembling. Her head was light.

"I—I'm all right, Giorgio. Let's go," she said after a few moments.

She declined his help as they went out into the busy Campo Santa Maria Formosa. With Giorgio silent and solicitous by her side, she walked a short distance around the church, looking in vain for the lace maker. Could she have ducked into a shop or private residence, or somehow managed during those few moments to take one of the eight routes that led away from the square toward San Marco or deeper into the Castello quarter? It seemed impossible, but nonetheless there was no trace of her.

She returned to the base of the *campanile* for one final look around the area.

"Do you want me to look for the old woman, Contessa?" Giorgio asked.

"No, of course not!" she said sharply. Then, more softly, "Go back to the boat, Giorgio. I'll be there in a little while."

Reluctantly, he left, walking with his slight limp and casting an occasional concerned glance over his shoulder.

The Contessa opened her purse and withdrew a small vial of perfume. She unscrewed the top and inhaled the musky scent. It somehow steadied her, and also dispersed the odor from the old woman that had been lingering in her nostrils.

She was about to follow Giorgio to the boat, when the monstrous, leering head at the base of the bell tower caught her attention. Its flat nose, grotesquely misshapen mouth, and protruding teeth transfixed her. It had on other occasions seemed almost like a cartoon figure, something designed to frighten children and the pathetically credulous. Now, after her encounter with Nina Crivelli, its leer was distinctly disturbing and strictly—all too strictly—personal.

An icy fear twisted around her heart. She couldn't shake it off in the privileged snug atmosphere of her sleek motorboat as it made its way back to the Ca' da Capo-Zendrini, nor later in the comfort of the *salotto blu*, where she hid herself away for the remainder of the day.

12

After her account, during which Urbino had not interrupted her to ask or say anything, the Contessa arose from the sofa with a sigh. Telling her story had taken its toll on her. She looked even wearier than she had before.

She went over to a small table, this one burdened with paperweights, and picked up a *mille fiori* ball. As she gazed into its crystal depths, she said in a resigned manner, "So you see, *caro*, it's a matter of blackmail."

She put the paperweight down and looked at him with an aggrieved expression.

"I definitely need a drink," Urbino said. "Or should I say *we*?" He went to the drink cabinet. "Sherry?"

"I give in. Yes, sherry."

The Contessa rang for the removal of the tea table, as if she wanted to clear the stage of a prop that had proved less useful than she had hoped.

After he poured out their drinks, they once again seated themselves. The Contessa took a sip of sherry. Urbino waited, but she remained silent and stared at him.

"My immediate reaction," he prompted, "is that Nina Crivelli doesn't seem the type to resort to blackmail."

"You speak of 'types'! You of all people! Hasn't your sleuthing shown you how little faith can be given to appearances when we're dealing with—with"—she struggled to find the right word—"the criminous!" she finished, somewhat lamely.

"Nonetheless, appearances do count for something."

Yet he admitted to himself that there had been a hard edge to the woman in the way she behaved toward her son, so different from her almost sycophantic speech to the Contessa and himself.

"You don't know her. I do!"

He might have used this as an opening to give her his own direct impressions of the lace maker, if she hadn't rushed on in a torrent of impassioned words.

"I saw deep into her soul, I tell you! It was dark, dark, dark! Don't I have the ability to see things for what they really are? You're the one with your head in the clouds! You're the one who can be as blind as a bat, whatever good your intelligence gets you. And your—your lotus days have done you not one iota of good, my friend, not one iota!"

Urbino was not surprised to have become the recipient of the Contessa's vitriol. It wasn't that he felt he deserved it, but that she believed he did. He took a sip of his sherry and waited.

"Tell me, *caro*," she said after a few moments, with all trace of irascibility now gone, "do you have any plans for dinner?"

It was less a question than an appeal, and even less of an appeal than an olive branch.

"No plans that I can't break for you."

"I do feel encouraged! I hope I'm not twisting your arm."

"You have my blind devotion, bat-like or otherwise."

"You're the prince of smirkers. Don't try to humor me. It won't work this time. The state of my nerves—"

The Contessa broke off when Vitale and Silvia came into the room in answer to her bell. She made strained, innocuous conversation in the ensuing minutes, while the table was tended to.

"The state of my nerves," the Contessa smoothly resumed as soon as Vitale had closed the door behind them, "is far beyond either your delightful humor or this sherry."

She nonetheless took a sip of the rich golden liquid before continuing.

"Nina Crivelli knows something about Alvise that she believes is damaging enough for me to want to pay her a large sum. She's making very obvious insinuations! It couldn't be more simple and more devastating!"

"But she didn't even mention Alvise's name."

"Ah, *caro*, even old women from Burano," she said with a cool air, as if a vast gulf of age and distance divided her from the lace maker, "even *they* have their subtlety! Do you think she'd breathe anything against Alvise? Do you think she'd give me any reason to accuse her of such a vile thing? Sometimes I think when you see a woman of a certain age—of a very advanced certain age, I should add—your filial instincts overcome you. Stop seeing the mother in them or, if you absolutely must, then admit that even mothers can—can"—she searched for the damning word: "blackmail!" She finished with obvious satisfaction.

The Contessa's reference to mothers reminded Urbino of what Nina Crivelli had said to him on the *motoscafo* yesterday about his devotion to his.

He got up. He needed what the Contessa called one of his meditative turns around the room as the two of them looked as squarely as they could at Crivelli's behavior in Santa Maria Formosa and as he silently ran through his mind his conversation with her.

"But how do you know she meant Alvise?" he brought out from the window with a view of the little bridge.

"I know, I know, I know!"

"It may be good enough for you, Barbara, but not for me. As I remember, and as I am sure you're thinking, you've been through something like this before. *We've* been through it together."

"Thank you for the *we*. Yes, you're right. I'm thinking of that summer."

"And it came to nothing."

They were referring to a difficult period of the Contessa's life that Urbino had helped her through, when she had had to confront the possibility that Alvise had cruelly deceived her.

"Nothing, you say! What about a murder!"

"I mean that it came to nothing insofar as Alvise was concerned, and my instincts tell me the same thing now." He thought for a few moments. "What was Giorgio doing at Santa Maria Formosa?"

"He said it was one of the churches he hadn't yet been in. He had some time on his hands and decided to see it."

"I suppose it sounds plausible."

"Are you suggesting he had another reason for being there?"

Actually Urbino wasn't sure what he meant.

"It's just that Crivelli seemed to get nervous when she saw who he was."

"You're ridiculous, Urbino. Giorgio didn't even know Alvise. He—"

"You're assuming that Crivelli has something to tell you about Alvise," he interrupted. "I believe you're wrong, as I said. If everything happened exactly the way you described it, Crivelli gave you some details about her information—if you can call them details—only when Giorgio was a few feet away, and in a voice that was louder than usual."

"I don't see how that involves Giorgio. She was determined to let me know that she had information of value to me. She practically named Alvise, as far as I am concerned."

"Perhaps." Urbino said it without any enthusiasm. He went over the sequence of events in his mind from the time Crivelli had accosted the Contessa until she had left the church right after Giorgio had come up.

The Contessa was giving him a sad, skeptical look.

"I can't help it, Urbino. I'm waiting for the next shoe to drop. I've been at my wit's end. I've wanted to tell you about it from the moment you returned but I couldn't. You were so caught up in being back and—and in other things, and I guess I kept hoping that I'd wake up one day to find that I'd been worrying about nothing. But the fear has only gotten stronger."

He took a sip of sherry. It was time to tell her about his meeting with Crivelli.

"I had a talk with her yesterday," he said abruptly.

"A talk with her? You knew about this all the while I've been going on?"

"What you've told me is completely new to me, but I met her on Burano. Habib and I went to Il Piccolo Nettuno. This is what happened."

As Urbino gave his account, without any embellishment or commentary, the Contessa was just as silent as he had been during hers.

When he finished, the Contessa was pale.

"I'm convinced now more than ever! She means me harm!"

"But she said she only wanted to help you—and to be helped," he added lamely.

"Take some clues from your Habib! You're always singing his praises until I'm deaf to anything else! He knows that she's to be feared."

Urbino poured himself another generous portion of sherry. He wasn't as sure about what he felt about Crivelli now as he had been a few moments ago.

"All that business about mothers," the Contessa went on, "and—and how much you like San Michele and cemeteries, even though you are such a young man," she emphasized. "Can't you see how crafty she is? How she was manipulating you? Did you ask yourself how she knew those things? She's the kind of person who makes a point of getting information, I tell you, of using information! I can only guess what she might know about you that's a deep dark secret even to me."

"Habib—"

"Yes, let's talk about Habib. Why is he so frightened of her?"

"He says she has the evil eye. You know he's superstitious."

"Yes, but why about Nina Crivelli?"

"Just look at her! She's frightening looking, as frightening as an evil fairy-tale character can be to a child. And Habib is in some ways a child, at least in his susceptibilities."

"Yes, yes, I realize all that. I'm not trying to cast any doubts on your young friend, believe me," she said with an air of innocence that didn't convince him, "but there may be more here than meets the eye. She could have approached Habib on some other occasion, and tried to get information from him. And information of a certain kind is power! It's money!"

Urbino resisted her implication that Habib might be lying to him, perhaps out of fear.

"It might be a good idea for us to see her together," he said. "No, I don't mean when we go to Frieda's, but perhaps we can get a message to her then. We might arrange to meet her at the Palazzo Uccello. A public place wouldn't be suitable, and she'd get the wrong idea if you saw her here. She needs to be asked some direct questions. Depending on what she says, we'll decide whether we need to go to the police." The Contessa gave a start. "I doubt it will ever come to that, and you should get it out of your mind that she knows anything compromising about Alvise. There's something else at work here. It's probably something easily explained."

He had spoken with more conviction than he felt, but it seemed to soothe her.

All the way back to the Palazzo Uccello, he kept turning over in his mind the strange sequence of events surrounding the old lace maker. It was a puzzling affair and he could understand the Contessa's distress. She very well might be in a vulnerable position, but he didn't think it had anything to do with the Conte—except, that is, for the great Da Capo-Zendrini fortune that was now hers.

Back home, he found Habib in the library, playing with the cat Serena. He had been considering asking Habib some questions about Crivelli, but the sight of him sitting on the floor and being so indulgent with Serena made him decide against it. He didn't want to spoil Habib's mood, at least not tonight, by bringing up a topic he knew was disturbing to him.

13

T here she is," Habib said to the dark-skinned young man by his side.

It was the next day. Habib and Urbino had gone to the Basilica of Santa Maria della Salute with one of Habib's friends. He was Jerome, a Senegalese in his twenties who had come to Italy to study at Perugia and was now at Habib's language school.

Habib was indicating the Byzantine painting of the Madonna and child on the high altar. Jerome's surprisingly blue eyes opened wide as he took it in.

"She's black," he said in disbelief. "Darker than you, Habib. Just like me."

"Yes! And it is stolen!"

"Stolen?"

"It was stolen hundreds of years ago. The Italians pray to it all the time."

Urbino listened in amusement. Habib was right. The painting of the Black Madonna was one of Venice's many holy thefts. The thief had been none other than the last of Venice's Doges, Francesco Morosini, who had brought it back from Crete in 1672 to adorn the newly built church. The Baroque Salute had been commissioned in thanksgiving to the Virgin for delivering the city from a plague. The ill and the infirm still prayed to her as the Madonna of Good Health. Every November she was honored by the Festa della Salute when a bridge of boats spanned the Grand Canal from the boat landing at Santa Maria del Giglio to the Salute.

"Will the church have to give it back?" Jerome asked.

"Oh, no! Urbino says that there are too many stolen things in Venice to give back. The city would be empty!"

"It is very strange."

"Yes. And there are also dead bodies that they stole away from churches and cemeteries. They put them in glass coffins and bury their bones in the walls of the churches. But there are none here." He lowered his voice even more. "It is a strange religion, Jerome."

The Senegalese nodded in agreement.

Before they left, Habib insisted that Jerome buy one of the small prayer cards at the sacristy, with a reproduction of the Black Madonna and a prayer for health in Italian on the back.

"I have one. It will help you with your Italian," Habib said. "And Urbino says it could help you if you get sick, God forbid it!"

Outside on the broad steps of the church, Urbino looked for the Contessa. The four of them had come to the Dorsoduro quarter in her motorboat. The Contessa had joined one of Frieda Hensel's friends at the nearby Pinacoteca Manfrediana after arranging for the collection to be opened for them.

Urbino didn't see the Contessa, but her boat, with Giorgio standing in front of it, was moored to the left of the church. A chill wind was blowing.

As they made their way across the little square to take refuge in the cabin and wait for the Contessa, a small crowd and raised voices by the *vaporetto* landing diverted their attention. Sitting on the damp stones was a thin, blond woman in her forties dressed too lightly for the cold weather. Two *carabiniere* officers stood above her in their full regalia. The woman was rocking back and forth, and speaking loudly in a language Urbino didn't recognize.

He approached the edge of the crowd, with Habib and Jerome behind him.

"Send her back where she came from!" shouted a tall man

in Italian. He held a little girl of seven or eight by the hand.

"How much more of this can we take?" an elderly woman with a muzzled cocker spaniel said. "They're just thieves, all of them."

"You're right," a bearded man said. "My cousin had his new car stolen right in front of his apartment in Milan!"

The blond woman raised her head and stared straight into Urbino's face. She started to speak to him in German in a desperate way. He was so startled that he responded in English and said he was an American.

She scrambled to her feet.

"Please to help me, mister!" she shouted in English.

She came up and touched the sleeve of his coat.

"I am come here to help the Italians. They must to understand that Mussolini lives in a building in the Vaticano!"

"What country are you from?" Urbino asked.

The woman stared at him blankly.

"I am artist! I make photographs!"

"Artists come from many countries. Germany? Holland? Where?"

"Don't waste your time," the bearded man said in Italian. "She's a crazy Albanian."

The woman started to cry, then she ran over to the quayside.

"*Sidi,* she will jump in!" Habib cried out as he and Jerome gaped at the unfolding scene. "She will drown!"

But the woman took off her shoes and started to dip them in the waters of the canal. She rubbed at them vigorously with her hand.

"Why are you doing that, signora?" the older officer asked. "Stop."

She put her shoes back on, and then scooped up water to splash against her pants.

"Why are you doing that?" the *carabiniere* repeated.

"Don't ask her," Urbino said, surprised at the sharpness of his tone. More softly he added, "There's no explanation. Can't you see that she's ill?"

The hostile climate against refugees and immigrants had become worse during the period Urbino had been out of the country. The newspapers were full of reports of how smuggling gangs were victimizing them and how many ended up dead or, at the least, discarded on Italy's shores and borders like human refuse. Perhaps this was part of this unfortunate woman's story.

"Look. She was very beautiful," the younger officer said. He held out a sheet of proofs to Urbino. "It was in her purse." All of the photographs were of the woman when she had been younger. She had indeed been beautiful. The officer pointed to one of the photographs. "Look. *Pazza*!"

In this photograph the Albanian woman held a pistol, with the barrel between her lips. There were other photographs of her with the pistol in various positions against her face.

"You have to take her to the hospital," Urbino said. "And call the Albanian embassy."

"Bah! The Albanian embassy," the older officer said in disgust. "They never help."

"You must."

During the past few moments Giorgio had approached to see what the commotion was about. When she saw his handsome face peering at her, she got up and started to come in his direction.

"He will to help me!" she screamed. "Yes! Yes!"

Giorgio looked startled and went back to the boat. The younger officer restrained the woman.

"We'll take her back to our post," he said to Urbino.

"Yes, and she'll be treated like a princess by the government," someone in the crowd said. "Just put her in a rowboat and push it off into the lagoon. Let her find her own way back."

"*Sidi*, you must help the poor woman!"

Although Urbino didn't think that Habib had understood everything that had been said so quickly in Italian, he was sure that he had caught its essence.

"She probably gave all her money to get here," Habib added.

His voice seemed full of the wisdom and sympathy of someone who could all too easily imagine himself in the Albanian woman's position.

Habib's response was an additional spur to Urbino's own solicitude.

"Don't worry, Habib. They'll help her," Urbino said, with more conviction than he felt. He knelt down by the woman. "Do you have any money?"

As soon as he asked it, he knew it was a silly question. He took out his wallet, and gave her most of what was in it. He wished he had more. She snatched the notes from his hand.

As Urbino was getting up, he caught the expression of disappointment clouding Habib's face before he averted it.

In the motorboat, no one was in the mood to indulge in light conversation, and the cabin fell into silence. As the Contessa was walking toward them from the direction of the Pinacoteca Manfrediana, Urbino said to the two younger men, "There was nothing more that I could do."

Jerome nodded. Habib didn't disagree, but an aggrieved look was planted on his face for the rest of the day.

14

F rieda Hensel was the kind of hostess who seemed determined that her guests were going to enjoy any party she
gave, even if it killed them. And the Contessa was her prime
victim this evening.

The Contessa, whose troubled mind had received no alle-
viation since the other evening, had a dazed expression as she
received the blows of the German woman's hospitality. Nonetheless, she managed to stand unbowed next to a large terres-
trial globe, elegant in her silver-green dress.

"I could never repay you, Barbara," Frieda said.

Her protruding, half-closed eyes gave her face a meditative
look that softened the effect of her blunt haircut. Tonight she
had foresworn one of her trademark colorful scarves, but had
compensated with an orange tunic over a vivid blue blouse.

Marlene Dietrich's throaty voice infiltrated the small room
from a player in the corner. Out of consideration for the different
nationalities represented in the room, Frieda had chosen one of
Dietrich's recordings in German, English, and French.

"Another sausage, Barbara?" Frieda urged as Dietrich started
to sing "Blumen Sin." In her eagerness to cater to the Contessa,
she had almost pulled the tray away from Silvia, who was helping out this evening. "I made them for you, special. What a
happy day when we met in Gstaad! From the snow-covered
Palace Hotel to this indescribably delightful doll's house!"

And indescribably crowded, Urbino thought, as he looked

around the tiny parlor with all its furniture. Everyone was positioned like statues, including Silvia, who, instead of circulat-
ing with her tray, was standing in the middle of the room and
extending it in different directions with mechanical movements.
The only exception to the rigidly posed guests was Oriana, who
had sunk regally into the depths of a sofa.

As new guests arrived, they obliged the others to move more
deeply into the room. Conversation was sometimes carried on
across a sofa or chair back, through the fringes of a lampshade,
or above the petals and fronds of the flowers overwhelming
their vases.

Habib, to his distress, had become separated from Urbino
almost as soon as they had arrived. He was pushed up in an
opposite corner against a large armoire that Urbino recognized
as having once graced the entrance hall of the Ca' da Capo-
Zendrini. Beside him was the gnome-like Marino Polidoro, an
art-gallery owner. Habib kept throwing pleading glances from
his expressive dark eyes in Urbino's direction. Urbino could see
no way to liberate him, short of climbing over the furniture and
squeezing around the other guests. At any rate, Polidoro was a
good person for the young artist to be stranded with on their
small island of worn carpet.

"Yes, I owe so much to our Barbara!" Frieda was saying yet
again as she thrust the plate in front of Urbino. "I would never
have known you, Urbino, and not your charming Palazzo Uccello. What happy hours there! So happy! I wished many, many
times that you wouldn't come back. Don't misunderstand me,
Barbara. I love your little green house. Now it is mine! *Mein
klein grünhaus*! It has made me a *hausfrau* for the first time. Every
morning I scrub off my stoop, on my hands and knees, yes!"

"You must not overdo it, Frieda dear," sang out Oriana. "The
Buranelli are very sensitive. Your neighbors might think you're
making fun of them with all your Teutonic energy. They don't
care for outsiders. Isn't that true, Regina?"

"Everyone loves Frieda," Regina Bella said.

Her face was somewhat drawn tonight. The green shade of

her well-cut dress made her look sallow even while it did the best for her full figure.

"But if anything is stolen, you can be sure she'll be the first to be blamed," Oriana said.

She drank down the rest of her champagne as if it were water and dangled her hand over the back of the sofa.

"We have very little crime on Burano," Bella said. She snuffed out her cigarette in the Murano ashtray with more force than was necessary. "Where would someone run away to?" She gave a nervous little laugh. "From time to time a rape, but they catch the person right away."

"I remember a murder and suicide some years ago," Oriana prodded.

Bella glared at her.

"A sad affair. A woman killed her mother over some dispute about a granddaughter. Then she killed herself. But she was part Sardinian."

"Yes!" Oriana exclaimed, pushing her oblong glasses further up her nose. "You see how Regina tells us that the murderer was not a Buranella! Probably the murderer's great-great-great-grandfather came from Sardinia back in the days of Garibaldi, and no one ever forgot it."

"Excuse me," Bella said. "I'd like to speak with Marino Polidoro."

"Hold your breath, my dear, and squeeze through," Oriana said.

Bella frowned as she moved away.

"Was this local murder one of your detective affairs, Urbino?" Frieda asked. "Barbara told me about your brave adventures."

"Bravery has very little to do with them."

"Urbino is driven by curiosity and goodwill," the Contessa clarified.

"But many times it is brave to be curious, yes? And good will can be the exact opposite for the criminal. You had something to do with the Sardinian woman?"

"Not at all. As Regina said, it was a sad affair that was only too obvious in its tragedy."

"You are not interested in the obvious?"

"What happened needed no further explanation, even if I had been so inclined."

"And of course you need to give your main efforts to your books. I understand that."

"You are a writer like Frieda?" asked a plain woman in her late fifties. From Urbino's angle it seemed as if her head, with its round face and green hat, was held aloft by a mass of white roses bursting from a brass vase.

"We are in good company," said her companion. She was about ten years younger and of considerably more height, so that she barely had to lift her noble-looking head to be seen—and to see—above a small, carved screen.

They were Marie Céline and Beatrix Bauma, who lived in Vienna and were wintering in Venice. Beatrix was an unemployed art teacher, and Marie was a milliner.

Urbino explained that, unlike Frieda, he wasn't a fiction writer. A little smile curved the thin lips of the German woman.

"He writes the most beautiful and inspiring biographies," Rebecca Mondador, an architect, said. She was an attractive woman with large eyes in a pale pointed face. "About Venezia, *la serenissima!*"

"I adore biographies," little Marie said. "I just finished one about Colette."

"Oh, our Urbino doesn't write biographies like that." Oriana's voice rose up from the sofa. In her hand was a replenished glass of champagne. "No sex and sensation. His are much more cerebral."

"All the more credit to him!" Marino Polidoro called out from his corner. "He leaves sex for the others."

Urbino was becoming increasingly embarrassed. The Contessa was still standing rather stiffly and silently beside the globe like an overdressed schoolmistress who had forgotten her geography lesson. No, there would be no help from her quarter, flashed through Urbino's mind. She was too abstracted by her own problems.

He took a sip of his champagne. Although it was of excellent quality, it didn't agree with him this evening. He put his glass down on a small table.

"Biographies of Venice?" Beatrix asked with a puzzled expression on her strong, haughty face. "What does that mean?"

"Yes, what are they?" chimed in Marie. "My English is better than hers—you know it is, Beatrix!—and I don't understand you."

"I write biographies about people associated with Venice."

"Associated with Venice for good or for bad?" asked Marie. "You must be clear, especially for Beatrix."

"For both good *and* bad, and sometimes at the same time!" Frieda said. "I read all your books when I was at the Palazzo Uccello. Wagner and Mann are my favorites!"

"That isn't surprising," Marie said with a little sniff. "And what are you writing now? Perhaps something about Venice and the French?"

"It's about Venice and women. There will be a chapter on George Sand."

"Oh! I hope you are writing about Rosalba Carriera," Beatrix said.

"I am."

"She is a very charming painter! And it would be interesting to write about Burano in your book, do you not think? It is like a woman, very feminine, with all the lace."

She glanced at the Contessa as if to acknowledge the striking example of femininity she made this evening in her shimmering dress.

"Feminine, Beatrix, yes, but also masculine with the fishermen," put in Frieda, with the plate of sausages still in her hand. "We cannot forget the men. Very traditional. One sex, one work, yes. No female fishermen, and no male lace makers!"

"Not yet," Beatrix said. "But perhaps someday."

"When everyone has forgotten how to make lace and there

are no more fish in the sea!" Polidoro said with a laugh.

"But what about the history of Burano, Marino?" Frieda said, putting down the plate. "History repeats itself. I've been reading about Burano in one of the books I bought at a shop in Dorsoduro. It wasn't always so strict and conventional. Men came here from Venice for their—their"—she searched for the word—"their affairs with both of the two sexes! Far from the eyes of Venice."

"You're thinking about the Barone Corvo and his gondoliers," Polidoro said with evident distaste. "But you are correct. Burano had that reputation in the old days."

"Are you planning to write something about Burano?" Urbino asked Frieda. "It must be a great temptation. I would be interested in reading it."

"Someday, perhaps. But now I'm working on something that will interest you even more."

Her eyes flickered in the direction of Habib, who still stood beside Polidoro.

Urbino had read two of her books out of curiosity when the Contessa had written him about his new tenant. One, *Der Zauberkünstler*, had been in the original German, and the other, *Open Sesame*, in English. Both were collections of stories, many of them only a few pages long and one of them barely of novella length.

His less than perfect German had been able to provide him with an adequate enough sense of the untranslated volume whose tales did seem the work of a conjurer, as the title stated. Also, if he could judge by these two works—Frieda had written five others—she retold folktales and legends from a satiric—at times, even sadistic—perspective.

The blurb on *Open Sesame* had said, "Hensel is a necromancer who transforms the familiar into the fearful, and creates a lot of fun in the process."

Although Urbino found the familiar often fearful enough, he had enjoyed most of the tales, especially the more cynical ones.

"What I'm struck by in your stories," he said to Frieda, "is how much they show your hatred of lies."

She gave him a surprised look.

"Do you disapprove? Although I don't know you well, your own books tell me that you yourself don't hate lies."

"My, my!" cried out Polidoro. "Urbino is very honest and sincere. Does he not unmask the liars and unveil the complete truth? In his books and in his inspections?"

"Please, Marino"—and Frieda held up her hand as if to fend off any further defenses of Urbino on the part of the gallery owner—"you misunderstand. That is not what I meant."

Before she might explain exactly what it was that she did mean, the Contessa roused herself from her abstraction to try to set things straight.

"Urbino believes that some lies are benevolent. Without them, so much, *too* much," she corrected herself, "would come crashing down." She looked a bit sadly and even fearfully around the room as if to assess the damage that might be done in its small, crowded perimeters by some unthinking truth telling. "There can be a high brutality in good intentions. I wish the thought was original to me, but I read it somewhere a long time ago. That's the way Urbino feels about stripping away some of the lies we all need." She gave him a weak smile. "But he can defend himself."

There was a silence. The Contessa's little speech seemed to have impressed itself on the gathering all the more because of her relative muteness since her arrival.

When conversation started up again, it did so suddenly and with an almost desperate air, as if everyone was making an effort to seem at ease. Words, phrases, and sentences were tossed through the heavy air from different corners of the parlor, negotiating their way above and around all the objects much more easily than the furniture-locked speakers.

"What a pleasant evening," Rebecca said.

"Your champagne, Urbino!" Frieda said. "Drink it all down in celebration of health and good company! My little party is not as grand as Barbara's ball will be, but we must do our best, yes!"

"I wonder if the fog has lifted," was Beatrix's offering as she looked in the direction of one of the closed windows.

"Just a little more," entreated Oriana to no one in particular as she held out her empty glass.

"Is there a draft?" Marie asked.

"A current of air carries to the grave," Polidoro intoned.

"I hope no one minds my cigarette," Regina Bella said from her cramped position between a little table and Silvia's elbow.

All the while, Dietrich sang, "Falling in love again what am I to do can't help it," as Oriana, her eyes closed now, moved her head slowly back and forth to the words.

15

A re you all right, Urbino?" Rebecca Mondador asked. "You look flushed."

"I'm all right, I think." Urbino had been feeling rather warm, and even a little dizzy, during the past ten minutes. "How can I tell? It's hot in here, don't you think? The Casa Verde wasn't made for so many people. Not in one room, anyway. And I can't say that I appreciate the cigarette smoke."

He turned his head in Regina Bella's direction. She was puffing away at another cigarette near the door. Their eyes caught briefly, and she looked away.

Rebecca gave Urbino a concerned look but didn't press him on the point. Instead she asked about the repairs on the Palazzo Uccello. He brought her up to date. Rebecca had been the first professional he had consulted about the damages when he had returned. Their friendship went back to the time of the Palazzo Uccello's original renovations when she had been starting her career.

Rebecca launched into some professional observations about the Palazzo Uccello's zoomorphically carved Gothic cornerstones. Urbino was beginning to feel more hot and dizzy.

Someone tugged at his sleeve. It was Habib. He had somehow managed to maneuver himself from the other side of the room, but not from the company of the tiny Polidoro. The gallery owner was still only a few inches away from him, lodged against an elbow chair and wearing a pained expression.

"*Sidi,*" Habib said in a loud whisper, "may we leave?"

"You're not enjoying the party?" Rebecca asked in a warm voice. She had become fond of Habib. They often went on outings together. "Where are your laughing eyes? Where is your smile?"

Habib ducked his head.

"It is a very nice party."

"And you've made a good connection, so you shouldn't be looking so sad. Do you realize what a talented young man you've been talking to, Marino?"

"You embarrass me," Habib said.

"That is too bad!" Rebecca scolded. "You are going to have to learn to sing your own praises, Habib, or you'll be left behind. And you mustn't squirm when people praise you. He's just like a child, Marino. He sees and feels things very clearly, and very intensely. Just a glance at one of his paintings will prove it. He has a marvelous talent. I said he's like a child, and that's true, but he also has force and vision. It's the most marvelous combination. Urbino and I find it a little like the Burano school, but much, much—"

"The Burano school was the Burano school," Polidoro interrupted. "It was almost a century ago; *last* century. And no amount of painting in the bright light and with the bright palette of Burano will turn yesterday into today, or today into yesterday, however I can say it! *Via col vento*, Rebecca! It is 'gone with the wind,' young man," he said putting a claw-like hand on Habib's sleeve.

Habib drew his arm away slightly. Urbino, knowing his superstitions all too well, assumed that he was disturbed by the man's unusual appearance.

"But I trust your opinion, dear Rebecca," Polidoro was saying, a little more subdued now. "I'd like to see some of this young man's work. We will arrange that, will we not, my boy? I agree with Rebecca. You must toot your own horn."

"What does it mean, *sidi*, to toot my own horn?" Habib asked anxiously in one of his stage whispers.

Mondador and Polidoro laughed as Urbino explained. His

head had become increasingly stuffy during the past few minutes. He made an effort at a smile, but it froze the next moment when he caught the alarmed expression on the Contessa's face.

Inconsequential pieces of her conversation with Frieda, Beatrix, and Marie had been drifting over to him, and weaving themselves into what Rebecca, Polidoro, and Habib had been saying. Now, however, he registered that the words *lace* and *lace maker* had occurred with some regularity in the last few minutes.

Marie was waving a lace handkerchief in front of her face.

"I can't breathe with all this smoke," she said.

But it wasn't her distress that was the focus of the women's attention but the lace handkerchief.

"Yes, it's a lovely handkerchief. You say that the old woman has one with the same design?" Frieda said. "The woman with thick glasses and very white hair? She wears gloves with the fingers cut off."

Marie nodded.

"She showed it to me when I was looking for one at a shop by the boat landing. I bought this one just to get away. She's frightful looking."

"You are a child," Beatrix said, but in a consoling tone. She touched her friend's wrist. "Put it away, *liebling*."

Marie stuffed the handkerchief in her pocket as Frieda was saying, "The old woman is harmless. It's not her fault that she looks the way she does. I tell you that she has a good imagination. That is what is important, yes!"

"What do you mean?" asked the Contessa.

Her voice sounded weak and somewhat tremulous.

"She tells strange tales," Frieda said. "Perhaps not as strange as mine. Ha, ha! But she could have been a writer, if all that is needed is the imagination. Regina must agree. She knows her better than any of us." She craned her head around the room, but Regina was now nowhere in sight. "Perhaps she's gone outside this time to smoke her cigarette," she said with a smile for Marie. "I am sure she saw you waving your handkerchief against the smoke!"

The tall Beatrix had a pensive look on her face. She stared at Frieda for a few moments.

"You must tell me something," she said. "Will you use her imagination?"

"Oh, you are speaking of the old lace maker! I have more than enough of my own, thank you!"

Her slightly protruding eyes regarded the Austrian woman without even a faint glint of humor.

"But other writers would steal," she added, "or pay much money for a good story! Artists are always sketching faces in secret. It is a kind of theft. And for a writer, everything becomes—how do you say it, Contessa?—meal for the mill?"

The Contessa nodded, her eyes locked with Urbino's. Any desire to supply the correct idiom was driven out by the discomfort so clearly reflected in her face.

"But I do not steal," Frieda went on. "I use what someone else tells me or something I read, and when I am finished with it, it is one hundred percent Frieda Hensel, yes!"

She then gave a colorful narrative of what she called the romance of lace that she seemed to be spinning out as she spoke. It was about a handsome fisherman from Burano who became shipwrecked, and was rescued and comforted by beautiful mermaids in a castle of coral. When the mermaids conveyed him back to Burano after many happy months, his pockets were full of the mermaids' seaweed. His wife, seeing the sad state of her husband, went to a wise old woman, who told fortunes and gave advice. The wife hurried home and started to copy the pattern of the seaweed with her needle and thread. And in this fashion lace making was born, and was forever associated with danger, seduction, melancholy, and love.

Urbino's mind had become less and less focussed as Frieda went on. He recognized some familiar elements in her tale from something he had read at one time or another, but, as she had just said, she had made them her own.

"Please, *sidi*, are you dreaming? You aren't listening to me!" came Habib's impatient voice. "I need good air! I do not feel well. We must go!"

Making his apologies to Frieda and arranging with the Contessa to meet her at the dock in half an hour, Urbino managed to extricate himself and Habib, both socially and physically, from the overcrowded parlor.

16

But once they were outside for a few minutes it was Urbino who didn't feel well.

It was a warmish night. Habib insisted on taking a walk. The fog drifting in from the lagoon soon swallowed the little green house behind them.

"This is better, yes, *sidi*?" Habib said after taking a deep breath.

He was wearing a dark brown burnoose, the capacious hood falling beneath his shoulders. It suited him, and in fact suited the damp, wind-swept *calli* of wintry Venice as it did the narrow street they were walking down now. Urbino, seized with a sudden chill, envied it. He drew the lapels of his tweed sport jacket against his chest and readjusted his scarf.

They were walking away from where Giorgio would be waiting with the *motoscafo*, but Urbino knew Burano well enough to take the proper turns that would eventually get them to their destination. As they moved closer to the open lagoon, the fog became thicker. At one point they had to grope their way for several feet.

Habib appeared to have regained whatever strength he had momentarily lost in the parlor. He began a spirited monologue about the deserted streets, the fog, the boots outside the entrances, the tolling of the church bell and the distant *put-put-put* of a boat's engine. He seemed seized with a nervous excitement

and his English came fluently as it usually did when he was
alone with Urbino.

Urbino made only an occasional comment as they walked
slowly past the shuttered houses, with the illumination leaking
through the slats. The more Habib spoke, the less Urbino felt
like saying anything himself, or needed to. And the more en-
ergized his burnoosed friend became, the weaker he felt.

They had been walking for about ten minutes when Urbino
was seized with a violent fit of shivering. He stopped. Habib,
caught up in a description now of the painting he was working
on, walked a few paces ahead before he realized that Urbino
had fallen behind.

"What is it, *sidi*?" he asked, retracing his steps.

Urbino was standing, or rather leaning, against the corner
of a building beneath the feeble glare of a lamp.

"Oh, my good God, you do not look good."

"I don't feel very good, either."

"Is your stomach running away? You should not have eaten
the sausages, *sidi*. It was pork!"

Urbino didn't feel like arguing that the sausages hadn't been
made of pork. In any case, he doubted it had been anything he
had eaten at Frieda's. He had been feeling a bit fatigued for the
past week or two, and especially today. From his first months
in Morocco he had occasionally been laid low by what he and
his doctors referred to as a stomach virus. He feared that he was
in for another bout.

"I have to sit down," he said.

Habib looked frantically around for something for him to sit
on. All he could find was a metal bucket. He turned it over, and
set it close to the building.

"*Sidi*, you sit here and push yourself against the wall."

He helped Urbino ease himself down on the bottom of the
bucket. Urbino's head was starting to swim.

"Here, *sidi*, you wear the burnoose."

He removed the heavy garment from his shoulders and
draped it over Urbino. He stared into Urbino's face and put a
cool hand against his forehead.

"Like a fire," he said. He nodded his head slowly. "I was wrong. It is not the pork. It is the old lady's evil eye! She threw it on us the other day, just as I said. I will be sick too, or have an accident. She is evil, and we are in her world now!"

He looked into the surrounding fog and darkness as if seeking out Nina Crivelli. Urbino could feel the Moroccan's fear and anger.

"Don't be foolish. It's just a return of what I had in Morocco. I'm afraid you'll have to go back to Frieda's. Barbara will have to have Giorgio bring the motorboat as close to here as he can."

Urbino lifted his head to read the name of the *calle* written on the wall.

"Can you remember that name?" he asked Habib.

"Of course!"

"But wait. Ring one of these bells. The people will know where Frieda's house is."

"We do not want to disturb anyone. Don't worry. I will take care of everything. The medina in Fez, it has many more turns and twists."

Before Urbino could protest, the fog swallowed up Habib.

17

On this same evening of Urbino's illness, as he waited for Habib to return, the Contessa paused at the open door of Il Piccolo Nettuno. Behind her fog was stealing away all forms and shapes. The restaurant was filled with distorted shadows.

"Is anyone here?"

Silence.

A sickening odor of food, soap, disinfectant, and a backed-up sewer assaulted her. The sharp sound of metal on crockery rang out from the kitchen. The Contessa started.

"Is anyone here? Signora Crivelli? It's the Contessa da Capo-Zendrini."

Her voice didn't sound like her own. A dull echo returned to her.

She had the feeling that she was being watched. She glanced behind her into the Via Galuppi.

It was deserted, at least what she could see of it through the fog. She quickly returned her eyes to the dark room. She sensed, rather than saw or heard, a movement from the back.

"Is it you, Signora Crivelli? It's the Contessa da Capo-Zendrini."

Once again the echo came.

She felt ridiculously frozen in place, poised as she was between the empty street and the dark room. For a few moments she had a feeling of paralysis, the way she did in nightmares when she knew she had to move but couldn't. Except that now she had the additional problem of not knowing if she should go into the restaurant or back into the night. Slow, phantom footsteps sounded behind her. Were they from the Via Galuppi or some alley behind the buildings?

She felt the wall on one side of the door, then the other. Her hand found the light switch. The restaurant became flooded in harsh fluorescent light. The upturned chairs were a thicket of arms reaching to the ceiling from the tabletops.

A figure in a dark garment suddenly swam into view ahead of her. The Contessa gasped and took a step backward. But it was only her own dismayed image.

Fear turned into irritation. She silently cursed the mirrors.

She walked into the room, slowly at first, then less hesitantly. She ignored, but only with effort, the reflections of her own progress from mirror to mirror. She riveted her eyes on the open kitchen door at the far end. Her foot stepped on something. There was a cracking sound. Beneath her foot was a pair of eyeglasses. One of the thick lenses had become dislodged from the frame. When she lifted her head, shadows flickered in the kitchen. She called out Nina Crivelli's name again. Silence.

She had no intention of going any farther.

It was then that she noticed another odor among the others. It was the smell of decay and death. It was a familiar smell. It was the smell of Nina Crivelli.

Her eyes fell to the floor again. There, a short distance away, lying face up between two tables, was the old woman. Her black shawl was twisted beneath her body. Her eyes, unshielded by her thick glasses, bulged out at the Contessa. Pressed against her mouth was a lace handkerchief.

Dishes crashed in the kitchen. A streak of gray rushed past the Contessa's feet and out into the Via Galuppi.

Cats and mirrors were nothing to be afraid of, the Contessa thought, but a dead Nina Crivelli, and what it might mean for her, filled her with dread.

She rushed out into the Via Galuppi.

PART TWO

A DELICATE FABRIC

1

A few evenings later the Contessa entered the library of the Palazzo Uccello.

Urbino sat on the sofa, bundled in a red-and-purple blanket with geometric patterns and slowly turning the pages of a large book. Perched on his head was a cloth cap with swirls of green and brown. Aligned on the carpet in front of the sofa were two green slippers with prominently pointed toes. The strains of Rimsky-Korsakov's *Scheherazade* floated through the room, a bit too loudly for the Contessa's taste.

Beside her invalid friend stood Habib. He was wearing a Missoni sweater that looked suspiciously like one of Urbino's, and an expression of solicitude that looked even more suspiciously sincere.

"It's time for another *tisane*," he was saying.

"It's good to see you, Barbara," Urbino said. "I wish you had come to dinner."

"I haven't had much appetite these days," she said, looking for a seat that wasn't littered with books and magazines.

"Would you like a *tisane*?" asked Habib, who had resolved the problem of whether to refer to her to her face as "Contessa" or "Barbara" by never using either.

"No thank you, Habib," she responded, having resolved her own little dilemma by choosing familiarity. "You just take care of Urbino."

"But of course!"

"I know what a difficult patient he can be."

She gave Urbino a knowing smile and started to seat herself in an oak armchair. Habib protested.

"It is too far from Urbino. Wait!"

He picked up the chair and carried it closer to the sofa. He grazed it against the mahogany confessional, damaged already from the neglect of Urbino's American tenants. Urbino showed no distress, but the cat, Serena, jumped from the confessional's maroon velvet seats, where she had been dozing, and resettled on the hearth.

"Thank you, Habib. You are very gracious—and very strong."

Habib took the book from Urbino and placed it on the refectory table, where it rested precariously on top of a pile of others. Then, at Urbino's request, he lowered the volume of the Rimsky-Korsakov.

"I will go now and make your *tisane, sidi*. You stay right there."

"It doesn't seem as if he has any intention of moving an inch. You do look better," she said to Urbino when Habib had left. "Much better than me, to be sure."

"How are you doing?"

"Miserably, *caro*. This is an absolute nightmare. And it's only just begun. Here I was waiting for the second shoe to drop!"

"You never should have gone there alone."

"Because I've put myself in a better position of being a murder suspect, or should I say worse?"

"Don't be absurd. First of all, Nina Crivelli died of a heart attack. No one is even considering the idea of foul play."

The Contessa was irked by his cool manner even though on most other occasions she had taken necessary shelter in it.

"And second of all?" she prompted as he stared at her from beneath his cap.

"Second of all, even if she didn't die a natural death, you would hardly be a suspect." He paused and added, "A serious suspect."

She gave a smile that she hoped communicated the peculiar

satisfaction that she felt. He was, at least to this extent, agreeing with her.

"And there's nothing about Alvise she could have black-mailed you with," Urbino went on. "We came to that conclusion after a lot of searching a few years ago, as I reminded you last week."

"It's lies I'm afraid of. Someone—maybe more than one person—could have been fed her lies. No," she said with a slow shake of her head, "it's not over yet."

Urbino gave a little tug at his cap that the Contessa interpreted as a sign of nervousness, unless it was self-consciousness about having been caught wearing it.

"Nina Crivelli was probably a disturbed woman who was trying to take advantage of you because of your prominence and your money. And she had a heart attack and died."

Even as he said it, he hoped it was as simple as that.

Scheherazade came to an end. In the sudden silence she heard Habib's laugh and Giorgio's voice coming down from the kitchen.

"They seem to get along quite well," the Contessa said.

Urbino made no response.

The bell of the Madonna dell' Orto tolled across the roofs of the Cannaregio. The Contessa's eyes wandered around the familiar room where she and Urbino had spent many enjoyable hours. Suddenly, her eyes stopped at a table beside the door.

"Where is that Faenza dish that used to be there?" she asked.

Her distress was not so much for the lovely blue majolica ware they had found together in Florence as it was a reflection of her own free-floating anxiety about things being confused and out of place.

"Oh, I hope those brutish Americans didn't break it! Forgive me, but they were! Or maybe you've moved it?"

"I'm afraid it was broken when Habib was playing with Serena."

"Beyond repair?"

"Not quite that, but it will never be the same, not," he added, "for those who know and can see."

As if to refresh her vision and her spirit, the Contessa stared at the Bartolomeo Veneto engagement portrait of a young lady, which Urbino had done such a good job of restoring several summers ago. This evidence of one of his talents encouraged her, all the more so because he had done the restoration while investigating something of great personal importance to her.

"You must help me," she brought out in a determined voice. "Humor me. Condescend to me. Be impatient, even angry with me, but *help* me."

"Help you how?"

"In the way you've done for me and for others before. Ask some questions. Get some answers. Settle this one way or another."

"As you see, Barbara, I'm not quite up to poking around at the moment."

"Oh, you will be soon, with such good care," she added as the sound of footsteps approached the door.

Habib appeared with a tray with three steaming cups. He went over to the Contessa first.

"Please, take one. It is not just for sick people. You must not be left out."

"How sweet of you. It does smell good."

"And for you, *sidi*."

He put the tray down on a low brass table beside an ottoman, neither of which the Contessa had ever noticed before. He went over to the fireplace.

"Tell me, Habib," the Contessa asked, "what does *sidi* mean?"

"It is a title of respect." He extracted something from his sweater pocket, knelt down, and opened his hand to Serena. She nibbled the treat and resumed her nap. "An Arabic word," Habib continued, "but like El Cid in the Spanish story. It is what I call my older brother, sometimes my father."

He seated himself on an ottoman, balancing the cup on his knee.

"I see."

Her eyes grazed Urbino's, and he looked away. She took a sip of the *tisane*.

"Very good. Did you get the herbs here in Venice? Maybe at that little shop in Dorsoduro? You know it, Urbino. By the Montin?"

"Oh, no!" Habib said with his engaging smile. "I brought them from Morocco."

"Smuggled them in, did you?" she asked.

Habib's smile faded. He looked at Urbino for help. When Urbino had explained, Habib turned back to the Contessa with an alarmed look.

"Contraband? I never did a thing like that! I never would go against the law!"

"Barbara was only joking."

Habib retreated into silence and his own cup of herb tea.

As she waited for conversation to pick up again, the Contessa glanced around the room. This time it was the absence of an eighteenth-century carved wood fire screen with an embroidered panel, one of her many gifts. However, she made no comment as she had before about the Faenza dish.

Urbino drew Habib out by asking about his progress in Italian at the language school. He spoke enthusiastically about his teachers and the new friends he was making. When Habib finished with a description of an itinerary of trips the school was planning for its students as far away as Rome, he got up and collected the empty cups.

"You must not stay up too late, *sidi*. The *tisane* steams your body much better when you are resting or asleep. Good night," he added with a slightly strained smile at the Contessa.

He departed with the tray, Serena trotting five feet behind him.

The Contessa stood up.

"It's good to see that he's adjusting so well."

"Yes. I'm pleased that he's making friends and feeling more comfortable here. I was afraid that he'd be isolated. I worry about him, of course—perhaps too much—but I am responsible for him."

"Indeed. I'm sure you'll find the proper balance between giving him his independence and looking after him. It's your way."

She looked at him warmly.

"I promise to ask a few questions here and there. I admit it might be a good idea to learn something about Nina Crivelli. Then your mind can be at ease."

"You're a dear! Let's hope for the best." She sighed. "Take care of yourself or, should I say, let yourself be taken care of. I see that there's no need for me to come running over with chicken soup."

She had aimed for a light, humorous note, but she wondered if the trace of regret in her voice were as evident to Urbino as to her.

"Bring it over whenever you want," Urbino said with a little smile. "It will be much appreciated. It's not in Habib's repertoire."

She paused at the door.

"He's an interesting boy," she said, almost before she knew she was going to.

"Even more so when you get to know him better. But he's not a boy."

"To me he is—and to you."

A plaintive female voice, accompanied by violins and flutes, drifted down the hallway from behind one of the closed doors.

"You know, *caro*, the Veneto portrait somehow looks more appropriate since you returned."

The young woman had a vague Oriental air in her large padded green turban.

"By the way," the Contessa went on, "is your own charming cap something you affect only in the depths of domesticity? I don't believe I've seen you in it before."

"I've worn it out on occasion," Urbino responded with what she was gratified to see was a touch of embarrassment. "Habib says that it's advantageous to wear it when I sleep—to keep my head warm during my convalescence."

"I see. To maximize the benefits of his delicious tea. Well, *caro*, you obviously won't have to spend very much time thinking of your costume for the ball. A few more well-chosen items should complete it! Good night."

2

After the Contessa left, Urbino went to the darkwood ambry. The small, enclosed cupboard contained neither alms nor chalices, although one of the latter stood on a nearby table, draped with a seventeenth-century lace cover. Like the confessional, the ambry served a very secular function although, in the case of the cupboard, there was some faint likeness to its original ecclesiastical purpose. He withdrew a glass and a decanter of Benedictine, and somewhat guiltily poured a generous amount into the glass. He needed something more conducive to meditation than Habib's *tisane*.

He sat on the sofa and arranged the Berber blanket around him. The dampness of the Palazzo Uccello, which all its radiators and insulation couldn't keep out, seldom bothered him, but his recent illness was making him feel the chill even more.

His thoughts turned to Nina Crivelli. Although the sudden death of a woman in her late seventies was nothing unusual, disturbing circumstances surrounded it.

From what the Contessa had told him and from what he had observed himself, Nina Crivelli struck him as a cunning woman. There was no question that she had acted as if she had a dark secret to impart to the Contessa for a good price. Whether it had been a secret worth paying for, or any secret at all, was more dubious.

She had managed, however, to throw the Contessa into fear and confusion. It was a power that, even in death, she still had.

Despite what he had said to the Contessa about unanswered questions, Crivelli's death had left too many for his satisfaction. It was not his nature—call it curiosity or nosiness or perhaps pride—to accept either provisional answers, or someone else's answers, to troubling questions. He needed to find out for himself.

He considered himself a student of human nature. His *Venetian Lives* as well as his sleuthing had developed his ability to detect the truth—or the truths—behind appearances. This didn't mean that he cavalierly dismissed appearances as lies. He had too much respect, and desire, for the truth to do anything close to that.

Urbino reviewed the events on the night of Nina Crivelli's death.

After Habib had left to seek help, Urbino had waited for what seemed an eternity. He felt all the oppressive weight of the deserted, fog-shrouded alleys as he sat on the overturned bucket, leaning against the building and hoping someone would come by. Increasingly weak, almost in a daze, he was hardly able to raise his head and certainly not his voice, at least not loudly enough to get the attention of any of the residents who were behind their shutters and in front of their televisions.

He lost all sense of time. At one point, a figure that resembled some spectral form in the early days of cinema approached him, all dark gray and indistinguishable as to sex or age. It seemed as if the figure was headed in his direction, but then, by some trick of the fog or Urbino's own distraught condition, it disappeared. Whether the person—for so he assumed it was, not sharing Habib's superstitions—had slipped noiselessly into one of the nearby houses or down an alley, or had turned around and retreated just as soundlessly as he or she had come, Urbino could in no way determine.

His next clear memory was of Habib calling his name anxiously, of footsteps, of Habib and Giorgio's faces, of strong arms lifting him and carrying him to the nearby *motoscafo*. Running through his mind as the craft made its way back to Venice and the Palazzo Uccello was the question of where the Contessa might be. She would have made her presence known by her comforting words.

Not until late the next morning, after he had been visited by a doctor and had regained some of his strength and mental concentration, did he learn her story.

She told it to him while the two of them were closeted alone in his bedroom. About five minutes after Urbino and Habib had gone out, Oriana had left, agreeing to drop Rebecca and Polidoro off with her motorboat that was moored nearby. Quick on their heels had been Regina Bella, who said she was expecting a telephone call. Beatrix and Marie then started to say their good-byes, politely refusing the Contessa's offer of Giorgio's services when Urbino and Habib would return. The two women said they would take the *vaporetto*, and made what seemed to her a rather hasty departure.

Only the Contessa, Frieda, and Silvia remained.

"Ten minutes after Beatrix and Marie had gone, I told Frieda I wanted to try to find you. It was a lie, but I didn't know what else to say. I wanted to see Nina, and have it all out, once and for all. Frieda said she couldn't let me go alone, but I insisted she stay. As I was leaving, she was helping Silvia clean up."

The Contessa made her slow way through the fog to the area where Nina and Salvatore lived. She needed the guidance of a middle-aged man who was inserting a key into his door as he returned for the night. He pointed out the second floor of a building indistinguishable from the others. Light glittered behind the closed shutters. She rang the bell, waited for a few minutes, and rang again. No one answered.

She then rang one of the other bells and had a conversation with the woman who came down to the outer door. She said that she couldn't possibly let the Contessa in at this hour. Both the Crivellis were surely asleep. She should come back tomorrow.

The Contessa then went to Il Piccolo Nettuno, on the remote chance that the lace maker would be there. Once again the fog slowed her down. As best she could estimate, it had been about twenty-five minutes since she had left the Casa Verde.

"I must have aged five years during those minutes in the restaurant. The noises in the kitchen and the cat darting past me would have been enough. But practically to stumble over Nina's body! What a dreadful sight! There she was on the floor, her eyes staring up at me and with the lace handkerchief against her mouth. And all those mirrors. I'll remember it for as long as I live!"

She had rushed out into the deserted Via Galuppi. A few frantic and stumbling minutes took her first to the *carabiniere* quarters beside the Church of San Martino. It was closed. Fortunately, she found a policeman keeping his lonely vigil in the station next to the Lace School.

An hour and a half later a *carabiniere* officer escorted her to Frieda's where she found the German woman and Silvia having a nightcap.

After the shock of learning about Nina's death, Frieda set the Contessa's mind at ease about Urbino. He was safely back at the Palazzo Uccello, she said.

She described Habib's hysterical arrival at the Casa Verde. To judge from his incoherent recollections, he had almost fallen into a canal and appeared to have crossed the causeway to the neighboring island of Mazzorbo. There, he realized his mistake, and he made his way back to Burano, where he eventually came upon two young men returning from the boat landing. They led him to *"la casa della tedesca."* It seemed that Habib had remembered enough Italian at the critical moment.

Frieda and Habib had gone in search of Giorgio and the motorboat. They found a moored motorboat that looked like the Contessa's, but assumed they were mistaken since Giorgio was nowhere around. They became lost in the fog, and were afraid they might be retracing their steps, when Giorgio suddenly appeared. He had heard their voices, he said. Thanks to his cool-headedness and sense of direction, they found the semiconscious Urbino. Frieda returned to the Casa Verde to wait for the Contessa's return while Habib and Giorgio took Urbino to the Palazzo Uccello.

"A sad and busy night on quiet little Burano," the Contessa

had said in a troubled voice. "Thank God, you didn't have to wait longer to be rescued, or things might have turned out even worse. Have you no idea who that person in the fog was?"

"I can't even be absolutely sure if there was anyone at all. I was in such a state. And then there was the fog. It was conspiring against us all that night."

"Not all of us. It was a friend of the murderer, and murder it was!"

She had given him a sage look and nodded her head.

Urbino turned off the lights and left the library.

He would do what he could to set the Contessa's mind at ease, and also his own. A few discreet questions here and there, coming from a concerned citizen of the serene city, might generate the needed answers.

Suddenly, music blasted down the hall. It was a male voice singing of love and fate, of a woman's eyes and death, of travels and loneliness. It was a familiar song from his time in Morocco, one he had heard in cafés and long-distance taxis. Habib had told him that the words, which he had translated for him, were from a famous Arabic poem. It was one of Habib's favorites. He often played it, and usually at high volume.

Urbino smiled to himself. The Contessa had said that Habib was a mere boy, and Urbino had disagreed, but in situations like these, with music blasting so late into the night, he was inclined to agree with her.

3

T he wake of the Contessa's motorboat frothed the steely gray
lagoon as it made its way toward Burano.

Although the Contessa had complete faith in Urbino's ability
to deal with the Nina Crivelli affair, she was impatient. She
wasn't the kind of woman to be content to sit back and leave
things to others, even if the other was someone as trusted and
competent as Urbino.

During this period after the lace maker's death, his illness
would make it impossible for him to do little more than think
and plan from the confines of the Palazzo Uccello. What she
needed now was some action.

She had decided, after hours of contemplation in her *salotto
blu* and an almost sleepless night following her talk with Urbino, to do a little sleuthing around herself.

It would begin with a visit of charity.

As soon as Giorgio left her at the landing, the Contessa
found herself face to face with the ghost of Nina Crivelli. Death
notices of a bespectacled, but much younger Nina lined her
route to the center of town.

The funeral had been a hasty affair. Services at the Church
of San Martino yesterday morning had been followed with burial in a cemetery on the mainland. If Urbino had been well
enough to accompany her, she would have gone, but she hadn't
felt up to doing it alone.

Of course, she thought to herself as she approached Il Piccolo Nettuno, here she was striking out on her own bit of sleuthing with Urbino nowhere in sight. She was being inconsistent, she knew, but her vigil at the Ca' da Capo-Zendrini had impressed upon her that precious time couldn't be wasted.

On the door of the restaurant, beneath another death notice of Nina Crivelli, a sign informed her that the restaurant would be closed until tomorrow in memory of the lace maker.

The Crivelli apartment was in a rundown building near the Church of San Martino. In the light of day, she could see that it hadn't been enlivened with a coat of bright paint in a long time, or with any paint or whitewash at all. The only sound she heard was a television behind the ground-floor door.

The front door was open today. On the chipped and peeling wall in the entrance was a crude, faded drawing of a hammer and sickle.

Next to it was another obituary notice. Beneath the picture someone had scrawled *Strega!* in large red letters.

Strega, witch.

It was what Habib had called the old woman.

The first door on the second floor bore the faded name *Crivelli* on a piece of cardboard. The Contessa picked up the knocker and rapped it against the door, first softly, then more loudly when she received no response. It was not quite noon. Perhaps Salvatore was out on errands.

She was about to turn away when the door opened a few inches. A slice of Salvatore's face from one dark-circled eye to his beard-stubbled chin was visible.

"*Buon giorno*, Signor Crivelli. It's the Contessa da Capo-Zendrini."

Silence. The eye stared at her.

"I've come to give you my condolences on the death of your mother."

The silence of the hallway and the echo of her voice reminded her of her night visit to Il Piccolo Nettuno. Salvatore's eye continued to stare at her. It was shot with red. Hot breath mixed with the smell of wine came through the narrow crack.

"I—I've come to give you something."

She fumbled in her handbag and pulled out a large white envelope. Did she notice some quickening of interest in the eye?

"It's a Mass card. From the Church of the Madonna dell' Orto," she said, hearing the tremor in her voice. "A Mass will be celebrated every year in perpetuity on your mother's *onomastico*. Her baptismal name was Anna. Annina, she was called, and—and Nina. Am I right?" She realized she was showing her nervousness. "So, you see, Signor Crivelli, on Sant' Anna's Day a Mass will be said in her honor." She waited for a response, then added, "Every year, as I said."

The door started to close.

"Here!"

She thrust the envelope through the opening but before it got all the way through, the door closed completely.

The envelope was stuck between the door and the jamb. She tugged at it, thinking she would slip it under the door, but it wouldn't move. More loudly than any words Salvatore might have used, its blank, white surface spoke to her of her failure.

4

The Contessa hoped to have more success with the two lace makers. So far things were going along well.

The Contessa was acquainted with Gabriela Stival and her friend, Lidia Invernizzi, from her attempts to establish the lace making scholarship. Before she had admitted defeat, a generous amount of liras had flowed not only into Nina Crivelli's greedy hands, but also into those of the two more amiable women.

The lace makers seated across from her in Gabriela's parlor were almost textbook illustrations of how age sees fit to expand some people while diminishing and contracting others. The two women had enjoyed a youth neither buxom nor lean, to judge by a photograph—their eyes squinting into the sun and their arms thrown around each other's shoulders—that Gabriela had proudly shown the Contessa.

Over the years, Gabriela had increased in size and roundness. Lidia, however, had dwindled down into something resembling a sparrow, but a sparrow with a distinct preference for clean white lace collars and cuffs.

Gabriela, for her part, wore no lace at all, perhaps because she had dressed the parlor with every last scrap and piece in her possession. Where it didn't drip from lampshades and embrace pillows, it adorned picture frames and crept across tabletops, only to gather more energy to cascade from curtain rods and foam out of vases.

The three women had managed to dispense with the

weather and Lidia's recent mishap with an unmuzzled dog, as well as a cup of coffee and a slice of hazelnut cake by the time they were ready for the topic of death on Burano.

"Poor Nina Crivelli," Gabriela said with a huge sigh.

She straightened her spotless white apron. The Contessa had never seen either of the two women without this traditional accouterment of their art.

"So young to die," Lidia chirped between bites of her second portion of cake. Every time she swallowed a piece, she closed her eyes and seemed to concentrate as it was sent on its way.

The Contessa made appropriate commiserating sounds.

"I suppose her heart was no better than her eyes," she said.

"Much worse," Lidia said with a cackle.

She peered at the Contessa through horn-rimmed glasses that dwarfed her face.

"We all come blind into the world and blind we leave, especially us poor lace makers," Gabriela said, suppressing a smile.

She pulled the bows of her wire frames back over her ears.

"Hearts can go any time," Lidia said. "Sometimes long before the body."

Gabriela nodded.

"At least she was able to work until the end," the Contessa said.

"Washing and scrubbing and sweeping was all she was fit for, and sometimes throwing a meal together. Lidia and I just began a *tovaglia*."

A tablecloth usually took ten women three years to put together. The Contessa's quick computation had her marveling at her companions' faith in their longevity.

She admired the elaborate stitching of net and flowers of the table centerpiece.

"Ah, yes, Contessa, you have always appreciated our difficult work," Gabriela said, stretching her apron across her lap. It immediately began to shrink back.

"You would have made an excellent lace maker," little Lidia added.

The Contessa hoped her slight regretful smile communicated what she had missed despite the richness of her life.

"But how impossible it would have been for me, dear ladies, to ever match your own excellent work, or that of poor Nina Crivelli, in her prime, I mean."

"Nina was never very good," shot back Lidia.

"Beware of a lace maker who works alone," Gabriela said. "They're crafty. God only knows what they're thinking."

"I see what you mean."

"Her mind was always wandering. When we work together, we talk, yes," Lidia said, "but it's our way of keeping our minds sharp, sharp, sharp on the work. Patience and concentration are the virtues of a woman dedicated to the stitch."

"That has always been my impression," the Contessa agreed.

"And Nina Crivelli, God rest her soul," Lidia forged on, "wasn't a woman dedicated to the stitch. To nothing but herself and her son." She darted a look at the Contessa. "That's why she didn't understand your good efforts on behalf of our art."

"I'm sorry to hear that."

All things come to those who wait. The Contessa inquired about the recipe for the hazelnut cake. She accepted another cup of coffee. She admired an antimacassar. She listened as Lidia gave her a lecture on *punto in aria*. She studiously examined a specimen of this difficult lace point in the form of a doily with wide volutes, flowers in relief, and borders of thick cording, as if she needed to memorize each detail.

Then Gabriela, with an air of exasperation, observed abruptly, "Nina Crivelli recited a poem over and over again. It was about you, Contessa."

"About me?"

"Exactly. *We've had our Contessa Marcello, and we want no Contessa Uccello.* Her own little poem. Just those words, weren't they, Lidia?"

The other woman bobbed her head.

"Lidia and I got very angry, and we argued with her. We told her what kind things you've done, and how good you could be for Burano and lace making, but she was impossible. She would hear none of it."

"The Contessa Uccello?" The Contessa was mystified. "She meant me?"

Uccello meant *bird,* as she well knew, and it was the name of Urbino's palazzo. The building had some vague association with the painter Paolo Doni, called Uccello. The fact that Lidia looked so much like a bird made the whole thing more confusing. She felt her face flush.

"You exactly, Contessa!" Gabriela confirmed.

"And the Contessa Marcello? What did she mean by that?"

"Oh, surely you know," Gabriela said. "The Contessa Adriana Marcello."

The Contessa had an almost irrepressible desire to reach out and shake the woman.

"The Contessa Adriana Marcello and Francesca Memmo," Gabriela supplied.

Then it was back to Lidia, who piped out, "Yes, La Scarpaiola!"

The Contessa felt as if half her wit and most of her Italian had somehow flown away and was nestling somewhere in the room amidst all the lace. Were they talking about a woman who made shoes? Maybe one who wore big boots? It was as if they were playing a maddening guessing game with her. Her irritation rose.

The two women, the one with her round fleshy face and the other with her sharp narrow one, stared at her with almost identical smug expressions.

The Contessa strained her mind as some associations, finally and thankfully, started to squeeze through. Before she could seize hold of them, Lidia began to explain with a quick, self-satisfied air.

"The Contessa Adriana Marcello helped to establish our lace school! More than a hundred years ago. It was through the kind support of Queen Margarita."

"I remember!" the Contessa cried out as if her life depended upon it. "And Francesca Memmo was the seventy-year-old lace maker who was the only person left alive who still knew the secret of the *punto buranese!*"

"*Brava!*" both women cried out at once.

"But why did she call me the Contessa Uccello?"

"Quite simple! Because of your Signor Urbino of the Palazzo Uccello!" explained Lidia.

The Contessa was aware of the deep pockets of resentment against her in Venice, where some people couldn't accept her marrying into the Da Capo-Zendrini family. She had enemies of a certain sort, men and women who cut her at social affairs, tried to undermine her work for local charities, and in general did everything they could to remind her that Venice could never be her home as it was theirs. Her close friendship with Urbino, whose relationship to the city was even more ambiguous in their eyes, only added fuel to the flames.

But this didn't answer the question of why Nina Crivelli, a lace maker from Burano, had felt animosity not only against her but, it appeared, Urbino as well. Even the grumblings about her failed lace making scholarships didn't explain things.

As if Gabriela read the Contessa's mind, she said, "It was all for no good reason that she could ever give. We told her that you had always shown the greatest generosity and kindness to us all, and that we had never heard a bad word against Signor Urbino."

"Nina had a mean spirit, God rest her soul," Lidia offered as a further explanation. "Always speaking against you as soon as your back was turned. She knew things about other people that they had forgotten themselves—or wanted to! She didn't have a friend in the world. To think she was a mother! Such a mother! Children didn't want to be within ten feet of her."

"Did she say anything against me in a specific way?"

"Of course not, our dear Contessa! What could she have said?" Gabriela protested. "And if she ever tried! We would have stuffed a *tombola* in her mouth, yes, wouldn't we have, Lidia?"

The laughter of the two lace makers had a sharp, malicious edge. The Contessa tried to show no emotion, neither inappropriate humor nor the consternation that was rising in her. The image of Nina with the lace handkerchief by her mouth, half in, half out, rose before her eyes.

"I saw Salvatore Crivelli today," she said, feeling tightness in her throat.

"How's that, Contessa?" asked Lidia.

The Contessa sensed a quickening of interest in the two women.

"I stopped by his apartment to give him a Mass card."

"A Mass card?" repeated Gabriela. "For Nina Crivelli? She wasn't a pious woman, and neither is her son. Her funeral was the first time in twenty years either of those two souls ever saw the inside of a church."

Lidia leaned toward the Contessa.

"Was Salvatore happy to get it?"

A smile quirked the corners of her lips.

The Contessa told them what had happened.

"What can you expect? It's bad manners, and more than that," Gabriela said. "He didn't have a tear in him all during the service."

"But more wine than the sacristy," Lidia added.

"He'll drink all the more now," Gabriela said. "To celebrate."

"They didn't get along?"

"Never!"

Gabriela's response was seconded by a quick nod from Lidia, whose eyes were closed as she took another swallow of cake.

"But we never heard him complain, did we, Lidia?" The other woman shook her head. "And there was plenty to complain about. She kept him all to herself in that house. I can imagine what it was like, having her as a mother, always at his elbow, following him to work, never giving him a moment's peace! A mother's love can be a curse when the mother is Nina Crivelli. Oh, he suffered, you can be sure. Suffered every day of his life since he was a boy. Mothers deserve respect, but she was impossible. Doesn't the Bible say to put aside your mother when you take a wife? He should have put her far, far away!"

"Salvatore was married?"

"*Is* married for all we know," corrected Lidia, her round eyes now wide open.

"Where is his wife?"

"You mean his wife and son," Lidia said. "Somewhere in Germany."

"Switzerland," Gabriela corrected. "Some more cake, Contessa?"

"No thank you. It's quite delicious, though."

"Germany! It was Germany," Lidia insisted.

"Switzerland! Roberto the mailman said Salvatore got postcards from Zurich."

"Berlin!"

"Berlin, and with a seven-year-old child? That's almost in Russia."

"When did she leave Burano?"

"Twenty years ago in May," Gabriela said.

"When she went to Germany!" threw in Lidia. "Your geography was always upside down. Berlin is nowhere near Russia! It's right up against the Contessa's England!"

The ringing of the doorbell ended the dispute. It was Gabriela's grandchildren. After admiring the two little girls and listening to them recite a poem together, the Contessa said her good-byes.

5

Y ou were wrong," the Contessa said to Urbino over the telephone from the Ca' da Capo-Zendrini that evening. "And as you see, you're involved yourself."

Her voice held a distinct note of satisfaction.

" 'The Contessa Uccello,' she called me," the Contessa said with quiet emphasis. "She disliked us both for whatever peculiar reason. A strange and unpredictable woman, no matter what you said the other night in her defense. But I'll agree about one thing. She didn't have anything to tell me—to *sell* me—about my wonderful Alvise. How could I have thought such a thing? Maybe it was you she was talking about!"

"Me?"

"And why not you? You're an eternal source of speculation. Going off to Morocco didn't help. You had almost become a familiar figure, but now people might be seeing you with new eyes! I know I'm flying off in all directions, but you need to get some focus yourself. And some proportion as well."

"All of which might be true," he conceded, "but at the moment we're concerned with Nina Crivelli."

"I'm trying to tell you that it all could be related. You and Habib and mothers and—and the rest," she finished, somewhat lamely.

"Habib?"

"Well, she singled him out for special attention, didn't she? And—and he called her a witch!"

"Not to her face."

"Oh, I know I'm not making much sense. How is the boy?" she asked, almost as an afterthought.

"Fine. He went to Vicenza yesterday with his language school."

"How nice. He doesn't seem the type to appreciate Palladian architecture, though."

"Perhaps not, but he seems to have had a good time. But to get back to Nina Crivelli, Barbara, aren't you forgetting that she was badgering you before I returned?"

"I'm not forgetting one single, solitary thing! She was a monstrous old woman," and then she added, somewhat guilty, "God rest her soul. Filled with venom and the wrong kind of mother love. And you can be sure she was spinning some fine web, and it wasn't made of lace! She collected information about people. Some do it for perverse amusement, but others do it to sell to the highest bidder, waiting for it to go up in value! The time had come for Nina Crivelli to market me! Or you! Or me *and* you!"

"At least you're leaving Habib out of it this time," Urbino said with dry humor.

"The Contessa Uccello, Nina said, and don't forget it. When you get on your feet, you'll have to start tending to things farther away from home."

6

U rbino had only a few moments to reflect about his conversation with the Contessa when the doorbell rang.

Natalia hadn't gone for the night. Shortly, she opened the door of the parlor after a discreet knock.

"Signora Hensel. Signora Bauma."

"But we are *signorine!*" Frieda called out as she strode into the room. She was carrying two small, brightly wrapped packages.

The tall, aristocratic-looking Beatrix Bauma, her hands behind her back, stood in the doorway and surveyed Urbino with a quick, amused glance.

He wasn't wearing the cap that had so preoccupied the Contessa several evenings earlier. The pointed slippers were on his feet, however, and he had donned an embroidered *jellaba* over a brightly colored pair of cotton pajamas in expectation of his visitors. Now that he was well on the way to mending, he enjoyed playing the invalid even more, especially with Habib's pampering.

"Would you like anything before I leave, Signor Urbino?" Natalia asked.

"No, thank you. I can manage."

Dressed in a long, belted dark-brown dress, Beatrix sauntered further into the room, her hands still behind her back.

"Oh, here, signora," Frieda said. She held out a woolen scarf, more muted than the silk one of bright blue-and-yellow tied flamboyantly around her head. "I forgot to give you this."

Frieda spoke in flawless, unaccented Italian.

Natalia took the scarf with something close to a strained little bow that Urbino had never seen her indulge in before. As she was closing the door, she threw a peculiar look at Beatrix's back.

"How comfortable you look!" Frieda said with a big smile. "And all prepared for Barbara's costume ball, I see. Ha, ha!"

"All I need is a mask," he said.

Beatrix looked as if she wanted to say something in response. Suppressed merriment danced in her eyes.

"You are better?" Frieda asked.

"Much better, thank you. Where's Marie?"

"She is tired from all the walking, poor little bird," Beatrix said. "She sends her greetings."

Frieda held the packages out to him.

"The one in blue paper is from me."

He unwrapped it. It was an elaborately decorated wax candle.

"I brought it from Munich. Maybe it will chase away the germs!"

"If I can bring myself to use it instead of keeping it as it is. It's lovely."

He opened the other package, which was wrapped in Venetian marbleized paper. It was a compact disc of Mozart's *Requiem.*

The Austrian woman laughed.

"Marie made a joke. I am happy to see you are far from a requiem! Where is Habib?"

"In his studio. Would you like a drink? Or perhaps some coffee or tea?"

"Some grappa," Frieda said.

"Red wine for me," Beatrix said.

When Urbino turned around from the bar with their drinks, a tall, frozen-faced dark figure was standing silently beside Frieda. A large cone-shaped beak concealed its nose and mouth.

A muffled moaning sound broke the sudden stillness in the room.

"Enough! Enough!" Frieda cried out. "He will need the *Requiem* if you continue!"

Beatrix untied the mask from her face and put it down on the table.

"I thought I would bring a little precaution in case you have something contagious."

The mask was that of a plague doctor, and could be found in any of the mask shops in Venice. Along with a black tunic, large black-framed glasses, full black gloves, and a thick wooden stick, it was one of the popular costumes for Carnevale. Centuries earlier, it had been the indispensable outfit for doctors taking care of plague victims. A piece of cloth soaked with a fumigating substance was placed in the cone to protect the wearer from the plague.

"She is always buying a new mask," Frieda said. "Soon she'll have more than you. But where have yours gone?"

Her slightly protruding eyes sought out the place on the wall where his collection of Venetian masks used to hang. A brightly colored carpet in a naive design now occupied the spot.

"I've stored them. They made Habib uncomfortable."

"A very impressionable and sensitive boy, yes."

She seated herself on the sofa next to Urbino. Beatrix was about to take the wing easy chair across from them when her eye was caught by something on a nearby table. She went over and picked up a carved wood diptych with miniatures of Giovanni Bellini's aloof Madonnas.

"Habib is lucky to have all these lovely things around him to inspire him." She replaced the diptych. Her eye quickly ran over some of the other objects in the room. "I would love to have a talk with him about his work. I didn't get a chance at the party to ask him what he was painting on Burano. He was there with his painting kit the day before."

"He was?" Urbino said. "He hasn't mentioned it to me, but it is an artist's paradise with all those colors."

"You say that he is working?" Beatrix asked. "Would you mind if I slipped out for a few minutes to see the boy?"

She was gone before Urbino had a chance to tell her which of the rooms was Habib's studio.

"You see how free Beatrix makes herself in your house," Frieda said after taking a sip of grappa. "I think she likes it even more than I do, if such a thing is possible."

"I'm happy you found it to your liking, and Beatrix too. Did you meet here in Venice?"

"Yes. We have become good friends, the three of us."

"Where are they staying?"

"Not far from here. In an apartment by the boat landing for Burano. But enough about Beatrix. You must tell me all about Habib. We writers like details, you know! How you met and such things. He is a delightful boy."

"We met in the medina in Fez. His family has a house there."

"And so?"

"One afternoon, when I was walking in the medina, someone pushed against me and I fell on the ground. Before I knew what had happened, my wallet and passport were gone."

"And this was Habib? I would not have imagined it!"

"Oh, not Habib. Quite the opposite. He came to my rescue."

"Most interesting!"

"He saw the whole thing from a café. He chased after the boy. A few minutes later he brought back my wallet and passport."

"And with all the money in it?"

"Yes."

"A very clever creature!"

Urbino gave her a sharp look.

"What do you mean by that?"

She looked embarrassed.

"It was quite clever of him to act quickly. Were the police involved?"

"Morocco isn't a country where you want to have much business with them, even when you're on the right side. That had been my impression. And Habib said it would do no good and could only draw attention to him—and to me."

"I see."

"The police there have a way of making a young man's life difficult," Urbino explained, disliking his defensive tone but unable to banish it. "I had a good example of that about a week later, also in Fez."

"Attention was drawn to him—and to you?" she asked, echoing his words.

"Yes, but he was the one in danger. It was when we were leaving the medina one evening. I stopped outside the gate to examine something I had bought. Habib walked on ahead. When I looked up, two policemen were talking to him. He was showing them his identity card."

Urbino poured himself more wine.

"I hurried over," he said as he reseated himself beside Frieda. "The policemen were taking him away. A police wagon was parked a few feet off. They cruise all over town, stopping to check identity cards. It's awful to see them filled with these young guys. I asked if he had showed them his university identity card. He was in his last year. He had, he said, but they didn't care. I don't know what came over me, but I actually started babbling in more Arabic than I thought I knew."

Frieda was drinking it all in with a writer's curiosity.

"Something popped into my head. He was my student, I said, and a good student. My Arabic was rather limited, but it worked. The policeman holding Habib looked at me closely, then at Habib. Without saying anything, he let go of Habib's arm. They got back into the wagon and drove off. I can't tell you how relieved I was."

"But you weren't his teacher, or were you?"

"It was a lie. I was putting my neck out. I suppose it would have been even worse for him, if they had bothered to check. It was a wild gamble."

"You saved him, and he saved you."

Frieda's imagination seemed to be giving the story a shape already. It made him feel uncomfortable.

Footsteps sounded in the hallway. Frieda stood up.

"I must get back to Burano, but I'd like to say good evening to your brave rescuer."

Beatrix re-entered the parlor.

"I cannot find Habib anywhere."

"I am sure you searched every corner, yes!" Frieda said. "Urbino will think you are a strange guest, my dear. But come. We must be on our way. Don't forget your mask! No, Urbino, you don't have to show us out. We know our way. You continue to get well so that you can visit me—you and Habib together."

7

U rbino's own search through the Palazzo Uccello revealed that Habib had gone out.

He often went for walks at night without telling Urbino. At first Urbino had been uneasy until he returned, but he had gradually become more relaxed about it. In Morocco it had been Habib who had been concerned by Urbino's unaccompanied walks into remote parts of the Fez medina.

Urbino returned to Habib's studio. The poster of Habib's favorite Arab diva stared out at him with her wide-eyed gaze.

Habib had tidied up the room. The paints and brushes were all in their places, the rags were arranged on the rack, the divan was made up, and the cassettes of Arabic music were in neat rows on the shelf. The ingenious storage and drying cupboards that Habib had constructed were closed and securely locked. Habib was jealous of his own space and became upset at any intrusion, whether it was by Urbino or Natalia. Urbino attributed it to the severely cramped quarters Habib had endured in his family's house.

In the library, he reclined on the sofa with a volume of Veronica Franco's love sonnets. Franco, a famous sixteenth-century courtesan and poet, who established a home in Dorsoduro for former prostitutes, was one of the women he was including in his new book.

He fell asleep before he had read through one sonnet, good

though it was. He was awakened by Habib's footsteps on the staircase.

"*Sidi*!" Habib exclaimed. "You are still up." He tossed his burnoose on the back of a chair. "It is late."

Urbino squinted at the clock. A few minutes past midnight.

"I hope you weren't worrying about me. I was fine."

Urbino started to close the lights and gather together some of his books and notes. Habib, however, was always a few steps or seconds ahead of him, and anticipated what he wanted to do.

"I walked all over the city, and went over all the bridges— or down the bridges, the way that you say in Italian! And I spent too much time in the Piazza."

"A lot of time, you mean. That is, unless you really do mean too much time."

"You are a little upset with me, I think. A *tisane* will help."

"No, thank you. By the way, Habib, have you ever been to Burano without me? Believe me, I don't care if you have. You know I want you to strike out on your own and do whatever you want as long as you're careful. But it might be just as easy for you to get confused here as it was for me in Morocco. You remember how many mistakes I was always making."

Habib nodded with amusement.

"But never any bad ones. Everyone liked you."

"I'm pleased that you think so. But listen, Habib, there are certain things about Burano that are on my mind these days."

"Because of the death of the old woman with the evil eye?"

"She's part of it. There might be problems for you, because of your association with me. I'm not saying you shouldn't go there. Just let me know when you do. Beatrix Bauma, the Austrian woman, said that she saw you there the day before Frieda's party. Did you go there to do some painting?"

Habib's dark, thickly lashed eyes met his and looked away.

"There is plenty to paint everywhere else, *sidi*."

"Does that mean you weren't there?"

"You make it sound like I would go there for a bad reason. I would never do that. You will not be disappointed in me. I swear to you."

There was an appeal and sincerity in his words.

But he hadn't said whether he had been there or not.

Urbino weighed his own desire to know with the need to trust him, his concern for Habib with his determination not to interfere where it wasn't appropriate. What had the Contessa said while he was recuperating? That he would strike the proper balance between encouraging Habib's independence and looking after him? At least she had faith that he would be eventually able to accomplish what didn't seem at all easy at the moment.

Habib looked weary.

"I'm only trying to look out for you. You know what that means, don't you?"

Habib nodded.

"Protect me."

"Right. Well, it's late." Urbino paused at the door. "I'll give you an easy one this time. The daughter of your brother's wife."

"My niece," Habib said with a smile. "But if his wife was married before, she is my stair-niece. No, my step-niece! Did you think of that?"

Urbino admitted he hadn't.

8

T o think this is the first place you want to see as soon as
you're well enough to get out," the Contessa said as she
stepped along the leaf-strewn path on Urbino's arm.

"It restores my sense of proportion," he responded.

It was three days after the Contessa had visited him at the
Palazzo Uccello. They were in the Protestant graveyard on the
cemetery island of San Michele. Old markers, eaten away by
time and weather, were scattered in the unkempt grass beneath
the twisted trees. Some of their surfaces were as smooth as the
wall that separated the area from the lagoon.

They approached an oval of grass and ivy with a squat urn
of fresh-cut flowers. It was the grave of Ezra Pound.

"How sad that Olga Rudge has gone too," the Contessa observed. "She could have been of help with your new book."

"If I could have believed what she told me. Tea with Olga,
from what I understand, involved listening to all of the reasons
why Pound hadn't been anti-Semitic, beginning with the fact
that his first name was the good old Hebrew one of *Ezra*."

"But isn't that your job, *caro*? To sort out the lies from the
truth?"

This wasn't the first time this morning that she had reminded him indirectly of his promise to try to get to the bottom
of the Nina Crivelli affair as soon as he had recuperated. She
also kept hinting about one or two things she wanted to tell
him, but he had so far succeeded in putting her off.

They continued in silence as they went out the door and passed beneath rows of burial niches. Another door, this one in a brick wall, brought them into the Orthodox section. It was simpler and more ordered than the Protestant graveyard, and not as overgrown with vegetation.

The Contessa proceeded down the path to Diaghilev's grave by the far wall. Beyond the wall was a marshy waste, and beyond that stretched the lagoon.

A ballet slipper lay on top of the tombstone, like an offering on an altar. It was moldy and misshapen, and resembled a miniature coffin filled with decayed leaves and withered flower petals.

"There's always a new one," the Contessa said. "Just once I'd like to see who leaves them."

"No, you wouldn't. It would destroy the romantic mystery."

She contemplated the slipper in silence, then turned to him.

"I do like romantic mysteries. But what we have is one that's not at all romantic, not like a slipper on a grave, and I *do* want to know. I *need* to know. You haven't even mentioned her name this morning. I've felt like screaming. *Nina Crivelli!*"

Her voice drew the attention of a lone woman in a large fur hat, who was a few feet away at the grave of Stravinsky and his wife.

"I've been trying to find out a few more things," she went on in a lower voice. "I went to Il Piccolo Nettuno for lunch the day after I spoke with Gabriela and Lidia. Salvatore was working. He didn't say a word that he didn't need to. I had really gone to see Regina Bella, but the cook said she went to Milan for a few days. Salvatore runs the place in her absence, so I assume she must trust him."

She linked her arm through Urbino's as they followed a path beside a wall. They were surrounded by tombs with Russian and Greek names, of princesses and various assorted aristocrats.

"I asked some questions of the women at the lace stalls. Oh, I was very careful, or I think I was. I could only get scattered information, since I didn't want to be obvious, but two women said exactly what Gabriela and Lidia said." She gave him a quick look to see if she had all his attention. "Nina wanted Salvatore all to herself. Her kind of love made his life a misery. She drove away her daughter-in-law and grandson twenty years ago, to Germany, they insisted. The two of them never came back to Burano."

"Or were never seen *if* they did."

She looked at him with a smile and patted his arm.

"Good boy! You haven't deserted me. You're thinking!"

He had been, indeed, but he wasn't ready to give her the benefit of what were, so far, unformed thoughts and vague suspicions. Yet he was sure of one thing. The mystery surrounding Nina Crivelli, which, before her death, he had feared would turn out to be banal, was surely anything but that.

When they left the Orthodox section, they took one of the paths that would eventually get them to the Da Capo-Zendrini mausoleum. January was a time when the Conte Alvise was on the Contessa's mind even more than usual, for it was the month they had married.

On their way to the mausoleum, the Contessa greeted some of the women and men looking after the graves of their loved ones. She stopped to have a conversation with a black-garbed old woman accompanied by a young girl of six or seven.

Urbino only half-listened. He was thinking about Frieda and Beatrix. He hadn't yet told the Contessa about their visit. There were one or two things about it that he needed to mull over in his own mind.

They resumed their slow pace in silence. The Contessa frowned when she caught sight of a field of graves in the grim process of being exhumed now that the dead's twelve-year tenancy was over. Many families only rented burial space for this relatively brief period of time.

Soon the impressive Da Capo-Zendrini mausoleum with its statues of weeping angels, St. Catherine of Siena, and St. Nicholas of Bari rose before them. The statues and the building itself had recently been cleaned and had a strange glow in the winter light. Urbino preferred them the way they used to be, but said nothing.

The Contessa seemed more abstracted than before. She must have been thinking of the recent November when she had come face to face with death and taken refuge in the mausoleum.

But when she broke the silence, it was to show that something else was on her mind.

"Seeing the signora's little granddaughter a few minutes ago reminds me of something I forgot to tell you. There was a girl about her age at one of the lace shops the other day. She heard her mother and me talking about Nina Crivelli. Nina had the *mal'occhio*, the little girl piped up. Remember what Lidia said. Children always kept their distance from her. She might have been a mother, but not the kind that had children running to her bosom! Quite the opposite!"

The Contessa took a large key from her purse and approached the iron doors. She paused at the steps and turned to him.

"That's also what Habib said. She had the evil eye," she reminded him.

9

T hat afternoon Urbino and Habib went into the Basilica San
Marco. Habib had arranged to meet two friends to examine
the bronze horses.

The Basilica had quickly become one of Habib's favorite
buildings, as soon as Urbino had assured him that there weren't
any bodies of saints displayed for public view. Urbino thought it
had something to do with the vaguely mosque-like quality of the
building, despite all of its gems, gold leaf, and brightly colored
mosaics representing the human figure. In fact, Habib loved the
mosaics, and he had a special preference for the animals and fish.
He enjoyed walking up in the stone balconies for a closer look.

"I'll wait until your friends arrive," Urbino said on this occasion. They were in the portico of the church. "Then I'll go to
Florian's. When you're finished, you can all come over, and we
can have something to eat. How's that?"

"Okay," Habib said.

"Maybe they're inside," Urbino said after a few minutes.

They went into the large domed and niched space of the
church and started to walk slowly around. There were only a
few other people.

"I don't see them anywhere," Habib said. After a few
minutes, however, he stopped searching for his friends and began to examine the mosaics.

Urbino seated himself in one of the chairs. He would let
Habib make a circuit on his own. Urbino sometimes found it

difficult not to give in to the temptation of an informative, but intrusive commentary.

The Basilica invariably put Urbino in a meditative frame of mind, and this afternoon was no exception. He stared up at the dome above him, and started to think about Nina Crivelli.

He hadn't proceeded far when his thoughts were broken into by raised voices coming from the direction of the Pala D'Oro. One of the voices was Habib's. Urbino rushed over. A well dressed, elderly man with a walking stick was berating Habib.

"A disgrace!" he said. "Begging in a Catholic church. The Basilica no less! Go to your own kind of church! And go back to your own country! The Cardinal is right!"

He was referring to the conservative archbishop of Bologna, who had singled out Muslim immigrants as a distinct threat to Italy. He began to spout some of the Cardinal's racist ideas in an outraged tone.

Fortunately, all of this was in Italian, and Habib couldn't understand most of it. But the man's venom didn't need to be translated. It was all too evident.

"What's going on?" Urbino said to Habib.

"This man is barking at me, *sidi*. I don't know why. I was praying, minding my own affairs. Can't a Muslim pray in your church?"

Urbino immediately understood. Habib had been offering his prayers with his palms upturned, in the Muslim manner.

The man now addressed Urbino.

"You know this person?"

"He's my friend."

The man gave a look that swept Urbino from head to toe, then back again.

"Indeed! Then take your friend out of here. It is disgraceful."

"It is you, sir, who are disgraceful. We leave you to your own prayers."

He put his arm around Habib's shoulder, and they walked away.

"Let's look for your friends."

"They are too late," Habib said in a low voice. "Let's go home."

As midnight neared, Urbino stood in sole possession of the Accademia Bridge.

He had left a morose Habib at the Palazzo Uccello. The episode in the Basilica that afternoon had depressed Habib, and then something Urbino had said that evening had somehow precipitated an even darker mood.

They had been reminiscing about a trip to Tangier, when Urbino had tried to get Habib to go swimming, and had started to pull him into the sea. Habib, who had once said that he knew how to swim, had fought back furiously. He hadn't spoken to Urbino for the rest of the day. Urbino had attributed it to Habib's remarkably strong will, which seldom asserted itself, but when it did, it did so with a surprising power.

When Urbino mentioned the episode tonight, Habib had started to tremble, with what might have been either fear or anger. Urbino had dropped the topic.

Urbino breathed in the cold air. It was a clear night. Stars, scattered above him all the way down the Grand Canal, seemed to find companions in the lights sparkling from the windows in the palazzi.

The resumption of his night walks was the best proof he could give himself that he was well. Although he had walked briskly, he was not out of breath, nor did he feel weak. When Habib had protested that he shouldn't go out tonight, he had assured him that he was up to it.

He looked out at the quiet scene. Hardly a building was without an association for him, whether it was historical, personal, or professional—or amateur, he reminded himself, since one or two of them had been related to his sleuthing.

He had gone to several receptions with the Contessa at the Palazzo Barbaro on the left. Browning, Sargent, and James had all been either guests or residents at the Gothic building. James had not only written a Venetian tale of greed and loneliness within its sumptuously decorated walls, but had also used it as a setting for a haunting chronicle of betrayal and undying love.

Beyond the Palazzo Barbaro, and standing in slight retirement from the edge of the Grand Canal, was a much smaller and far more humble structure, the Casetta delle Rose. The controversial poet, Gabriele d'Annunzio, had lived there. It carried Urbino back to an autumn when he had done a bit of delicate sleuthing that involved two brutal murders on the Rialto and an aristocrat under the spell of d'Annunzio. This had been when the Contessa had scrambled for her life into the family tomb, as he had recalled that morning.

On the opposite side of the canal was the imposing Palazzo Contarini-Polignac, whose landing stage was being washed by the wake of a *vaporetto* making its way to Santa Lucia. He had spent many hours gazing at its Renaissance facade while writing his biography of Proust, who had been a guest of the Polignacs.

Further down was the eighteenth-century Palazzo Venier dai Leoni, known to Venetians as the Palazzo Incompiuto, or the *unfinished palace*, because nothing beyond a ground floor had ever been completed, giving it a decidedly odd look. Peggy Guggenheim had bought it after the Second World War to house her pioneering collection of modern art.

For Urbino, however, the palazzo was indelibly associated with the murder of a beautiful young artist's model, whose drowned body had been washed up on its steps while he was visiting the collection. Only after considerable effort had he been able to sort out the dark secrets that had led her to that end.

As he leaned on the wooden parapet of the bridge, he allowed his mind to play over some of the aspects of this case, which had touched upon the Contessa as his present one was doing.

The death of the young model had seemed to be a suicide, but Urbino's sleuthing had exposed it as a murder. Now he was face to face with the apparently natural death of an old woman, and all of his intuition cried out that this too was murder.

A chill wind gusted up the Grand Canal. He gathered his cape more securely around him and walked down the steps of the bridge into Dorsoduro.

He struck out with renewed vigor through the funereally silent Campo Carità and around the edge of the Accademia Gallery. He then entered the network of alleys and bridges that would eventually bring him to the Church of Santa Maria della Salute.

The only sounds were the lapping of water against stone and the hulls of moored boats and an occasional cry of a cat or muted laughter from one of the apartments above him. He went beneath the dark windows of the Palazzo Cini with its neglected collection of Tuscan paintings, across the Campo San Vio, and down a *calle* to a quay beside a small, picturesque canal.

On the other side of the canal was Polidoro's shuttered gallery. He reminded himself that he needed to visit the art dealer and pursue the topic of Habib's paintings.

He didn't slow down until he reached the corner of the bent *calle* where the Palazzo Venier dai Leoni had its entrance. The gate was closed, but its graceful wrought-ironwork with embedded, colored stones, hinted at Peggy Guggenheim's taste that was more flamboyantly displayed within.

He was about to resume his way when a sudden realization struck him. He had been wrong about the relative silence of the night. Footsteps had been sounding behind him; quiet, cautious, but persistent. They had stopped when he had paused at the gate.

It wasn't an unusual occurrence. On other occasions footsteps would sound behind him as if they were following him and keeping pace with him. It was one of the deceptive tricks of the stone and water of Venice that the footsteps could turn out to be your own, or those of someone unseen walking ahead of you, or down a parallel or intersecting *calle*. And yet Urbino was sure that this wasn't one of those occasions.

He lingered in front of the gate. Should he retrace his steps or continue to the Salute?

The decision was made for him when someone turned the corner from the canal embankment. Dimly illuminated was a tall figure. Urbino stood without moving as the figure came closer and resolved itself into a man in a wool cap. He was walking unsteadily. At one point he leaned against the wall of the palazzo garden.

Urbino waited. The man approached. He lurched toward Urbino, who moved away. The sour smell of wine struck his nostrils. The man gave Urbino a quick, sidelong glance as he passed. He weaved down the narrow *calle* toward a bridge that crossed to the Campiello Barbaro.

Urbino made his way slowly in the same direction, keeping his ears sharp for any unusual sound. The air was colder as it blew toward him from the canal ahead.

When he reached the other side of the bridge, the drunken man was nowhere in sight. The darkness, however, could have concealed him in any number of places.

Urbino hurried past the garden wall of the little square, down another bridge, and plunged beneath a dark, damp *sottoportego*.

It was here that footsteps sounded behind him again, but whether they were the same ones as before, he couldn't tell. They sounded the same—soft, slightly hesitant, but persistent. He quickened his gait through the enclosed passageway. Although the *sottoporteghi* scattered throughout the city were picturesque and rather unusual features that he enjoyed seeking out, they weren't the safest places on dark, lonely nights like this, especially when someone might be stalking you.

As soon as this thought registered on Urbino's consciousness, his momentary fear gave way to a vague feeling of embarrassment. He nonetheless hurried past the de-sanctified

Benedictine church and monastery, went down another small bridge, and finally gained the Campo della Salute. The white dome and scrolls of the church rose dimly above him, conveying a sense of peculiar comfort.

The *vaporetto* was pulling away from the Salute landing on its slow trip to the Cannaregio. Urbino strained to hear beyond the sounds generated by the boat, but heard nothing other than its comforting throb and the wash of its wake. When these had subsided, he was once again surrounded by the melancholy, brimming silence that was nighttime Venice.

His mind wandered back to the thoughts of murder, Nina Crivelli, and the Contessa that had absorbed him on the Accademia Bridge.

Was it possible, he asked himself as he listened for any unusual or unexpected sound, that the Contessa was in fact indirectly responsible for Crivelli's death—for her murder, he quickly corrected himself? He needed to keep his mind focused on this probability. Nina Crivelli had been murdered.

Could the Contessa's two visits to Burano have set into motion a desperate attempt to discourage further questions about the lace maker and her death? Urbino, as her closest friend, with a well-known reputation for sleuthing, could also have become a target. And even Habib could be in some kind of danger, if the murderer thought he was snooping around Burano on Urbino's behalf. Beatrix had said she had seen Habib on Burano, but Habib had neither confirmed nor denied it. It was possible he had been there on many occasions. But if he had, why wouldn't he have told Urbino about it? It didn't make sense. On the other hand, what reason might Beatrix have had for saying she had seen Habib there when she hadn't? Was there any way that she might profit by such a lie?

The immediate fruit of all these thoughts was Urbino's decision not to seek out the Punta della Dogana on the other side of the church as he had originally planned. The area, with its serene view of the Basin of San Marco and the Giudecca Canal, was never so isolated as at this time of night.

The Santa Maria del Giglio *traghetto* had stopped ferrying

passengers hours ago. The *vaporetto* would take him the short distance across the Grand Canal. From there he would make his long walk back to the Palazzo Uccello.

He seated himself on a bench with his back to the Grand Canal. It gave him a view of the looming mass of the Salute and its *campo*. He was reminded of the episode with the emotionally disturbed woman, which had upset Habib so much.

Occasionally his eye strayed to the bridge, obscured by shadows, which led to the former Benedictine monastery. In all the time he sat watching until the boat arrived, he saw nothing but a scene as still as a photograph.

11

The part of the Dorsoduro quarter that Urbino had walked through late the night before looked different in the light of day. The dark theater set was now illuminated beneath a bright mid-morning sun in a blue sky, and alive with residents and a scattering of tourists, who went about their respective affairs with a sense of purpose.

After having *tramezzini* sandwiches and a coffee near the Accademia, he made his way to Marino Polidoro's art gallery. Last night it had been all shuttered and closed in on itself. Now its sign was clearly visible, as were the carefully selected items behind its large windows.

It had an ideal location near the intersection of two canals behind the Guggenheim Museum. The front room was crammed with art, furniture, and various objects from the sixteenth to the nineteenth century. Urbino had no reason to doubt the authenticity of any of them. The provenance of whatever he and the Contessa had bought from Polidoro had been well documented and beyond any question.

And yet rumors circulated about his unscrupulousness in getting his hands on something that he wanted. Urbino had discounted much of the gossip as either the expected backbiting of his profession or an unsympathetic reaction to the man's appearance. For there was no doubt that Polidoro was not just ugly, but grotesquely so because of his small, misshapen body.

"I thought I'd drop by since I'm in the area," Urbino said.

"Very good! I have something special that has come my way. It's been waiting for your appreciation."

And my money, Urbino said silently to himself, for although he believed Polidoro was maligned, no one had ever exaggerated his love for money.

Polidoro handed Urbino a miniature pastel portrait of a lightly powdered old woman with a fan. The color and the expression were delicate.

"Rosalba Carriera?" Urbino asked.

"It's been attributed to her. What do you think?"

"It's possible. How much?"

Polidoro named a sum that Urbino wasn't prepared to pay. He looked at it for a few more moments, then handed it back.

"It would help inspire your book. Carriera is included, you say."

Urbino nodded.

"I'll think about it."

He moved around the large front room, then the smaller one that opened off it, admiring Polidoro's newer acquisitions and flirting with ones he had seen before. There was a room in the back that Polidoro used for his art exhibits, but it was empty at the moment. Urbino glanced at a corner table with an assortment of cups and saucers, scent bottles, a Saxony coffee service, delicate vases of pink and blue, and—somewhat incongruously placed amongst all the china—a commedia dell'arte marionette similar to those in the collection at the Ca' Rezzonico.

After examining an eighteenth-century commode with marquetry of different woods, he brought up one of the topics that were on his mind.

"I'd like you to take a look at Habib's work." Then, remembering Polidoro's dismissive comments when Rebecca Mondador had mentioned the similarity between what Habib was doing and the Burano school, he added, "It's very original."

"I'm sure it is, if both you and Rebecca recommend it." Nonetheless, there was hesitancy in his agreement. "Have him bring over some of his work. Better yet, why don't I stop by the

Palazzo Uccello? It's been too long since I've reacquainted my-self with the things you practically stole from me."

Polidoro's suggestion suited Urbino, but he added that it might be better to wait until some of Habib's other work arrived from Morocco.

"We have a Spanish friend in Tangier who runs a gallery. He's been successful in selling Habib's work and has sent off some smaller paintings he's been holding for us. They should be arriving soon."

"Very good. I'd like to help the boy, if I can."

And if he could make a good profit at the same time, Urbino thought.

"So you're the boy's benefactor?" the dealer asked with a twisted smile.

"And perhaps you can be too. There's only so much I can do for him."

"I'm sure you've done a great deal already. Let me think." The dealer screwed up his face into an even more grotesque shape. "This isn't a Biennale year, so perhaps I could show some of his work in the back room in July. That is, if it's half as good as what you and Rebecca have been saying!"

"Thank you, Marino. I'm sure you won't be disappointed."

"I hope not. Good day. And if anyone shows an interest in the Rosalba Carriera, I'll let you know. Perhaps we can come to an understanding."

12

Urbino didn't find Habib at the Palazzo Uccello when he returned. He had left shortly after Urbino had, Natalia informed him, taking his painting case.

"I'd like to clean his studio, Signor Urbino, but he insists I stay out."

"Don't worry about it, Natalia."

He stepped into Habib's studio. Tubes of paint, most of them almost completely depleted, littered the table. The stretching frame wasn't in its usual spot beside the door, and a palette knife and a canvas-cutting knife lay on the floor. Rags had fallen from the rack, and the spread covering the divan was rumpled. Cassettes were scattered around. Habib must have left in a hurry.

When Urbino had returned to the Palazzo Uccello last night, Habib had been out. He had probably gone to walk off his strange mood. The studio, which Urbino had checked, had been in order then.

Urbino looked through Habib's paintings. There were Venetian scenes, a landscape of Umbria, and a portrait of Urbino. They were all vivid, even to the point of distortion and exaggeration. Some of them had true coloristic brilliance, especially a series on the flat-bottomed *bragozzi* boats of Chioggia, with their primary colors and almost cabalistic designs. The portrait of Urbino, reclining on the sofa in the parlor, was treated in a broad manner, with few details of his face, and communicated an almost haunting, contemplative mood.

Yes, they were good, very good. Polidoro was sure to be pleased.

Urbino opened a small wooden box on the table. Inside it were envelopes with letters from Habib's family and friends. He closed the lid.

He went over to the drying cupboards. They were locked. When he found himself looking among the room's unaccustomed clutter for the key, which Habib might have forgotten to take with him, he stopped himself. It was too much like snooping.

Habib didn't return for lunch. Before going to Morocco, Urbino hadn't minded eating alone. In many ways, he had enjoyed it. But this afternoon he felt Habib's absence keenly. He couldn't interest himself in his book, and soon closed it.

To Natalia's chagrin, he left most of his meal untouched. He brought the bottle of wine to the library. There, he gave himself up to thinking about Nina Crivelli, especially about how she had accosted the Contessa in the Church of Santa Maria Formosa.

Ten minutes later he called the Contessa.

"Yes," she said. "You got the right impression. She did seem different once she saw it was Giorgio."

"More nervous?"

"Yes."

He could tell from her tone that she was reluctant to admit it.

"Yet she spoke clearly and confidently enough when she said that the person she had to tell you about was dead."

The Contessa said nothing for a few moments.

"Actually, she even spoke loudly. Giorgio couldn't have helped but hear. It embarrassed me. But he's behaved perfectly about it. I have no complaints about him."

"But you said not long ago that you weren't too pleased with all the changes at the Ca' da Capo."

"With the changes as changes, is what I said."

A slight edge had come into her voice.

"And I also said that Giorgio is as good as Milo ever was,"

she went on, "even if he doesn't know the canals as well. And Vitale is perfect for the job." She paused as if waiting for him to agree, then rushed on: "I believe it was Silvia I was concerned about. And still am. All her little peculiarities and lapses of memory are irritating, but considering this business with Nina Crivelli, none of that seems important anymore."

"Nonetheless, it all bears some looking into."

"Silvia? She's Lucia's cousin. I've known her since she was a little girl."

"Not so much Silvia, but certainly Giorgio and Vitale. You hired them when I was away. You never mentioned the circumstances."

"Not that you would have been interested in them at the time. As for Vitale, he placed an advertisement in the *International Herald Tribune*. He was working in Switzerland at the time—Geneva—and wanted a position closer to his family. He's from Bologna. The advertisement gave a phone number and an address. I contacted him and he came for an interview the next week."

"References?"

"Four. Impeccable. My agent in Milan usually takes care of these things, but this time I wanted to do it myself. I'm not quite sure why."

Urbino, however, had a good idea that it might have had to do with his absence. She might have needed to prove that she could take care of things without the help he usually gave her.

"You checked them?"

"Every single one."

"And what about Giorgio?"

"Ah, Giorgio! Well, I have Oriana to thank, there. She met him on holiday on Capri last May. Without Filippo, I might add. An elderly gentleman there employed him. Giorgio was looking for something different, preferably in the north. Oriana told him that a good friend of hers needed someone to see to the *motorboat* on a regular basis, and occasionally the car."

The Contessa had a Bentley that she kept at her summer villa in Asolo.

"And just like that you hired him?"

"Not at all! Oriana met his employer, a Signor Mazza. He had nothing but good words about Giorgio, and *his* beauty didn't blind her. According to Oriana, he's far beyond her acceptable age limit. But don't think I only depended on her," the Contessa went on with a defensive air. "I asked for a proper reference, and even telephoned Signor Mazza myself. He was most helpful. And I interviewed Giorgio and gave him a trial run. You don't think that I might have been susceptible to his charms?"

"He is rather Byronic with his limp."

"But, really, *caro*, I'm sure you think Giorgio can be trusted since Habib has been spending time with him now and again."

"He has?"

Urbino's response was spontaneous. He immediately regretted it.

"You don't know? Well, it hasn't been that often, but Vitale did say he went up to Giorgio's rooms about an hour ago."

The Contessa didn't pursue the point.

Urbino said he would stop by for tea that afternoon to take a look at Vitale's and Giorgio's recommendations, and the advertisement Vitale had placed.

13

By the time Urbino left for the Ca' da Capo-Zendrini a few hours later, Habib still hadn't returned. He took the main route, since Habib was unfamiliar with the confusing shortcuts. He didn't encounter him.

The Contessa looked festive in the embroidered silk *gilet* he had brought back for her from Morocco. It was gold-sequined, with a geometric design in red and green.

"Habib left an hour ago," she informed him without having been asked. "He went over the bridge. He had his painting kit."

"Yes," Urbino said noncommittally.

She stared at him, then said, "Here you are." She handed him a cardboard file box. "I think you'll find everything in order."

Urbino declined tea and poured himself a sherry. He seated himself across from the Contessa and opened the box.

On top was the advertisement from the *International Herald Tribune*. There was nothing unusual about it. It was an explicit request for employment, preferably in the Venice or Bologna areas, as a "butler-majordomo or personal assistant." It gave a phone number, an address in Geneva, and Vitale's full name.

The three letters of reference all seemed in order.

"I spoke with them all," the Contessa said. "They corroborated everything in the letters."

Signor Mazza's letter on Giorgio's behalf was more detailed than Vitale's. It was written by hand, and the penmanship was thin and shaky. It had a slightly old-fashioned quality as would seem to befit the elderly man whom the Contessa had said had written it. It wasn't a general letter of reference, but instead one specifically tailored for the position Giorgio was seeking as the Contessa's boatman and driver.

"Very much to the point," Urbino observed. "You spoke with Mazza?"

"As soon as I read the letter. I telephoned him."

"What was your impression of him?"

"Very polite. He said that Giorgio was sure to suit me as he did him. A fine young man, he said. He joked about wanting to keep him almost enough to lie about his competence and honesty, but he didn't want to stand in his way."

"I think I'll give him a call myself."

The telephone code was the Naples district, which included Capri. He got a recording that told him the number had been disconnected. He then called information in the Naples area, and asked for the number of Ugo Mazza. There was only an Umberto Mazza. No Mazza was listed simply under the initial *U*.

"It doesn't mean anything," the Contessa pointed out. "Oriana said he was thinking of leaving Capri and the Naples area completely. Not only was he old, but Oriana said he looked rather ill. His voice seemed weak over the phone. It's been eight months."

"Not a long time."

"Long enough to take a turn for the worst and die."

Urbino neither agreed nor disagreed. He called Oriana. Without telling her why, he said he would be dropping by the Ca' Borelli in an hour.

"I'd like her firsthand impressions," Urbino explained as he got ready to leave. "And could you arrange to have Giorgio take me to Burano tomorrow morning, if you have nothing planned for him?" Sensing that she was about to ask if she might come along, he added, "It would be better if I went alone. You did an excellent job yourself. Now I need to do a few things on my own."

"And why do you need Giorgio?"

"It will make things more convenient. Good-bye."

As he was leaving, he had a few words with Silvia in the downstairs hall. She said that on the night of Frieda's party, the German woman had helped her clean up for about a half hour, and had then gone upstairs with a headache. She had come back down in response to Habib's frantic arrival.

14

Despite its slingshot chairs, glass cubes of tables, and the concealment—if not the total banishment of almost every object remotely nonutilitarian—the living room of the Ca' Borelli would always be dear to Urbino's heart. How could it be otherwise, with its magnificent view from ceiling-high windows of the Basilica and the Doges' Palace across the expanse of the lagoon?

The Borellis—these days, only Oriana—lived on the Giudecca, an island shaped like a fish bone that was separated from the Dorsoduro quarter by a wide, deep canal. In July, during the Feast of the Redeemer, a temporary bridge of boats stretched from the Church of the Redeemer, only a short distance from the Ca' Borelli, to the Zattere embankment on the other side. Urbino and the Contessa usually watched the fireworks display from just where he was sitting now.

Urbino asked Oriana to dim the lights for the sake of the view on this clear January night.

"You seem preoccupied," Oriana said. "Is it Habib?"

"Why do you ask that?"

"Why do I ask it indeed! Because you worry about him too much sometimes. I assure you, he's doing fine. I bumped into him at the Rialto market the other day. He was with friends from his school. He knows his way around very well, much better than you probably did in Morocco! And he was full of praise for you. I can recognize gratitude and devotion when I see it, as long as I'm not romantically involved with the person. And then, poor Oriana!"

Urbino smiled.

"I think you see clearly in all circumstances. No, it's not about Habib, though it's good to know that you think he's doing so well. It's about Giorgio."

"A mission from Barbara! She wants me to keep my distance. But there's nothing between us. I must be on my best behavior if Filippo and I are to patch things up."

"It's about Giorgio's former position in Capri. You know how upset Barbara has been about the changes at the Ca' da Capo. I'm trying to set her mind at ease. I'm looking into her new staff, as I would have if I'd been here at the time she hired them."

It was rather feeble, but unless he told Oriana more about Nina Crivelli than he or the Contessa thought was appropriate, it was the best he could come up with.

Oriana gave him an assessing look and a little smile curved her lips. She lit a cigarette. When she spoke, it became clear that she was going to take him at his word.

"Ah, yes," she brought out after blowing a stream of smoke over her left shoulder. "Poor Barbara was quite at a loss without you. She didn't like it one bit. Perhaps this is one of her ways of making you suffer. But I assure you, I was looking out for her even more than usual. That's precisely why I found Giorgio for her."

"How did you meet him?"

"I was in a café in Anacapri with my friend, Camilla. Giorgio was with two men at a nearby table. It was all very convivial. We started to talk about the sea and boats and Capri and Venice. Camilla mentioned Barbara, or rather the Da Capo-Zendrini name, and how the family was originally from Naples. One of Giorgio's friends remembered hearing that Alvise had married an *inglese* who was living up in Venice."

"Did Giorgio tell you what he did?"

"Just that he was a mechanic and a chauffeur. When Camilla and I met him alone a few days later, he said that he took care of the boat of a *napolitano* who lived on Capri part of the year. That's when I got the bright idea about seeing if I could help both Barbara and him. She needed someone to replace Milo."

"She could have found any number of men here."

"Could have, and would have, but it almost seemed like fate. Here was this available young man who was looking for a new position and—"

"When did you learn that?"

She gave him an amused look.

"My, my, aren't you playing the sleuth! Forgive me if I suspect there's something else going on here than doing penance for our Barbara! But I can see that you have no intention of telling me more than you have already. To answer your question, Giorgio told me—told me and Camilla," she emphasized, "that he wanted to move on to a new position. Somewhere other than Naples. He's from Sicily, so I assumed he wanted to work his way up the entire length of the country!"

Oriana went on to explain how the idea that Giorgio might apply for the position had come to her after this second meeting and how she had discussed it with Camilla, and then with the Contessa. It had only been then, she insisted, that she had broached the possibility to Giorgio. From that point on things had moved along quickly.

"I met Ugo Mazza at the Gran Caffè. A pleasant, quiet-spoken man. Illness was obliging him to give up his villa and his boat. He was moving from the Naples area."

"To where?"

"He didn't say, but he mentioned he wanted to be near his daughter. Or was it his son? He had only good things to say about Giorgio. Completely reliable, an excellent mechanic, polite and well brought up. He understood that Giorgio needed to move on, and he wanted to do everything he could to help him. He gave me the letter of recommendation that day."

"Did he tell you how he originally came to employ Giorgio?"

"No."

"Did you ever go to his villa?"

"No. Giorgio said that he was a very private man."

She stubbed out her cigarette with more force than was needed and stood up.

"I admit I was struck by Giorgio's drop-dead good looks. My God, he's a fine specimen! But I would never have had him put in such a responsible position right in the heart of Barbara's home if there had been the slightest doubt about him."

15

Habib was tidying up his studio when Urbino returned from seeing Oriana.

"I'm sorry I missed you at Barbara's this afternoon," Urbino said.

"You were there, *sidi*? I didn't know you were going. There we were in the same place at the same time. You went to see her and I went to see Giorgio."

"I know. It's too bad that you didn't have a chance to say hello to her. She would have liked to see you."

"Sometimes I think she does not like me. Am I foolish?"

"No, you're not foolish, Habib, but you're wrong. It may be one of those cultural confusions we sometimes have even between the two of us. Barbara likes you, but perhaps she will think you don't like her if you don't say hello when you go to her house."

"I like her, too, *sidi*. She is a very gracious lady, and she always wants to help. And she is your best friend. Friends like her are as precious as rain in the desert. But I was making a visit to Giorgio in his part of the big house. You like Giorgio, don't you? Remember how he helped both of us on the night you got so sick?"

"I have no reason not to like him."

Habib turned on his engaging smile.

"Listen to yourself, *sidi*. Sometimes you say things in a funny way."

Urbino smiled in return.

"I suppose I do."

"Giorgio helps me." Habib gathered the cloths from the floor and started to arrange them on the rack. "With my Italian. He is patient. And he has sympathy for Arabs and North Africans." He paused, then added, "Just like you. He is from Sicily. It has many Arab traditions. It is too close to North Africa."

"Very close," Urbino corrected.

"And Jerome thinks he is nice, too. Jerome is interested in boats and the lagoon. You remember how Giorgio explained so much about the lagoon when we went to Burano."

"Yes."

To help Habib, Urbino picked up an edition of *Il Gazzettino*, the local newspaper, that was lying on the floor. It was folded in half. He would have placed it on the table immediately, but his attention was drawn to one of the articles. Words were circled in red pencil, and there was writing in the margins in the same red pencil that he identified as Arabic script. It was an article about the accidental deaths of illegal immigrants who had suffocated while being smuggled into England in a truck.

"I see that you're studying your Italian vocabulary, but don't you think it would be better to translate the words into English instead of Arabic?"

Habib took the newspaper from his hands and put it on the table.

"You always try to make things more difficult, *sidi*. But I know it is for my own good. I am doing my best."

"I know you are. Did you find this article interesting?"

"Very interesting, and it has many strange words. But it is very sad." A melancholy expression crossed his dark face. "It reminded me of that poor woman by the Church of Health. I hope that she is safe. Maybe it is better to read stories with easier words, and with happy things in them. But I am hungry, *sidi*. I think that Natalia will lose her patience if we keep her waiting any longer."

16

Early the next morning Urbino went out to the shops to buy a few items to loosen one of the tongues on Burano. When he returned to the Palazzo Uccello to meet Giorgio with the boat, he found him talking with Habib.

"Would you like Giorgio to take you to the school before we go to Burano?"

"No, thank you, *sidi*. I will walk. Good-bye."

Giorgio maneuvered the motorboat out of the canals and headed it across the lagoon, where fog was creeping over its flat, steely-blue expanse. They made their way between the wooden poles that marked the channel through the shallow waters.

Soon Burano appeared with its cubes of colorful houses and leaning campanile. No longer could the island beckon Urbino with its colorful stage set of apparent normality. Now it was all too real, and bristling with troubling questions whose answers threatened to disturb the surface calm of both the Ca' da Capo-Zendrini and his own Palazzo Uccello.

He needed to proceed delicately, but he also needed to do it with an open mind and open eyes. Otherwise, his efforts might do more damage to the Contessa, himself, and, yes, perhaps even Habib, than might be done if he just left things alone.

Giorgio brought the boat to the main landing area on the Fondamenta Squeri. He seemed more cool and professional than usual. When he touched his white cap as Urbino got out, Urbino had a sense of confusion. Had there been a touch of irony in the act, or only the man's customary deference? He couldn't decide.

Urbino arranged a time to meet Giorgio at the same spot.

"You will not need me until then?"

"No."

"Very well."

Giorgio remained standing on the deck of the motorboat. He didn't leave for all the time that Urbino kept him in sight, unobtrusively, he hoped, as he made a point of examining the lace goods in some of the stalls.

17

Y ou've brought some temptations from Marchini," Carolina Bruni said from the sunken comfort of her sofa. On her lap slept a fluffy white cat. " *'Love me with a little love, a childlike love!'* " she screeched. "Turn down the volume. Put all the goodies out. I don't want to disturb Mimi, do I, little one?"

She shouted some more of Ciò Ciò San's lines from the love duet of *Madama Butterfly* down at the cat. Mimi stirred, then buried her head more deeply into the folds of her mistress's bright yellow dress.

Carolina was Natalia's cousin. Ten years ago Urbino had helped her sort out a problem that had threatened to deprive her of her house on Burano.

Even without Mimi on her lap, Carolina would have been reluctant to get up. This was not because of her age—for she was barely sixty and in fairly good health—but her size. She reminded Urbino of nothing so much as a Buddha, a resemblance increased by the vague oriental cast to her face and her preference for robes of rich design.

The fact that she seldom left her house didn't prevent her, however, from doing as good a job about gathering information as the spies of the notorious state inquisitors had once done in the sixteenth century.

The parlor was furnished with very few pieces and was unadorned with any knickknacks, except for signed photographs of Luciano Pavarotti and Renata Scotto, displayed on a table beside the record player. What was most striking by its absence was lace of any kind. Carolina might just as well have lived on a remote desert island in the south Pacific for any sign that her house displayed of Burano's feminine art.

Urbino seated himself in an armchair across from the imposing woman, who gave him a broad smile as she stroked Mimi. She was attractive, despite her size, and would have been even more attractive if she didn't exaggerate her features, already obvious enough, by the generous application of makeup and an ink-black hair dye.

"And my favorite drink to wash them all down with!" she exclaimed as she held up her cup of Prosecco Rosé. "But there's no need for such kindness. You swept me off my feet a long time ago. That is not so easy to do!"

She delivered her excruciating version of an operatic laugh.

"I'm glad you brought the bigger ones." She dipped a pastry in her cup. "The little ones aren't worth anything. You can hardly taste them."

Urbino sipped his wine. To please her, he, too, was drinking it from a cup. She held out hers for more. The rim was smudged with her lipstick.

"No need to pretend with me! It's about Nina Crivelli that you've come."

"It's on the Contessa's behalf. She'd like to do something in memory of Signora Crivelli." He had planned to use this pretext, even though Carolina would know it for what it was. "She thought of a Mass card, and offered one to Salvatore, but—"

"I heard all about it from Gabriela and Lidia. I'm sure Salvatore ripped it up and threw it in the trash." She waved a pastry in the air. "Shhh! Listen!"

It was "Un bel dì vedremo." She didn't follow her own advice, but joined in for several moments that seemed unusually long to Urbino and apparently to Mimi, who stirred uneasily.

"He's not a pious man?" Urbino asked when she had finished.

She raised her big brown eyes to the ceiling.

"Pious! Like mother, like son! But even if she had been Santa Maria Goretti, he would have torn it to shreds after what she made him suffer through. She might have thought she loved him, but she made his life a misery just the same, even if no one ever heard him complain. Not even when he got something for himself and she destroyed it. His wife and son, I mean. She won in the end. But I'm sure the Contessa told you everything Lidia and Gabriela told her."

She gave him an amused look.

"I smell something more than the Marchini pastries! But why you should be snooping around about Nina Crivelli, I don't know! Let the dead alone, especially miserable ones like her! But she suffered for the misery she caused. Always swallowing pills. A terrible way to live, or die! I told Dottore Rubbini—he was Nina's doctor too—that if I ever have to eat pills instead of food, he'll have to put me out of my misery. Give me these any time!"

The pastries were rapidly disappearing.

"Pills, pills, and more pills. For her heart and God knows what else! Thank God for Regina Bella, or she wouldn't have known what she was taking, or when she had to take what!"

"Regina Bella was in charge of her medication?"

"Did I say that?" she responded with something like anger. "She reminded her from time to time. Did you take this pill, did you take that one? Salvatore didn't care one way or another. But Regina wasn't always around, skipping off the way she does to Milan, Rome, God knows where. Always thinking she's a queen, just like her name. Regina Bella. But she isn't a queen and she isn't beautiful, but you can't tell her that. Always wearing the latest fashion. All the profits from that place are on her back. There's a man behind it all, someone she slips off to see. Call it a woman's intuition."

"She was kind to look after Nina when she could."

Carolina shrugged her big shoulders.

"Maybe kind, maybe something else. Nobody can tell why people do half the things they do. You should know that! Years back, a woman went to her husband's grave on San Michele every day. Most people thought she was praying for his soul, but she went to laugh and curse."

Carolina attacked another pastry. Urbino decided to change the direction of her information, or rather return to a topic she had mentioned earlier.

"Salvatore couldn't help being angry if his mother broke up his marriage."

"She was a wicked woman, God rest her soul. Always scheming, putting her nose in other people's business."

She emitted another operatic laugh.

"I don't mean like you, Signor Urbino, even if you spent a fortune on Marchini pastries and Prosecco to get me to babble about Nina Crivelli! No, I see from your sweet face that you're about to apologize. I won't have it. How can I so easily forget your kindness which, wretched slave to my problem that I was, I welcomed in rapture like a ray of the sun?"

This sounded vaguely familiar to Urbino. Was it from *La Traviata? Aida?* Because it might herald another burst of song, judging from the deep breath the woman was now taking, he asked if she might tell him something about Salvatore and his wife.

A wounded look came over Carolina's face.

"After all this time in Venice, you're still in a rush like all the other Americans! As you wish! Listen carefully!"

Carolina then hurried through the story of how Salvatore had met Evelina when she came to Venice from the mountains near Udine on vacation with her family. It had been an immediate attraction between the blond, German-looking Evelina and the handsome young Salvatore.

"But she should have looked further than his face. She had no idea what life would be like on Burano, isolated, everything either lace or fish, fish or lace. And with Nina in the same house! Evelina nagged Salvatore to leave Burano, but he's never been able to defy his mother." She took a sip of Prosecco, smacked her lips, and added, "Well, he doesn't have to worry about that anymore, does he?"

"What about the son?"

"Gino. Such a darling boy! Even when he was eight, you could tell he'd grow up to be a fine specimen of a man, even with his problem. Twenty years it's been."

She sighed heavily, with a big heave of her bosom, and shook her head.

"What do you mean about Gino's problem?"

"A clubfoot. Nina blamed it on Evelina's side of the family."

"I agree that something like that doesn't have to be a handicap." He paused, wanting to choose his words carefully. "Take Giorgio, the Contessa's new chauffeur. He has some problem, but it hasn't held him back in his profession."

"He has a clubfoot?" Carolina asked.

"I don't know if that's what it is. He does have a limp. Have you ever seen him?"

"No, but I've been told he's very handsome."

"Getting back to Evelina, what brought her to run off?"

"No handsome man like this Giorgio, if that's what you're thinking! She just couldn't take it any longer. Gino almost died one winter from appendicitis. As soon as he recovered, she took him away with just one suitcase between them. Salvatore and Nina were out. Nina threw all their things in the street afterward. All Salvatore could save was a little vase. Evelina had treasured it. It was a family heirloom, she said, but she probably picked it up in some junk shop. Salvatore kept a fresh flower in it all the time, maybe he still does. You wouldn't think he was sentimental, but there you are. For the first year he heard from her every month or so. She never said much, and what little she said was public knowledge. It was all spelled out on postcards."

"Postcards?"

"Yes! Can you imagine! She didn't even have the decency to write a letter. Probably thought she was tempting him with pictures of Germany. And the cards all said the same thing. That Gino was well and Salvatore shouldn't worry. Eventually they stopped. Oh, I could see the strain on him, but he hardly ever raised his voice to Nina. He went away for a few months a year after she left."

"Went away?"

"Nina said he was helping some cousin in Naples but it was the first and the last time we heard a breath about any cousin down there or anywhere. My guess is that he went to some clinic to get his nerves back. Nina must have managed the whole thing."

"Was he better when he came back?"

"Who knows? He's sly. You don't know half of what he's thinking or feeling. He can keep a secret to the death. Nina probably thought he had forgotten about Evelina and Gino, but as far as he's concerned, he's as married as the day she left. He probably still expects her to return. Nina would have croaked if that had ever happened when she was alive!" Her eyes twinkled with malicious amusement. "And the thought of Gino must be a knife in the heart. I hope he'll be happier now, but Nina's death isn't enough. He'd need Evelina and Gino, but that won't happen, not in this life."

Urbino needed one more piece of information.

"In what way did Nina poke her nose into other people's business?"

"Enjoyed hurting people by revealing their secrets. Sometimes she tried to make money from it. My friend Bettina gave her a sack of it to keep her from ruining her daughter's reputation. About something that happened all the way in Bologna! I would have told her to scream it from the top of the church tower and then jump off!"

"She needed money so badly?"

"Wanted it! And wanted to make people suffer one way or another, either by forking it over or being tortured and shamed. Probably thought she was going to live forever on pure meanness and a good bank account. I figure she was storing up a pile to buy out Regina Bella."

"Does Regina plan to sell the restaurant?"

"She'll have to, the way she spends money! Nina wanted to be *padrona* and lord it over everyone. And it would have been security for Salvatore. No matter what he thought about her and how nasty she was, she loved him. He was the only thing she had."

"When did Signor Crivelli die?"

"A long time ago. Kidney disease."

Urbino got up to turn the record over. As the orchestral interlude started, he asked her why there wasn't any lace in her apartment.

"I could never learn one stitch! It's better not to be reminded of one's failures."

They listened to the interlude. Carolina closed her eyes and hummed along in excruciating accompaniment with the chorus, stroking Mimi. When the music imitated the sound of birds, the cat's ears perked up, but she remained sleeping.

"Poor Butterfly!" Carolina said. "Soon she'll be dead—all over again!"

"I'm afraid I'll have to leave you to face the sad occasion on your own."

"Will you see the German woman? She brought something for me the other day. Took me by surprise. In and out in a few minutes. I don't want it in the house!"

She indicated a cassette box of Wagner's *Tristan und Isolde* on the mantelpiece.

"But it isn't too much different from *Madama Butterfly*, is it?" Urbino asked with a smile. "Love and death."

Carolina didn't look convinced.

He slipped the cassette box into his jacket pocket.

"One thing more," Carolina called out when he reached the door. "Tell the Contessa that no one on Burano would have believed Nina if she had said anything against *her*."

Her brightly painted lips curved in a smile.

"But did she?"

"*I* never heard anything, and as you know, Signor Urbino, I hear everything, one way or another!"

U rbino approached the door of the Casa Verde. Before he had a chance to ring it, the Contessa's tenant from the purple building next door called out a greeting. She was shaking out a rug from an upstairs window. She informed him that "the foreign lady" had gone out an hour before and hadn't returned yet.

He slowly made his way in the direction of the central square. The fog had grown thicker and was invading the scene around him. It was seeping through the drying nets and swirling around the upturned boats.

He mulled over what he had learned from Carolina Bruni. She had been a rich source of information, especially about Salvatore's marriage, Nina's role in its breakup, and Salvatore's behavior afterward. Urbino saw no reason to question most of what she had told him, at least up to a certain point. One of the tricks of both his sleuthing and his writing was figuring out what that point might be. Going beyond it could be disastrous. A whole biography, or large parts of it, could be tainted.

As for these investigations that he had become more and more involved in over the years, the stakes were nothing less than life and death.

Nina Crivelli was already dead. Salvatore's wife and son had disappeared twenty years ago, and had never returned to Burano, or so it seemed. If one or both of them had died, surely some word would have reached Burano. The content of every postcard Evelina had sent Salvatore had been common knowledge. Yet Salvatore had his secretive side, according to Carolina. His mother's eyes and those of Burano were ever vigilant, but they could have been deceived.

What would Salvatore do to get his wife and child back? What might he already have done? That he might have harmed his own mother was a possibility that Urbino needed to confront, disturbing though it was to his sensibilities. But he couldn't allow himself to be hampered by this blind spot anymore than by others he knew he had to guard himself against. Salvatore's life with his mother, from all reports, had been a torment. If he had done something as monstrous as kill Nina, what had brought him to do it? To say that he might have snapped after all these years wasn't enough for Urbino. There would have to have been something outside the small confines of their apartment that had triggered it.

That there had been a trigger, Urbino was fairly certain, but Salvatore was far from being the only one it could have set off.

By this time Urbino had reached the Piazza Galuppi. A mother and her little girl smiled at him as they walked past. Both of them had the delicate faces and masses of bright hair that Burano has long been famous for. A few moments later, the sight of two handsome men lounging against one of the buildings reminded him that the island had once had a reputation for something in addition to feminine beauty, lace, and fishing. Men, both Venetians and foreigners, had often sought their illicit assignations here. The Baron Corvo, buried on San Michele, had spent many languorous hours with his gondolier of the moment, as Frieda had drawn attention to on the night of her party.

Urbino stepped into the Oratorio Santa Barbara. As he contemplated the huge Crucifixion scene by the young Tiepolo, he considered, with almost a sense of relief, something unrelated to his previous line of thought.

It was the Contessa's encounter with Nina Crivelli near the portrait of Santa Barbara in Santa Maria Formosa. Nina's behavior had been more or less consistent until the entrance of the person who, a few minutes later, revealed himself to be Giorgio. What might this mean? What secrets might she have had from him? Or could Nina have been sly enough to deflect the Contessa's suspicions on to Giorgio in this way? If she had, however, it hadn't had its desired effect.

Urbino turned his speculations to Giorgio's presence in the church. Was he there by chance or had he been in search of Nina, perhaps to prevent her from saying anything against him? That he might have gone to Santa Maria Formosa to protect the Contessa from Nina was not inconceivable, except that Urbino felt himself resisting the idea. He took note, once again, of another one of his blind spots. He wasn't well disposed toward Giorgio and might be too willing to think ill of him. How much of this was because of Habib's obvious admiration of the boatman was not clear in his mind.

After leaving the Oratorio, Urbino went to the Lace School a short distance away. A sign announced that the museum was closed for repairs until March. Urbino was disappointed. He had hoped that the women who sat making lace as part of the museum's exhibits might have been encouraged to tell him a few things he didn't already know about Nina and Salvatore.

Out in the square again, Urbino skirted the Church of San Martino, where a fishing net was drying on one of its walls. He looked up at the leaning campanile.

It was from here that Carolina had said Nina could have shouted out whatever secrets she knew about her for all Carolina cared, and then jumped off. Urbino agreed with the spirit, if not exactly the letter of Carolina's comment. The only effective way to deal with blackmailers was to break the tyranny of fear and silence they thrived on.

No sooner did he have the thought than its naiveté struck him. Most people in the power of a blackmailer saw no escape except through money or murder. Carolina's friend Bettina had paid up for the sake of her daughter's reputation. How many other people in Burano, or even Venice, had done the same? And had some desperate person, perhaps even innocent of any crime or indiscretion, seen no choice but to remove Nina from the scene completely? And had the lace handkerchief been his, or her, way of showing that her mouth had been stopped forever?

The bell sounded the noon hour. Urbino went down the Via Galuppi to Il Piccolo Nettuno.

Two tables were set out on the pavement. At one was an elderly couple, both with white hair and elegant clothes. Muffled in scarves, but otherwise giving no sign that it wasn't the warmest of months, they spoke enthusiastically in German. Salvatore came out with a tray of steaming plates. He glanced at Urbino, but didn't give a flicker of recognition.

Inside, only one table in the far corner was occupied. A thin woman in her seventies, wearing a faded blue shawl, sat alone. A plate of pasta and a half-filled bottle of wine were in front of her. She nodded to Urbino, and returned to her meal.

Urbino seated himself at the same table he and Habib had lunched at a few weeks before. Low voices came from the kitchen. He ran his eye over the menu. He wasn't hungry.

Salvatore came inside. He poured more wine into the woman's glass and brought her more bread before coming over to Urbino.

"My regrets on the death of your mother, Signor Crivelli."

"Thank you, signore. Would you like some wine?"

Urbino chose a Bardolino.

"I'll have a salad and a plate of the same pasta the woman over there has. She seems to be enjoying it a great deal."

Salvatore made a little face. It might have been a frown or an attempt at a smile.

"Very good, signore."

He nodded and walked into the back of the room. He appeared to be steady on his feet today. Perhaps now that his mother was dead he was drinking less. This possibility was quickly driven from Urbino's mind, however. In one of the mirrors he caught a glimpse of Salvatore raising a small bottle to his lips, then thrusting it into the deep pocket of his apron.

Urbino had known that he wouldn't be likely to have much conversation with the man other than whatever was natural between a waiter and a customer. Surely Salvatore knew about his relationship with the Contessa and, even more to the point, his reputation as an amateur sleuth. On both counts he wouldn't be receptive, whether or not there was good reason to suspect him in the death of his own mother. He had already had enough meddling in his life. It would be natural for him to resent any more.

There was another way of arguing it, however, Urbino reminded himself. If Salvatore were guilty, he would probably be inclined to put Urbino off the scent by being friendlier, to both him and the Contessa. Instead, he was doing the opposite.

And it was also possible that, with his mother now dead, resentment had faded. In its place there could be regret that he hadn't been a better son, even if he had deserved a better mother. Even Urbino, who had often been told by his own parents and others that he was a good son, had suffered his own peculiar kind of guilt when they had both died in an automobile accident. Urbino had seen too many ways that grief could manifest itself, and in the most unlikely of people, to feel secure about easily identifying its true expression. He—

"Urbino, how nice to see you!" Regina Bella broke into his thoughts. She wore one of her stylish outfits. She looked as if she had lost weight since Frieda's party. "I hope you're enjoying the meal? Why only salad and pasta? You're not still ill, I hope? What brings you here? Are you alone, or is Barbara somewhere? And Habib?"

Her questions came so thick and fast that at first he could do little more than smile and nod. She was filled with nervous energy.

He asked her to sit down.

"Just for a few minutes," she said. "Would you mind if I smoked?"

She lit up a cigarette and seated herself. But the next moment, she was up again to greet five French tourists, whom she escorted to a large table in the back.

When she returned, they chatted briefly about Burano and a project to drain its canals. Then he mentioned that he had visited Carolina Bruni. Regina stiffened and colored. She stubbed out her cigarette, and made a joke about the woman's voice.

Salvatore came to clear the table. Urbino ordered a coffee.

"Salvatore is back at work, I see. It's good to return to a regular schedule after a bereavement, if one feels up to it, of course. Considering that his mother had her heart attack right here, though, I thought he might have some reluctance."

Regina followed Salvatore with her eyes as he went into the kitchen. Before she brought them back to they glanced down at the floor a few feet from their table.

"It's the way he wanted it. I suggested that he take more time off. You'll have to excuse me, but I want to catch the next boat."

"I have the Contessa's boat. Giorgio could drop you anywhere you like. You'd get there much quicker."

"That's all right." She got up. "You enjoy your coffee. Have some of the tiramisu—on the house. Nella made it this morning. *Ciao!*"

Urbino decided against the dessert, but he lingered over his coffee. A few more customers came in. Salvatore was busy. Although there weren't many tables, it was a lot of work for one person. Nina had frequently helped. In the light of her death, Il Piccolo Nettuno would see some changes, but not, Urbino suspected, the kind that the old lace maker had hoped for, if she had lived.

A few minutes later, when Salvatore was outside, Urbino walked toward the back of the room, feeling slightly disoriented by the mirrors. He entered the kitchen.

It was small and cluttered, and filled with a pleasant mixture of food aromas. A back door led into a courtyard, which was connected to the Via Galuppi by a narrow *calle*.

Nella, a small, rounded woman in her forties, was spooning tomato sauce into the middle of a plate of rigatoni. He introduced himself and thanked her for the meal.

"But you didn't eat much, signore."

"It's still a little early for lunch for me. I'll save the tiramisu for the next time."

"I've already wrapped you up some. Salvatore was going to bring it to you."

She reached for a bag tied with red ribbon on the counter by the courtyard door. Next to the bag was a stiff-brimmed white cap.

"You can return the bowl the next time."

"How kind to wrap it so nicely when you're busy like this. You must miss Nina Crivelli's help. There's a lot to be done, with just you and Salvatore."

"Don't forget Signorina Regina. We manage."

Footsteps approached the door. It was Salvatore. A distinct scowl marred his good-looking, but haggard face. His eyes fixed on the cap for a few seconds, then looked away.

"Here." Nella handed him the plate of pasta. "I gave the signore his tiramisu. Enjoy it, Signor Macintyre. If you'll excuse me, I have to prepare the risotto."

Urbino was now eager to return to the motorboat. Salvatore, however, took a long time to bring him his bill and return his change. When he was about to leave, he was further delayed by one of the French tourists from the back of the restaurant, who called him over to their table. She excused herself and said that she recognized him from the photograph on his biography of Proust. She had it with her. He signed it and chatted with them for a few minutes, hoping he didn't show his impatience to leave.

By the time he reached the motorboat, Giorgio was standing at attention in his white cap and dark blue jacket. A slightly mocking smile seemed to curve his well-formed lips.

19

The next day was bright and sunny, and Urbino and Habib made an outing to Murano, where Habib wanted to do some sketching. Urbino left him at the Ponte Vivarini, while he wandered around the island, stopping in the Glass Museum and the Basilica of San Donato, which held vivid memories of his first case. For most of the time he kept thinking about what he had learned on Burano yesterday. It had been a great deal, and he was trying to sort it out.

For the last hour of his ruminations, he sat at a café near the Ponte Vivarini and idly watched Habib go about his sketching. Habib was so caught up in his work that he didn't even notice. When Urbino rejoined him, he proudly showed his sketches of the bridge and the Palazzo da Mula a short distance away. They were quite good.

Before they went for lunch at Urbino's favorite trattoria on the island, they stopped by Bartolomeo Pignatti's glass factory on the Fondamenta dei Vetrai.

Ten minutes later Habib was watching Pignatti with child-like wonder as he went about his art. The glassmaker was like some muscular priest officiating before a tabernacle of fire and making all the ritualistic gestures that would help him fashion a precious offering. Even his occasional grunts and mumbled words and phrases suggested scraps of mysterious prayers and supplications. Urbino followed the man's movements with his own fascination as the iridescent lump of molten glass at the end of a long tube began to swell from the force of Pignatti's lungs.

Eventually, with the application of pincers, spatula, and the artistry of the maestro, a shape emerged. Urbino, who had spoken a few quick words to Pignatti after they had discussed the Palazzo Uccello's damaged chandelier, was able to recognize it before Habib.

"A squirrel!" Habib said.

Squirrels, along with cats, were his favorite animals.

Pignatti placed the little glass animal in an oven to cool.

"He's making you a whole family. We'll pick them up when we finish lunch."

20

Urbino was finishing dinner that evening when the telephone rang. It was the Contessa. He was alone in the Palazzo Uccello and looking forward to an evening of quiet reflection. Habib had gone off to see Jerome shortly after they had returned from Burano and had said that he wouldn't be back until late.

"I had success with Corrado," the Contessa said with a thrill of excitement in her voice.

Corrado Scarpa, the Contessa's friend, had a connection with some of the police officials at the Venice Questura. Over the years Urbino had benefited from information he had passed on. Yesterday afternoon, after returning to the Palazzo Uccello, Urbino had asked the Contessa to look into a few details. He hadn't filled her in yet, however, on all he had learned.

"I told him I needed to settle some questions in my own mind since I was the one who found Nina Crivelli's body. I said that I keep telling myself that if only I had got there earlier, I might have saved her. I doubt if he believed me, but he agreed to read the reports and talk to Dr. Rubbini. There's no doubt she had a massive heart attack. No evidence of anything else, except a bruise on the back of her head, caused by her fall. She died almost instantly. From what can be estimated, less than an hour before I found her. A local couple left the restaurant with Salvatore and the cook at nine-thirty. He locked up. Nina must have arrived shortly after to clean."

"What about the lace handkerchief?"

"The medical examiner's report mentioned it only to say that it couldn't have been in any way the cause of death and that she probably had a coughing fit before the attack that killed her."

"But it doesn't quite make sense. The handkerchief was part-way in her mouth."

"But not stuffed into it. Horrible idea!"

"Maybe it had been, but it had come out somehow."

"Or because of someone."

"Was any medication found on her?"

"No, but it seems it wouldn't have saved her anyway because of the severity of the attack."

"And there was no autopsy," Urbino reminded her as well as himself, "so no one would know if there were traces of any medication in her body."

"But Dr. Rubbini confirms that she had a long-standing heart problem, and that she was taking medication for it."

"And Regina Bella?"

"Rubbini praised her. She often accompanied Nina on her visits. Salvatore couldn't be depended on. Carolina Bruni was right. Regina tried to make sure that Nina had her pills with her all the time. She even went to the pharmacy to get them."

"Did Nina take her condition seriously?"

"It appears she did. She was determined to do everything and anything to keep herself alive and well as long as possible. Rubbini said it was for Salvatore's sake."

21

B ecause of his investigation into the Nina Crivelli affair, Urbino had put aside his *Women of Venice* project. After his conversation with the Contessa, he went to the library and started
to sort through his notes on the book. He often found that by
keeping one part of his mind at work on something unrelated
to a troubling problem, another part was freed to attack it.

He read through some material on the Contessa Isabella Teotochi, who had kept a literary salon at the Palazzo Albrizzi in
the San Polo quarter. Teotochi, whom Lord Byron had called the
De Staël of Venice, was one of his and the Contessa's favorite
figures, but this evening he couldn't concentrate on her or any
other aspect of his project. His thoughts kept returning to the
lace maker.

He took down his books on lace making and Venetian lace,
and started to page through them. He wasn't looking for anything in particular, but he felt that the information and illustrations might put him in a receptive frame of mind. Accounts
about mermaid's lace and the collar made for Louis XIV out of
white human hair and Cencia Scarpaiola, who had once been
the only person alive to know the secret of *punto in aria*, amused
and informed him. It wasn't until he came across a definition of
lace in one of the books, however, that he felt he had found
something of relevance: *Lace, a slender fabric, made of thread, incor-
porating holes as an intentional part of the design.* The fact that it was
the definition by a woman named Earnshaw made it all the

more interesting, because of the name's association with passion, death, and betrayal. Emily Bronte's tragic heroine, Catherine Earnshaw, was one of Urbino's favorite characters.

Urbino smiled to himself. It didn't take too much of a stretch of his imagination to realize that this definition uncannily described his own method of sleuthing. The fabric he was threading was indeed slender, even delicate, and there was no question it was full of holes. Whether he could make these holes a part of the design remained to be seen. More likely, the holes, this time around, would make no design possible, and would only contribute to the disintegration of what he was working so hard to achieve.

He checked his wristwatch. It was a few minutes before ten. Habib was out with some friends from the language school. He decided to take a walk.

Before he left, he telephoned Frieda and mentioned that he had something that was hers.

"That's strange. However did you find it?" she said in a puzzled tone.

"Find it? Carolina Bruni gave it to me."

"Carolina Bruni?" Frieda repeated. "But I don't—oh, of course, *Tristan und Isolde*. No, no, you don't have to bring them here. Tomorrow morning at eleven? Caffè Quadri? Bye-bye!"

Out in the damp night air, Urbino walked first as far as the Rialto Bridge, deserted of its shoppers, but not of tourists in the form of an elderly French couple. They were standing in the middle of the bridge where Urbino had stood a few weeks before. They too were looking out at the broad nighttime expanse of the Grand Canal, over which a mist was starting to thicken.

From the Rialto landing, he took the local *vaporetto* to the Salute stop. Only Urbino and an old woman got off. The Salute's snowy cupolas and towers loomed above him, but he didn't linger. He walked past the wide steps of the church and down the *fondamenta* on the Grand Canal side to the isolated Punta della Dogana.

He never tired of the view. It had been his destination the other night, when his walk, unlike now, had been haunted by the sense that he was being pursued. Tonight things were different. He felt that he had overreacted before.

The Punta della Dogana was where the Grand Canal, the lagoon, and the Giudecca Canal met. On his right floated the small island of San Giorgio Maggiore, with its Palladian church quietly gazing at the excesses of the Doges' Palace and the Basilica across the water.

The leaden clanging of buoys and the bleat of a solitary foghorn were carried on the sharp wind blowing in from the lagoon and assaulting the weather vane statue of Fortune on the Customhouse Building. He pulled his cape more securely around him.

He gazed out at the stretch of dark water, punctuated here and there by boat and buoy lights and gave himself up to his thoughts.

He no longer had any doubt that Nina Crivelli had been murdered, and that it had been done in a way that had blinded the authorities. The circumstance of the pills was a confusing—but crucial—element in the picture. Regina Bella had taken it upon herself to see that Nina was supplied with them. But Nina hadn't been in Regina's company all, or even most of the time. Certainly far less than Salvatore. He should have been the one to look after his mother, but it appeared that he had neither the desire, considering his resentment, nor the ability, given his frequent bouts of drunkenness.

By answering some questions about the pills, Urbino might be closer to knowing what had happened to Nina, and who had killed her. They were one of the many holes that he needed to incorporate into his design.

Why were none found on her body? Had she taken any before the attack? When had Regina most recently checked on Nina's supply of pills? And who else knew about them, other than Regina and Salvatore and Dottore Rubbini?

Carolina Bruni knew, he reminded himself. And this probably meant that it must have been common knowledge among Nina's acquaintances.

Urbino also considered the lace handkerchief in relationship to the pills. The handkerchief had been pressed against her mouth when the Contessa had discovered her body. Could Nina have kept a supply of pills tied up in her handkerchief, as Urbino remembered one of the nuns in his high school used to do?

From the pills, Urbino passed on to Salvatore and his wife and child. After suffering from his mother's emotional abuse over the years, Salvatore had lost what he treasured most because of her. And then he had gone on living in the same house with her, day after day, obliged to listen to her complaints, gossip, and protestations of a love that must have become hateful to him.

It wasn't a pleasant thing to contemplate, let alone endure.

Casting one last look out at the dark waters of the lagoon, Urbino abandoned the Punta della Dogana for the Zattere embankment with its aloof villas and the former salt warehouses, where art exhibitions were mounted during Biennale years.

Through the mist he tried to make out the lights of the Ca' Borelli on the Giudecca across the way. He had no reason to accuse Oriana Borelli of anything more than having had her head turned by Giorgio's handsome looks. But he did suspect Giorgio, more and more now. It was possible that he had cleverly contrived to meet Oriana down in Capri because of her closeness to the Contessa.

And what had his cap been doing in Il Piccolo Nettuno's kitchen? That it might not have been Giorgio's cap would be too much of a coincidence.

Had he stopped by to see Regina or Salvatore? If so, had it been an amiable visit? What business might he have with them? The possibility that he might have wanted to see Nella was a bit far-fetched, unless he had become accustomed to getting a quick meal in the kitchen whenever he took the Contessa to Burano.

Then there was also Giorgio's barely perceptible limp to consider. It endowed him with a romantic aura, especially because he was otherwise so obviously healthy. It also made him more difficult to confuse with a man of similar appearance. Was this the reason he seemed to try to conceal it, or was it vanity?

Urbino kept pulling and drawing on his thread, snipping it

here and there. It was slow, patient work, but he had done it
many times before with success. His thread was fine, and it was
white, as white as the background he was working it into, as
white as the fog on the night Nina Crivelli had been murdered.

Urbino entered the Fondamenta Ca' Bala, and continued in
the direction of the Grand Canal to the Campiello de Ca' Barbaro,
which he had crossed the other night. Here he encountered one of
the few other people he had seen so far on his walk. The young
man was walking a muzzled cocker spaniel, and greeted Urbino
with a nod as he passed.

Urbino made a detour that had him going back toward the Salute, until he took a turning that brought him down a narrow *calle*
to the edge of the Grand Canal. Above him were the windows of
the palazzo where a friend of Henry James had thrown herself to
her death over a hundred years ago, perhaps in unrequited love
for the cool Master.

Whenever he was in this part of Dorsoduro, he usually came
here out of a mild compulsion. He liked to stand where the
woman had met her death, partly as a reminder of a tragic event
with such reverberations in the life and work of a favorite writer
and partly for reasons he had never tried to figure out, and didn't
want to.

He looked across the Grand Canal to the illuminated Palazzo
Contarini-Fasan, with its pointed arches and Gothic balconies.
Like the building he was standing beside, this palazzo had its
own associations with love and death, for legend had sentimen-
tally identified it as the House of Desdemona.

Inevitably, Urbino started thinking about dark-skinned
Moors, jealousy, and handkerchiefs. Of all Shakespeare's trage-
dies, he responded most emotionally to *Othello*. It touched something close to his own fears and insecurities. Nobility in the grips
of the powerful, demeaning green-eyed monster was a terrible
thing to witness, and certainly a more terrible thing to experience.

He turned away from the Grand Canal. In a few minutes he
came to the canal where Polidoro had his shop and residence.
When Urbino noted that, unlike the other night, a second-story

window was unshuttered and lit, he had a sudden desire to speak with the art dealer. The shop was closed.

He rang the brass bell. When there was no answer, he rang again. He wouldn't have been so persistent at this hour if the light weren't on. When there was still no answer, he backed a few feet away and looked up at the window.

One of the curtains darkened as if someone had approached it. The shadow went away. A few moments later the light was extinguished.

Urbino didn't ring again. Several minutes later he jumped on a departing *vaporetto* headed toward the Cannaregio.

It was almost midnight when he got back to the Palazzo Uccello. Habib hadn't returned yet.

22

"H ow does this sound to you?" Urbino asked the Contessa the next morning before his rendezvous with Frieda. They were in the sun-washed morning room of the Ca' da Capo-Zendrini.

"I'm afraid to hear it." The Contessa lifted her cup of *caffèlatte*. She was seated across from him in a matching armchair covered in Fortuny fabric. "The expression on your face is so intense, and I must say you look a bit knackered."

"I'm fine. I just didn't sleep too well last night."

Habib hadn't returned until one-thirty. He had gone to his studio where Urbino had heard him puttering around. Urbino had eventually fallen asleep half an hour later. When he had awakened later than usual, Habib had already left.

"Are you all right, *caro*? Not a relapse, I hope?"

"No, I'm all right."

"Is there anything the matter with Habib?"

"Why do you ask?"

She shrugged and took a sip of coffee.

"I'm just concerned. So what is it you're so eager to pour into my ears before I'm barely awake?"

"It's about Giorgio."

"Indeed? What exactly?"

"Just listen. Don't say anything until I'm finished."

He told her about Salvatore's son Gino, who had been born with a slight clubfoot and who would be twenty-eight years old now. Giorgio, he pointed out, was about that age and had an obvious limp no matter how he tried to conceal it. He also had the kind of good looks that the child Gino might have grown up to possess. Giorgio had joined the Contessa's staff in a rather suspicious manner. It was possible that Oriana's infatuation had played into his hands in some way. Urbino also expressed his doubts about Giorgio's former employer, Signor Mazza, who had been so helpful and forthcoming in Capri. Now, no trace of him could be found, it seemed.

"Not long after Giorgio appears on the scene," he continued, avoiding looking at the Contessa, "things start to become strange. Nina Crivelli begins to follow you around. She accosts you in Santa Maria Formosa. She tries to get money out of you. Is it blackmail, extortion, or some clever swindle that takes advantage of your love for Alvise and your concern for his reputation? Or is it something else that we haven't even thought of? She also tries to enlist my help once I return. Then, on the night of Frieda's party, she ends up dead. According to the medical examiner, it's from natural causes, but it could be from something very different. There's all that business about the pills. And there are ways that a death can appear to be natural, but be very much the opposite. Sometimes even an autopsy doesn't get at the truth, and of course there was none done here."

He took a sip of mineral water before going on.

"Then, on that same night of Nina's death, Habib and Frieda can't find Giorgio. They come across a motorboat they think is yours but Giorgio is nowhere to be seen. A little while later he suddenly appears, and my rescue is under way. Could Giorgio have been the figure I saw in the fog, who approached me and then turned away?"

"You yourself have said you're not even sure if you saw anything! And Giorgio is not required to be with the boat every single moment. And it's the dead of winter!"

He didn't allow any of these comments to deflect him.

"Then, when I'm on Burano yesterday, I see what must be his cap lying on the counter of the restaurant kitchen. By the time I get back to the boat, his cap is on his head. And there's a smile on his face that seems to be more of a smirk.

"He had enough time to retrieve the cap and return to the boat before I got there. I had no clear view of the Via Galuppi from where I was in the restaurant, and no view at all of the *calle* that runs to the courtyard. He could have slipped into the kitchen by the back door, gone down the *calle* to the street, and then to the boat. Why is he hanging around the restaurant? Could Giorgio be Gino, come back for no good reason? For a very bad one, in fact? To punish his grandmother Nina Crivelli, who was responsible for all the troubles his mother and father suffered? Nina somehow recognized him after all these years and was going to tell you, if you gave her enough money. Then something goes very wrong, and he kills her!"

Having spelled it all out for the Contessa, he had to admit to himself that it sounded far-fetched. Yet his experience with other cases had shown him how bizarre human behavior could be, and how an almost incredible combination of chance and design could deliver a victim into the hands of a murderer.

"All the blind lace makers in Burano couldn't have stitched together a sorrier piece of material!" the Contessa burst out.

"Full of holes but no design?" he asked, mocking his thoughts of the night before.

"What? Well, yes, exactly! Maybe we should ask Oriana if she's ever been intimate enough with him to see an appendicitis scar! And as if his having one or not would prove anything either! I can think of a dozen inconsistencies. Why is he still hanging around the restaurant if he killed Nina? Don't give me any nonsense about a criminal revisiting the scene of his crime! And where is Salvatore in all this? Did he recognize Giorgio too?"

"Salvatore might very well have played a twisted and malicious role either alone, or in collusion with Giorgio. He—"

"And there's something else," she broke in. "Why would it have been worth a pretty penny to me to have Nina reveal that Giorgio was Gino?"

"Not worth anything to know that an employee in close contact with you, one with a great responsibility, had secured his job under false pretenses? That you were harboring an impostor here at the Ca' da Capo?"

As he said this, however, Urbino realized that it wasn't at all quite good enough as an explanation.

"Not worth what she probably wanted!" the Contessa shot back.

"I'm not saying she was thinking clearly, not if she recognized Giorgio for who he really was," he went on, with less and less conviction. "She would have known his return threatened her with the loss of what she needed most, Salvatore."

"I still don't see it. She would have dealt with him herself. *Caro, caro*, you're building a house of cards." She shook her head slowly. "It would make more sense if Giorgio had been killed, and you were arguing that Nina was the murderer! You have to rethink it. If you had told me everything you learned from Carolina Bruni right away instead of brooding over it the way you do over things, you wouldn't have lost yourself in such a maze! Giorgio's cap, for example! Maybe he did leave it there! So what? He might have become friendly with Nella during my visits to Burano and my meals at the restaurant. She probably had him dine royally for nothing while he was waiting for me. Or the cap could belong to any number of men. Giorgio's not the only man in Venice to wear a white cap."

Urbino started to pace around the room. He went to the fin de siècle Viennese piano and played a few notes at random. He knew the Contessa was right to be skeptical. So much in his scenario was incredible—mainly, of course, that Nina could have hoped to get money from the Contessa for revealing that Giorgio was Gino.

"I know you're worried about me," the Contessa said, breaking into his thoughts. "The way I'm so vulnerable here at the Ca' da Capo. I suppose I bear some of the responsibility for planting these suspicions about Giorgio in your mind. No sooner had you returned than I was complaining about all the changes here. But, as you know, you can set your mind at ease about Giorgio stalking me through the building with a monkey wrench at odd hours of the night."

"What are you talking about?"

"You don't know?" She held his gaze for a few moments, and then looked away. "As of yesterday evening, he's not living here anymore. He moved into that empty ground-floor apartment in my building in the Calle Convertite. I'm seeing that he gets a phone immediately so that he can be here quickly if I need him when he's off duty. To be honest with you, I can't blame him for wanting to be on his own. A good-looking young man like that needs more privacy than he was getting here, although I never interfered. I assumed Habib would have told you. He was here last night helping Giorgio move things to his new apartment. They did it quite late."

The Contessa was now looking intently at him. His own eyes went to the mantel clock. To his surprise, he saw that it would be impossible to be in the Piazza San Marco at eleven unless he rushed.

"I have to be going. I'm meeting Frieda at Quadri's."

He threw on his cape.

"All I'm asking you to do," he said, "is to think about what I've said."

"And you, *caro*, should think about what *I've* said."

23

Urbino arrived at Caffè Quadri at five minutes past eleven.
Frieda, in a suit of jade and plum, was seated at a table
beneath a large oval mirror. Her blunt-cut hair, uncovered by
one of her scarves, showed a lot of gray. Circles ringed her eyes.

"I was ready to leave."

"Leave? I'm not worth waiting more than five minutes for?"

"Five minutes? You're more than an hour late!"

"Didn't you say eleven?"

"Ten."

Urbino didn't press the matter.

"I'm sorry. May I sit down? I won't delay you much longer.
Would you like something?"

"I've already had a coffee."

Urbino ordered a Campari soda.

The room, with only two other tables occupied, was filled
with light. Compared to Florian's across the Piazza, Quadri's had
an open and airy feel with its trim little lamps, floral stucco
patterns, cream and light-green walls, and blue-green tiled floor.
It wasn't as popular as Florian's, and never had been. The Aus-
trians, during their occupation of the city, had favored it,
whereas the Venetians had shown their solidarity by frequent-
ing Florian's.

Urbino handed Frieda the cassette box of *Tristan und Isolde*.

"I see that I failed to convert Burano's resident diva."

"You tried. It mustn't be easy being a stranger on Burano."

"I haven't had many problems. Being Barbara's friend is an advantage. There is much respect for her."

"You've found that to be the case?"

She gave an amused smile.

"If you were not so devoted to her, I would think that you are surprised."

She might have meant this to be playful but it struck his ear as a bit frosty.

"You are thinking about that poor lace maker," she said, looking at him more intently. "She was an exception."

"Did she ever say anything against Barbara?"

"To me, no. But I have heard talk. There has been more of it since Barbara visited the lace makers who live by the church."

"You know them?"

"My neighbor Loretta does. I heard something about Barbara requesting prayers in church for the old woman, and about establishing a scholarship many years ago and trying to get the woman to return money. I am sure it is only gossip," she added in a dismissive tone. "Barbara is a kind and generous soul, yes! She is like a sister I have never had. And what she means to you is very evident."

"How well did you know the old lace maker?"

"I met her once, or maybe it was twice. She was very nice. I asked her about lace making. Oh, she had many stories to tell. The legend of lace, all about lost sailors and mermaids. You remember? It was the story I gave you all at my party. She told me about a Dogaressa's dress made of lace, and someone she kept calling the 'Michelangelo of the bobbins,' and the difference between needle lace and bobbin lace. She described stitches and threads, *filo tirato* and *reticello*, and *punto in aria* and *controtagliato*. She was more intelligent than you might think from looking at her."

"Your Italian pronunciation is excellent, and you must understand Italian very well to have learned all that from her. Did she ask you any questions?"

"Ha, ha! You know us writers, Urbino. We ask questions but we don't answer them if we can."

She was now staring out into the arcade. She opened her slightly protruding eyes wider.

"Oh, look! Marie and Beatrix!"

She dashed out to fetch the two women, and was soon shepherding them into the room.

The tall Beatrix, with her regal bearing, wore a long, dark coat. A hat perched on top of Marie's round head. It was a whimsical fabrication of leather and fur, and resembled an acorn. Both women were flushed.

"Where are you going?" Frieda asked.

"The Querini-Stampalia Museum," Beatrix responded. "To see the Gabriele Bella paintings about eighteenth century Venetian life! Regina Bella is related to him."

"I want to go to the Fortuny Museum. Beatrix says she is not interested in a lot of old fabric. And I say that I am not interested in the eighteenth century!"

"There's more than just Fortuny's fabric designs at his museum," Urbino said with a glance at Beatrix. "And the Gabriele Bella paintings at the Querini-Stampalia are interesting as well," he added, not wanting to take either side in their dispute.

"More old paintings," the plain-faced milliner said with a sniff.

"You never complained before," said the younger woman.

"Because I never saw so many old paintings all at once before," Marie shot back.

"You can go to the Fortuny Museum another day," Frieda said.

"I want to go today."

"So silly, my little one," Beatrix said. "I promise that we will stay for only an hour. Then we will have our celebration meal."

"What are you celebrating?" Urbino asked.

"Ten years of looking at old paintings!" Marie put in.

"There are worse things, my dear. Perhaps the two of you will join us? We are going to the Antico Martini."

"That's kind of you," Urbino said, "but I have plans. Perhaps some other time."

"I must go to the Biblioteca Marciana," Frieda said. "I may have left something there."

"But it is only on the other side of the Piazza," Beatrix pointed out. "You can still have lunch with us, after we go to the Querini-Stampalia."

"If it isn't at the Marciana, then I must turn the city up and down to find it."

Urbino remembered how pleased she had sounded yesterday evening when she first heard that he had something for her.

"It is very important then," Marie observed.

Frieda gave Urbino an embarrassed glance.

"Yes. Please excuse me."

She pulled on her coat and was gone before the topic might be pursued any further.

"We must be going as well," Beatrix said. "Come, Marie. Only an hour for old paintings, I promise. Good day, Urbino. Please give our greetings to Habib."

As Urbino finished his Campari soda, he mused over what it was that Frieda thought she had misplaced, and what it might have to do with him, given her look at him.

The other plans Urbino had mentioned involved Rebecca Mondador. There was something he hoped she could give him the answer to. She always had her midday meal at the same trattoria near her offices in San Polo. He passed through the archway under the Moors' Clock Tower. Above him the two brawny, dark-skinned bronze statues started to strike noon.

As he walked along the crowded street with its clothing stores and souvenir shops, he remarked to himself that everyone who spoke about Nina Crivelli, either to him or the Contessa, didn't have much good to say, except for Frieda. Could this be because she had barely known the woman, if that was indeed the case? Or did she have no better opinion of her than anyone else, but was holding herself back from saying so? Might not Nina have accosted her about the Contessa just as she had Urbino?

What also nagged at his mind about Frieda was that she was German, and that her Italian appeared to be quite good. Germany seemed to be where Salvatore's wife Evelina had run off to with their son. But what was he thinking? That Frieda might be Evelina returned after all these years? She was about the right age, just as Giorgio was the age that Gino would be now. But, for that matter, so was Beatrix.

Urbino could easily imagine the Contessa's ridicule if he confided these random thoughts to her.

First Giorgio, she'd say, and now Frieda and maybe even Beatrix?

It did sound as if he were conjuring up something like a Shakespearean masquerade. But he often needed to go off on tangents and consider extremes, and even contemplate what seemed to be the impossible. Eventually, it had been his good fortune to find a balance in this way, a balance that had him realizing with a sudden awareness and understanding what the truth was.

And, on one or two rare occasions, experience had shown that the extreme and the impossible were not that at all. They were instead something quite normal in different dress.

He stopped in the Church of San Zulian. A few tourists were examining Veronese's *Pietà*. Two elderly women in black were sitting in front of the simple altar.

As he looked up at the ceiling of carved and gilded wood with its paintings, his thoughts returned to Frieda. What might she have left at the Biblioteca Marciana? The most likely thing was something she had written. Could it be related to the case?

No matter how he turned around all these unanswered questions about Frieda, however, he couldn't come up with anything that might link her with Nina's murder. Living on Burano hadn't necessarily given her more contact with her than anyone else. All her guests that night had been in just as good a position, if not better, to do the ultimate harm to Nina. And the opportunity to murder Nina would have to take final place after motive and means. Both were, in this case, far less than straightforward.

As Urbino stepped out of the church, a friend hailed him. They hadn't seen each other since he had returned from Morocco. All the way to the Rialto, they caught up on things. Vittorio, a history professor at Ca' Foscari, suggested that they have lunch with some other friends who were waiting for him at Al Graspo de Ua.

But for the second time today, Urbino was obliged to decline lunch, and they parted in front of the restaurant.

When he reached the trattoria where Rebecca had her midday meal, her colleague, a small man in a black suit, was sitting at her customary table. He informed Urbino that Rebecca had been called unexpectedly to Rome on business and wouldn't be back for a week.

25

When he returned to the Palazzo Uccello an hour later, Natalia said that the Contessa had called several times and asked him to get back to her as soon as possible. He was reaching for the telephone when it rang.

"Urbino! Finally! I've been trying to get in touch with you ever since I heard."

"Heard? About what?"

"Marino Polidoro. He's in the hospital. In a coma. It's not certain that he'll pull through."

"What happened?"

"No one knows. His cleaning woman found him unconscious in his shop this morning. Things were all broken up around him. They don't know if he was hit on the head, or injured himself when he fell or was pushed."

"How did you find out?"

"When I called my dressmaker for an appointment. Everyone is talking about it in Dorsoduro."

Urbino told her how he had walked by Polidoro's building late last night and had seen the window in his apartment lit only to have it extinguished when he rang the bell.

"Why did you want to speak with him?"

"It was on the spur of the moment. I was on one of my walks and happened to be in his area."

"Happened to be! On one of your walks! As if you take those walks for exercise! Well, keep it to yourself! Maybe I don't want to know if it's even half as bizarre as what you've been thinking about Giorgio. But whatever it is, you'll probably have to tell the police. Your good old friend Gemelli."

Gemelli, the commissario at the Questura, considered Urbino a meddler, but he couldn't ignore that Urbino had been a help to him in the past. In fact, Gemelli had occasionally taken the credit for the successful resolution of some cases in which Urbino had played a crucial role.

"He needs to be approached at the right time and with a stronger theory than I can give him now."

"But you do think what's happened to Marino is related to Nina Crivelli?"

"I need to think it through a little more."

"Don't take too long! Who knows what could happen? You may be able to convince him that Nina didn't die from natural causes, or at least arouse his suspicions. We can only benefit from that."

"That means you're no longer torturing yourself about your relationship to the whole affair. Not that I ever thought it's anything but an indirect one."

"Not even considering your theory that Giorgio is Gino Crivelli returned from Germany to kill his grandmother?"

"What I mean is that I don't think now, nor ever did, that it had anything to do with the Conte."

He chose his words carefully, wanting to keep Giorgio out of the picture for the moment.

"Even if it does, I have to face the truth. It's better to do it sooner than later." She brought this off with an air of bravery that carried across the line with the residue of something directed more personally at Urbino. Like many of her insinuations since he had returned to Venice, it seemed to brush its wings up against his relationship with Habib. "I'm depending on you to make things as easy for me as possible. But if there's anything more I can do, let me know. I don't like to be put on the shelf."

"You could never be put on any shelf! As a matter of fact, there is something you can do. It's about Regina Bella. Carolina Bruni suspects she's having a relationship with some man and wants to keep it a secret. Try to find out more about it. Being a woman, you would have an easier time of it."

"Because we women are such meddlers and gossips that it wouldn't draw as much attention. I'll see what I can do."

"There's another thing. Exactly how did you and Frieda meet at Gstaad?"

"Even poor Frieda comes under scrutiny after taking such good care of the Palazzo Uccello?"

"I sensed that you were a little suspicious of her yourself the night of her party."

"Whatever do you mean?"

"When she mentioned Nina and said that she had a lot of imagination."

"You're wrong. I was suspicious of Nina and what she might have said about me. But Frieda has never given any sign that she's heard any gossip. If I'm suspicious of anything about Frieda, *caro*, it's that she's a writer. God only knows what such people can be up to!"

She paused. Urbino could imagine her smiling at this gentle jab at him.

"You can strike her off your list with a very strong and black line," she went on. "I was the one to approach her. I overheard her ask the concierge to make reservations for her in Venice. That night at dinner we were both sitting alone. I introduced myself and asked if I could join her. I told her I lived in Venice. It was only then that I learned who she was. I can't say that I had ever heard of her, but that doesn't mean anything, since her books aren't my cup of tea. We hit it off right away, though, and I never felt in the slightest way that she wasn't what she seemed. I'd never have given her the responsibility of the Palazzo Uccello or the Casa Verde if I had."

26

When Urbino was about to sit down to what was now a rather late lunch, Natalia told him that Habib had also called two hours earlier. He had decided to go to Verona on a trip organized by the language school and wouldn't be back until after ten.

Despite the meal of *sarde in saor* with grilled polenta, which was one of Urbino's favorites, he didn't have much appetite.

He went to the library where he tried to work on *Women of Venice*, but once again, as had happened last night, he couldn't concentrate. His mind played over the various aspects of the Nina Crivelli case. He wrote names on a sheet of paper and then connected them, sometimes with firm lines, other times with dotted lines and question marks. The effort brought him nowhere. He crumpled up the sheet of paper.

He called the hospital. Marino Polidoro's condition was the same.

What had happened? Had someone broken in and attacked him? Or had a late-night rendezvous gone wrong? Was the attack related to his business or to Burano? Or possibly to both at the same time? Urbino speculated about how Polidoro's life-threatening coma could be related to Nina Crivelli's murder. Last night he had assumed that the dealer himself, after seeing him in the street below, had extinguished the light in his window. It was completely possible that the figure behind the curtain hadn't been Polidoro, but the man—or woman—who had attacked him.

The attack seemed to have taken place during Urbino's walk through the Dorsoduro. It wouldn't be easy to find out where certain people had been during this same period. For example, had Salvatore, Regina, and Frieda all been on Burano? If any of them had come to Venice, the night boat crew might remember, since the water bus between Burano and Venice was infrequent during those hours. But there was the possibility that someone could have hired a water taxi or even have had a private boat at his or her disposal, in which case there would be no trace.

As for Beatrix and Marie, they were within easy striking distance of the Dorsoduro from their apartment on the Fondamenta Nuove.

But all of these people could have been behind their own doors or in their own beds, with pleasant or troubled dreams, during the crucial hours. The only two who Urbino knew for sure had been out and about last night were Giorgio and Habib, sometimes together, at other times alone.

Urbino regretted that Rebecca was out of town. If he were lucky, she might be able to provide a necessary piece of information. He called her office and learned that she was staying at the Hotel d'Inghilterra.

The hotel informed him that she was out. He left a message for her to call him.

27

At ten-thirty that evening Habib's quick steps bounded up the staircase. He first went into his study for a few minutes, and then, in search of Urbino, he came to the library. When he entered the room, he stopped short.

"Something is the matter, *sidi*. I can tell from your face."

"I'm fine. How was Verona?"

"It was interesting, *sidi*. I decided to go at the last minute. We saw Juliet's balcony. But I think you are angry that I am late. You would have been proud of me! I spoke Italian for almost the whole day. I learned a new Italian song. Do you want to hear it?"

"Not now. I have a few questions I want to ask you."

Habib's expression was pained, as if he'd been wounded. He dropped into a chair and stared at Urbino from under his long dark lashes.

"The answers are important to me, and also to other people. Tell me, Habib, how often have you been to Burano? In addition to the time we went alone and when we all went to Frieda's party."

"That German lady!" Habib burst out. "She is strange the way she looks sharply at me with her eyes squeezing out of her head. She looks at me, then she looks at you."

"Have you been to Burano more than the two times?" Urbino asked again, refusing to be sidetracked. "As I said before, it doesn't matter if you have, but I'd like to know."

For a few moments Habib's face became set in thought as he seemed to contemplate the arabesque patterns on the carpet. Then he looked up with an expression that was a little wary.

"Yes," he admitted with a sigh. "Three or four times, *sidi*. But I had a good reason to go and also a good reason not to tell you. You must believe me! Or else I will be too sad."

His voice was wistful and a little defeated.

"Did your reasons have something to do with Giorgio?" Urbino pursued. "You've been spending a lot of time with him. You helped him move to his new apartment last night. Did you spend all those hours going back and forth between there and Barbara's?"

"First you ask me about Burano. Now it is about Giorgio! I am sorry, *sidi*, but I am not accustomed to count the hours and the minutes the way that you are!" A note of truculence had entered his voice. "I helped Giorgio and the time passed, and then I came back here. There is nothing wrong with Giorgio. You have bad feelings against him. He is good to me," he added with what was now almost a defiant air.

"I believe that you think he is. You have an open nature, but not everyone does, Habib. And you have to realize that I can understand people here better than you can. It's like the way I had to depend on you in Morocco, when I didn't understand things properly because it wasn't my culture. And if you haven't told me the whole truth—"

Habib sprang to his feet.

"No!" He swiped at a pile of books on the table and sent them flying to the floor. "You say I lie and deceive you! It is unfair! You don't trust me. You don't believe my words. I will show you instead. But then everything will be spoiled! And I am finished forever with that island of bad luck!"

He bolted out of the room. A few moments later the front door slammed.

28

Urbino remained seated, half-expecting Habib to come back. When he didn't, he gathered together the books and stacked them on the table again. He poured himself a generous portion of whisky and drank most of it down quickly.

He had done it all wrong, he berated himself. He should have known what Habib's reaction was going to be.

He remembered the time in a gold shop in the Fez medina when the owner had asked Habib to turn out his pockets. Habib had shouted and pushed the man against the counter. It had frightened Urbino because he was worried that it would get Habib into trouble with the police, but the episode was soon smoothed over. The ring was found, and fifteen minutes later all three of them were having tea in the back room.

Urbino went to Habib's studio. His satchel was lying on the divan. Inside was a photograph of a smiling Habib and two of his fellow students. Urbino recognized them as French girls whom he and Jerome hung around with. The picture had been taken in Verona, probably by an itinerant photographer who had an instant camera. Above their heads Urbino could make out Juliet's balcony.

On the table were Habib's passport, his Italian residency card, and his identity card from the language school, which he had forgotten in his haste. He carried them with him almost all the time. It was a habit he had formed in Morocco where any policeman could arrest you if you didn't have them—or even if you did, as Urbino too well remembered from the time he had managed to avert this from happening in the Fez medina.

It made him nervous to think of Habib being out of the house without them, even here in Italy. As an American, Urbino had never become accustomed to the need to carry around his own residency card all the time.

He checked his wristwatch. Habib had been gone almost half an hour.

What had he meant about showing Urbino something and everything being spoiled? When he had stormed out of the house, it had been with an aim in mind. And, Urbino realized, a destination.

He telephoned the Contessa. She picked it up on the second ring.

"Giorgio's address? You know the building, don't you? In the Calle Convertite right off the Fondamenta Pescaria. But why do you want it at this hour? Are you—"

"I'll explain tomorrow."

He scribbled a hasty note to Habib on the off chance that he might return while Urbino was out. He put Habib's documents into his cape pocket and left the Palazzo Uccello.

It wasn't far to the Fondamenta Pescaria, which was along the Cannaregio Canal. He took the quickest route, which someone inexperienced with Venice like Habib would have considered the back route. It would gain him perhaps five minutes.

As he emerged on the embankment from beneath the Sottoportego del Ghetto, a blue police boat with its light flashing was visible in the canal. He hurried in its direction. Two policemen were leading Habib, handcuffed, to the boat.

"*Sidi*! Please help me! I did nothing wrong! He was dead when I got there. Giorgio is dead!"

As the policemen helped Habib into the boat, he threw Urbino a wild and desperate look. Unlike the time in Morocco, Urbino knew that nothing he might say to the policemen, in any language, would get them to release him.

PART THREE

PUNTO IN ARIA

1

On the second morning after the scene on the Fondamenta Pescaria, Urbino bought a copy of *Il Gazzettino* from the kiosk on the Strada Nuova. The events on the edge of the ghetto had occurred too late to reach the paper yesterday morning.

But Urbino didn't open the newspaper in the middle of the busy thoroughfare, tempted though he was. He was on his way to the Ca' da Capo-Zendrini. He would wait until he and the Contessa could read it together.

The past two days had been almost total confusion. The police were detaining Habib on suspicion of the murder of Giorgio. It was feared that if he were released before the full investigation was completed, he would escape to Morocco.

Urbino had failed, despite the services of one of the best lawyers and the intervention of Corrado Scarpa, to secure Habib's release. He hadn't been allowed to see or speak with him, or even send him a note.

Luigo Torino, the lawyer, said that Habib was being treated in the same manner as the other prisoners, which was intended to be a consolation. Urbino was tortured, however, by the thought of Habib locked away in a cell that he imagined not much more comfortable than the ancient ones attached to the Ducal Palace.

Three policemen had come to the Palazzo Uccello yesterday afternoon and gone through Habib's possessions. Urbino had opened the cabinet with the spare key. Nothing inside had looked even remotely suspicious to Urbino, but the policemen had taken away letters, photographs, a small appointment book, and, for some reason, Habib's language school notebooks.

Urbino was oblivious to the scene around him on the Strada Nuova. He returned greetings from friends and shopkeepers mechanically. He almost upset a table of socks displayed for sale, and collided with several people walking in the opposite direction.

Weary, distracted, he dropped into a chair in the Contessa's morning room and opened the newspaper. He found the piece on Giorgio's murder on the first page of the Venice news and read it out loud:

BOATMAN MURDERED IN CANNAREGIO

Signor Giorgio Fratino, 28, of Venice and formerly of Naples was found bludgeoned to death in his apartment in the Calle Convertite on Thursday evening. Dr. Franco Brilli, the medical examiner, pronounced Signor Fratino dead on the scene at 12:17 A.M.

Residents of the area reported hearing an altercation. A suspect, Habib Laroussi, a Moroccan national of 24, was restrained by two of the residents of an adjoining apartment and subsequently arrested. He remains in police custody.

Signor Fratino had been a resident of the city for the past eight months and was employed as boatman and chauffeur by the Contessa da Capo-Zendrini. Before moving to his quarters in the Calle Convertite, he occupied rooms at the Ca' da Capo-Zendrini.

Commissario Gemelli of the Venice Questura did not wish to comment on the investigation except to say that all proper procedures were being followed in their attempt to determine what brought Signor Fratino to his untimely end.

It was the Contessa who broke the silence after he finished reading.

"They would have to mention my name twice. I'm sorry," she added. "That's a terrible thing to say. How's Habib doing?"

Urbino stared at her and shook his head slowly.

"The Moroccan embassy still hasn't sent anyone up from Rome. Habib in prison! It's inconceivable!"

The Contessa patted his hand.

"We'll get him out soon."

"If I could only see him! He probably thinks I've abandoned him."

"Stop this nonsense! He knows you're doing whatever you can. Here, have some coffee."

Urbino declined. His nerves were already in a terrible state.

"I'll have some anisette."

He poured himself a generous portion.

"Who do you think killed Giorgio?" the Contessa asked.

"All I know is that it wasn't Habib, and that whoever did, probably also killed Nina Crivelli."

"You'll have a hard time convincing Gemelli of that. Be prepared for what he'll say. That you're blind to the truth. That you've lost a proper sense of proportion. That you're grasping at straws. You—"

"How easily all that comes off your tongue! I have no doubts about what he'll say. Gemelli and I have been on opposite sides of questions before, and once or twice it was because of your own interests, don't forget! Now I have something at stake."

"Don't let it carry you away. Try to keep some kind of proportion."

For the second time the Contessa mentioned his danger of losing a sense of proportion. It was good advice, of course, but even as he took it in, he feared that, although so short a time had passed since he had seen Habib hustled off by the police, he was already too far down the road to stop himself. He wasn't even sure that he wanted to. His need to believe in Habib was a rock that he clung to.

He tossed down the remainder of his anisette.

"I have to be going. I'll call you after I see Gemelli."

"Why don't you come for dinner? Even better, why not spend the night, or as long as you like? Your room is always waiting for you."

She sighed, for she must have been reminded of the last time he had slept in the room. It had been during a house party when the Ca' da Capo-Zendrini had been buffeted by the terrible storm and one of the other guests had been murdered.

"I don't want you to be alone."

He gave a hollow laugh.

"Don't you think I'm used to it?"

"Things are different now."

"Yes, well, at any rate, I don't think I'll be wandering around the Palazzo Uccello like some pathetic soul."

2

B ut that was exactly what he did when he got back home. He roamed through the rooms, feeling oppressed by all the objects that used to give him so much pleasure. He sank into an armchair only to get up a few moments later. Natalia watched him silently with a sad look on her face whenever his steps carried him into the kitchen.

Knowing he wouldn't be able to eat a full lunch today any more than yesterday, she was preparing his favorite fillings for *tramezzini*. The scent of baking *pancarré*, however, gave him more pain than pleasure, for he remembered how much Habib delighted in the little sandwiches. He told Natalia he would eat in the library.

He went to Habib's studio. The Arab diva stared down at him with a vaguely melancholy look. Under a chair were Habib's slippers, at odd angles to each other, where he had kicked them off. They seemed to speak of the abruptness with which he had been snatched away from safety.

Urbino picked them up to add to a suitcase of clothes and other items he would bring to the Questura for Habib. He could hardly remember what he had tossed into the first one he had entrusted to Torino.

On a little table was the family of glass squirrels that Pignatti had made for Habib. Two of them had fallen on their side. Urbino straightened them.

As he was leaving the studio, a large book lying on the floor and partly concealed by the drape of the cover of the divan, caught his attention. It was the German–English dictionary from the library. He bent down to retrieve it and exposed a large manila envelope behind it. The flap of the envelope was unsealed. Inside was a folder with several sheets of paper. Without examining the sheets, he took the envelope and the dictionary to the library.

On the refectory table was a tray with a plate of *tramezzini*. There was also a pitcher of fresh orange juice, which Natalia believed was a cure for everything from a headache to liver ailment. He doctored the pitcher with vodka. He knew he should keep a clear head for his meeting with Gemelli that afternoon, but he also needed to get through the intervening hours as well.

Inside the folder were several sheets of unlined paper covered with German writing in a large, sprawling hand. He took a shrimp-filled sandwich and started to read. It was slow going at first, both because of the handwriting and also because of his less than firm grasp of German.

He had no doubt he was reading something that Frieda Hensel had written. It was in the manner of some of her other tales. He made a rough translation into English in his mind as he read, stopping often to look up unfamiliar words in the dictionary. He realized that his loose and inexact translation didn't do justice to Frieda's haunting style. The story went something like this:

> In a kingdom of ice and snow, the young prince ordered all the mirrors destroyed. "From this time forward," he announced, "let other people be our mirrors."
>
> The guards went throughout the kingdom smashing mirrors large and small, and threw the fragments into a deep well in the mountains. No guard, not even the most trusted, was allowed to seek out the mirrors in the palace.
>
> The prince himself went through all the three hundred and sixty-five rooms, for each had its mirror, large or small, round, oval, square, and rectangular. He broke all of them, except one.

This mirror had stood in the nursery since before he was born. He would take it out to sea and send it to the dark depths where every fish is blind.

He bid a sad farewell to his ailing father and held up the last mirror in the kingdom to show the old man his reflection.

"Go, my son. I will be dead before you return."

No more, no less than three days' journey in the kingdom's mightiest ship brought the prince to the enchanted spot. While the captain and the crew watched in silence, the prince dropped the mirror off the stern into the steel-blue waters.

No sooner did it slip beneath the surface than a storm began. The ship was hit by gales from the north. Stones of ice fell on the deck. It was seared by the hot, dry winds of the south. Sand collected in the furled sails.

Little by little the ship was driven toward the black magnetic rocks feared by all seafarers. The captain, a brave and experienced man, threw his turban into the sea and said that they must all now make their peace with God.

The magnetic rocks pulled all the nails, one by one, from the ship, and added them to thousands and thousands of others. The sailors were tossed into the sea as the ship fell apart. Everyone was drowned except the prince.

He was tossed by the wind and carried by the waves for three days and three nights. He lost all sense.

The prince awoke to find himself on an island of golden sands and green trees. He ate bananas and dates, and drank the milk of a coconut, and then fell asleep.

He awoke to see a ship sailing toward the island. At first his heart leaped at this timely rescue. Then he climbed to a treetop and concealed himself among its leaves.

The ship anchored. Seven slaves emerged, each with a silver shovel over his shoulder. They stopped beneath the prince's tree and began to dig until they uncovered a little door. They opened it. Seven more slaves came from the ship, burdened with all manner of foods and spices bursting from sacks and piled high in baskets. Even chickens and sheep were among the bounty they carried to the door and down into the ground. Then came fur-niture, and carpets, and robes and slippers. All disappeared through the door.

Out of the ship emerged an old man with a long, white beard. Beside him was a boy of great beauty, with smooth cin-namon skin and the eyes of a gazelle. This boy, who possessed the grace and innocence of a young animal, enchanted the prince. He was seized with an uncontrollable love. The conceal-ing leaves of the tree, brushed by a warm breeze, didn't quiver any more than he did himself.

The prince watched with all his senses keen as the old man and the boy disappeared through the door and into the earth.

And then the procession from the ship to the door was re-versed. The slaves returned, empty-handed, and the old man slowly made his way on board, but not with the beautiful boy. Slaves covered the door with dirt once more. The ship departed.

Within moments the prince was clearing the door of earth and lifting it, not even feeling the effort. A spiraling staircase, encrusted with seashells and coral, carried him downward, then downward still.

There a large, oval chamber blossomed before him. It was as richly decorated as the palace in the kingdom of ice and snow. No space was unadorned. Carpets lay three deep on the floor, and tapestries of sylvan scenes hung from the walls. Books and musical instruments, embroidered ottomans and golden cande-labra, were in lovely disarray. Braziers wafted the scent of myrrh and bergamot and ambergris. From the lofty ceiling on a chain of gold hung a censer, also of gold, out of which licked blue, orange, and violet flames.

Nowhere was there a mirror.

In the middle of the oval room, seated on a divan of ebony, with a canopy festooned with flowers, and surrounded by can-dles and a rich variety of fruits and sweets, sat the boy holding a jewel-encrusted fan. His large dark eyes flared up in fear. He fell backward against the cushions

"Do not fear me, beautiful young man," said the prince in a whisper. "I have been brought a long distance to rescue you

from this death beneath the earth. I give you love more precious than water in the desert, or the sun in my kingdom of ice and snow. You will be my friend forever."

"I see by your gentle voice that you mean me no harm," said the boy. His voice was like a liquid. "Come sit next to me."

The prince did as he was bid. He soon was drinking in at closer sight the boy's gentle beauty.

"You are mistaken, good sir," continued the boy. "I have been brought here not to die, but so that I might live. I am the only son of a rich jeweler. When I was born, a soothsayer told him that a prince would kill me after he threw a mirror into the sea and survived the wreck of his ship. For sixteen years he kept me hidden from the world. But then, three days ago, he heard that such a man had approached the edges of our kingdom. He brought me to this place, which has been awaiting me since the year of my birth. The prince will not be able to find me here. In forty days my father will return. All will then be well."

Upon hearing this story, the prince, who had always believed in soothsayers, cursed them silently for their lies and foolishness.

"My dear boy," he said. "No one could ever be so cruel to one so beautiful. I will keep you company for all the forty days, and when they are passed, you will come to my kingdom to be my friend and my heir."

And so the prince and the boy stayed together until the fortieth day. The prince served the boy the most delicious foods. Lamb and pine nuts. Duck in pomegranate sauce. Salads of oranges and dates. Olives and preserved lemons. Rose-flavored apples and cakes of honey. He bathed him in perfumed waters. And every night he slept with him in the canopied bed to show his love and protection.

The day arrived on which they eagerly awaited the coming of the boy's father and the beginning of their life together above the earth. The prince bathed the boy as had become his treasured habit, and carried him to the divan. He presented him with his favorite lime-pistachio sherbet.

> *After a honeyed nap, the boy wished for some watermelon to eat. The prince climbed on the bed to get the knife hung on the wall. At that moment the boy, in his playfulness, tickled the leg of the prince.*
>
> *All control was lost because of this sweet mischief, and the prince fell on top of the boy and drove the knife straight through his heart. The boy died in the arms of the prince.*
>
> *The prince became mad with grief. He tore his garments and cursed the workings of fate. When the old jeweler arrived with his retinue, he found the prince as motionless as the boy he was clasping in his arms.*

Frieda had written two lines after this, but they had been crossed out and were undecipherable.

Urbino felt chilled. He poured himself another drink.

With an unshakable certainty, he knew that this story was what Frieda was searching all around Burano and Venice for.

His mind went back, as it was doing so often now, to the night of Frieda's party. When he had asked her if she were planning to write something about Burano, she had said, rather mysteriously, that she was working on something that was sure to interest him even more. And then she had glanced at Habib.

It didn't take too much effort to figure out that she must have been referring to what he had just read, with its distorted, camouflaged similarities to his relationship with Habib. It had only been after her party, however, that he had told her the circumstances of his first meeting with Habib in the Fez medina. The story's conception, if not its composition, seemed to have come before either of the two murders as well as before his own confidences.

The story spoke of responsibility and all too clearly and painfully of Habib's vulnerability. The boy in it had trusted not wisely, but too well, and had ended up dead because of it.

How had the story ended up in Habib's possession? Frieda hadn't given it to him. If she had, she wouldn't think she had lost it.

Did the story have anything to do with how Habib had

rushed out of the Palazzo Uccello, apparently in search of something to show him? Something that, once shown, would spoil everything, as he had said? And could all of this be related to the altercation at Giorgio's apartment that the neighbors heard before Habib was arrested?

The German dictionary indicated that Habib had been reading the story. How far had he gotten, and how much had he understood?

And why hadn't he told him about it? It appeared as if he had been trying to conceal it beneath the divan.

Could he have taken it from the Casa Verde? Habib might not be a murderer, but was he a thief?

Urbino cried out a silent protest.

There were holes everywhere, holes that could never contribute to any design, it seemed to him, no matter how skillfully and patiently one plied the needle. They were holes big enough to fall into.

He was overwhelmed with an even greater urgency than before to help Habib.

If to help was to harm, as the tale said in its sinister way, then they were already doomed.

3

Urbino had never gone to the Questura with more trepidation and anger than he did at four that afternoon. He didn't know if all the alcohol he had drunk was going to prove to be a handicap or not, but at the moment he was grateful for its comfort. He felt forlorn as he sat in Gemelli's outer office, the valise for Habib on the floor beside him.

Fortunately, Commissario Gemelli didn't keep him waiting long.

As soon as Urbino seated himself on the other side of the metal desk, Gemelli switched on the tape recorder. He was a dark, good-looking man in his early fifties, with a military bearing.

"We meet again, Macintyre. Too bad our paths don't cross socially as well."

He picked up a crushed pack of cigarettes and gestured with it in Urbino's direction.

"Still not smoking? Even now?"

He took a cigarette out, smoothed it, and lit it. Gulls screeched outside the windows.

"You're not looking well. Much worse than your Moroccan friend, as a matter of fact. But perhaps that's not so strange considering the difference in your ages. How well do you know Laroussi?"

Habib had always been happy that his name sounded Italian. It made him feel less a stranger in the country. But he wouldn't be pleased with Gemelli's tone. No sooner did Urbino think this, than he reminded himself that by now Habib had probably become all too familiar with the commissario's tone.

"Quite well."

"And for how long?"

"Sixteen months."

Gemelli took a drag on his cigarette.

"What exactly is the nature of your relationship?"

"As you just said, Habib Laroussi's my friend."

"Friends across the ages and across the seas, but, obviously in this case, not across the sexes."

Urbino remained silent for a few moments, then said, "Call it a very particular friendship."

"I assume you want to help your particular friend, Macintyre. Going all evasive isn't the way."

"He could be further endangered if I'm not careful about what I say and how I say it. I wouldn't withhold any information that I believed would be of help to him, no matter what it might be, but I have no intention of telling you anything that might be used against him."

"So we'll call your relationship with Laroussi a particular friendship. Knowing you as I do, it tells me enough, but only for the moment, I assure you. How did you meet?"

Urbino told him the story he had told Frieda, about how Habib had come to his rescue when he had been mugged in the Fez medina. He could see from Gemelli's expression that he was even more skeptical of Habib's motives than Frieda had been.

When he finished, Gemelli said, "The oldest scam in the book. Two guys working over the dupe. The bad one and the good one. And you showered Laroussi with all your trust and a good deal of money. You were ripe for the picking as soon as you stepped into that Arab street looking like someone from the pages of *L'Uomo Vogue*."

"You're mistaken."

"I am? Tell me. What did the Fez police say when you filed a report?"

Urbino shifted uneasily in his seat.

"I didn't go to the police."

"Indeed? And why not?"

Urbino wanted to shout that he hadn't gone because the police there were even ten times worse than Gemelli himself was, which was pretty bad to begin with. But he kept his silence.

"Let me answer for you. You didn't because Laroussi said it wasn't a good idea. They would harass him, he said, and he didn't want them to bother you either. You had your wallet, he pointed out. There was no need to get the police involved. Something like that, was it?"

Urbino said nothing. Gemelli shook his head.

"I thought you were a smart guy, Macintyre. Who's smarter? You or Laroussi, who's now here in Italy and living with you at the Palazzo Uccello as your very particular friend? Oh, but I forget. He's not there at the moment, is he? He's being detained on suspicion of murder in his own private little cell. On very strong suspicion."

"You don't even have circumstantial evidence against him."

Gemelli gave an unpleasant smile and snuffed out his cigarette in the stub-filled ashtray.

"Don't be so sure of that."

Urbino waited for him to say more, but it soon became obvious that he wasn't going to be sharing this kind of information, if, in fact, he had any. Gemelli lit up another cigarette, went to one of the windows, and pushed aside the curtain.

"Luigi Torino has filed all the papers and is petitioning to have Laroussi released under your supervision, Macintyre, but it's not going to happen. Not even if the representative from the Moroccan embassy has a letter tomorrow from his ambassador. Laroussi is going to be staying there a while longer." He paused, still looking down at the canal with its police boats. "A whole lot longer."

"You can't keep him there forever. He's innocent."

Gemelli dropped the curtain and turned back to Urbino.

"I can't believe how American you still are after all these years. Let's assume that he's as innocent as the lamb you think he is. His chances for staying in Italy are less than zero, with the way things are in the world these days. We know them all too well down in Sicily, believe me, Macintyre."

"Them?" Urbino repeated with a challenge

"North Africans. Arabs. Muslims. Illegal immigrants."

"Signor Laroussi is not illegal, and he's not an immigrant. He has a valid residency permit."

"Which can be revoked at any time, especially under the circumstances, and even if he is a lamb. Even your own land of freedom isn't too favorable to his kind. This isn't America, but it isn't Morocco either. That's why young men like Laroussi will do anything to get here. And stay. Take his brother, for example."

Gemelli looked at Urbino closely.

"Which brother? He has two."

"But he had three."

Urbino tried to conceal his surprise.

"His brother Lotfi died three years ago," Gemelli went on. "He was in a small boat with twenty other North Africans. They had got to Malta. From there they were promised passage to the golden shores of Italy by one of our industrious immigration gangs. For a very generous sum, of course. When the Italian coast guard approached, he jumped into the sea, and drowned off the coast of Sicily."

"How terrible!"

"A common enough story these days. As I said, those people will do anything to get here. I guess Laroussi's brother didn't have any luck crossing over to Spain from Morocco."

Urbino's heart was pounding. He was a confusion of thoughts and emotions. Gemelli's revelation put in a new light Habib's distress over the Albanian woman who he thought had been about to throw herself in the Grand Canal and possibly drown. It also explained his fascination with the article on the accidental deaths of the illegal immigrants in England.

"You'll never find out who really killed Fratino if you can't see any farther than your own prejudices!" Urbino broke out.

His anger brought an amused look to Gemelli's face.

Urbino stood up.

"Look for a link between Fratino's murder and the death of the former lace maker, Nina Crivelli, two weeks ago on Burano."

To Urbino's satisfaction Gemelli now seemed puzzled.

"Are you saying that this woman—what was her name? Crivelli?—was murdered?"

"The medical examiner says it was a massive heart attack, but she was murdered. I'm sure of it."

"As sure as you are of Laroussi's innocence? We'll do some checking up, if only because you've been right a few times before. I'll grant you that. But let me tell you something. You may be opening another can of worms and dumping it right in Laroussi's plate. Some link between Fratino's murder and the murder—or so you say—of this lace maker? Laroussi could be that link. Three paintings of Burano were found in Fratino's apartment. Laroussi admits to having painted them."

"*Admits*? I'm surprised you don't say *confesses*. Do you have someone who speaks Arabic? Or are you managing to confuse the poor boy completely?"

"He understands us well enough, believe me. But maybe your Torino with his Ermenegildo Zegna suit should have thought of that himself. At any rate, tomorrow or the next day the official from the Moroccan embassy will be arranging for someone from the university here to do the translating."

"By which time you will have managed to get him to say anything! I want to see him as soon as possible!"

Gemelli took a long drag on his cigarette.

"You know, Macintyre, I actually feel sorry for you. For the first time since we've been squaring off against each other. Yes, you can see your particular friend, Laroussi. I'll make arrangements for tomorrow morning after he meets with the Moroccan official. And I'll see that your lovely little valise is delivered to him this evening."

4

Exactly how he got back home Urbino didn't remember. He had a jumbled impression of squares and bridges, of twisting alleys and dark passageways under buildings, of looming statues and cluttered market stalls. Lone gondoliers at the foot of bridges, desperate for commerce in this period between the New Year and Carnevale, called out "Gondola! Gondola!" mistaking him, perhaps because of his distracted air, for a tourist. He returned the greetings of acquaintances mechanically and hurried on.

The house seemed cold and empty. Serena greeted him at the top of the staircase as she usually did, but even she seemed bewildered. Her plume of a tail drooped at a discouraged angle. He gave her a generous portion of her favorite canned food sent by a friend in London, but she only sniffed at it and padded away.

A note from Natalia said that Rebecca had telephoned and would be back at the Hotel d' Inghilterra at six o'clock. It was twenty-five minutes past five.

After a quick shower, he poured himself a glass of Corvo. He then telephoned Frieda from the library. The pages of her story were still scattered over the surface of the refectory table.

"It's Urbino. We have to talk," he said as soon as she had picked up.

"Urbino! I was just thinking about calling you. I need—"

"Did you find what you thought you had left at the Biblioteca Marciana?"

"No, I—"

"I believe I have what you're looking for. A manila envelope with a story about a prince from a kingdom of ice and snow who kills a jeweler's son."

During the long moment of silence that descended on the line to Burano, Urbino could feel the German woman's surprise. Or was it fear?

"You have it? I don't understand."

"Neither do I. I have some questions I need to ask you, but not over the phone."

"I have some questions as well." She had regained some of her composure. "As well as something to show you. That's why I was about to telephone you."

"I'll come over tonight."

"No, no! I will come to the Palazzo Uccello. I am having dinner with Marie and Beatrix at their apartment." The two women had rooms on the Fondamenta Nuove, about a fifteen-minute walk from the Palazzo Uccello. "I will also spend the night with them. I will see you at nine o'clock."

She hung up before he could tell her that Habib had been arrested. But perhaps she already knew and in her confusion and relief had forgotten to mention it.

5

W hat's going on up there?" was the first thing Rebecca said. "First Marino is attacked. Now Barbara's boatman has been murdered and Habib is arrested!"

"Everything seems to be falling apart. Marino's still unconscious. No one knows what's happened except that his shop was broken into. As for Habib, he was in the wrong place at the wrong time."

He was too weary and preoccupied to go into all the details. He also felt an urgency. He needed information.

"I get the picture. Habib is a convenient scapegoat. His skin color and nationality, not to mention his religion, fit the bill these days. I can imagine how you must be feeling. You know what I think about him. He deserves all the efforts you can make on his behalf. And given the backlash we've been seeing against immigrants in this country and against anyone who even looks Arab or is suspected of being Muslim, he's going to need them. The boy has a temper, yes, but murder!"

"What do you mean about his temper?"

"It's nothing against him. I just hope he controls it when they interrogate him. He can get very angry. One time on the *vaporetto* he almost threw a fit when the attendant accused him of trying to get a free ride. Habib couldn't find his Carta Venezia transport pass. I thought he would push the man into the Canal."

Like the time in the gold shop in Fez, Urbino thought.

"He has a sense of justice and fairness," was his only response.

"Of course that's what I meant. But, Urbino, when you called a few days ago it wasn't about Habib, was it? This whole thing hadn't happened yet."

"It was about Marino. Does he have any connection with Burano?"

"A connection with Burano? Well, he knows Frieda Hensel, of course. They met through Beatrix Bauma, who's a client."

"What about lace?"

"Lace? Marino isn't the type for lace, unless we're talking about something like that chalice cover you bought from him. Then he'll sell it for ten times more than he paid. But you know that about Marino. He's got a good eye for quality and an even better one for money. But now that I think about it, I did see him talking with an old Buranella once or twice. You don't think she could have a *dogaressa's* robe hidden away in a chest somewhere, do you?"

"Where did you see them?"

"On Burano last month. I went there about the renovation of a building off the square. From the window I saw Marino talking to a woman in the street. She must have been in her seventies. Snow-white hair, glasses, and black, fingerless gloves."

"Did you mention it to him?"

"Not until the night of Frieda's party when I saw them talking together again. She approached him as I was ducking into a shop to get Frieda a card. When I came out a few minutes later, she was walking away. I made a joke about how persistent the lace makers were. I explained how I had seen him talking with the same woman in December. He said I was mistaken, and that was that." She was silent for a few moments. "But I'm sure it was the same woman. She's rather hard to forget. Just as hard to mistake for someone else as Marino is."

"Did the woman trace her finger in the air as she spoke?"

"Trace her finger in the air? No, I would have noticed that. But wait a minute! Wasn't there talk about a lace maker the night of Frieda's party? Yes, and I remember something about gloves without any fingers. It must be the same woman and"— Rebecca was making quick connections—"could it be the woman who died the same night? Is that why you're interested in her? But she died before Polidoro was attacked. And before Barbara's boatman was murdered. What does it all mean?"

"That's what I need to find out."

After talking with Rebecca, Urbino called the Venice taxi service and spoke with Natalia's cousin, who worked for the company. The last time a taxi had been hired either to or from Burano had been by an American more than six months ago.

6

When nine, then nine-thirty had come and gone, and Frieda hadn't arrived, Urbino suspected she might be paying him back for keeping her waiting at Quadri's.

Then, at a quarter to ten, the doorbell was pushed several times in rapid intervals.

"Finally!" Frieda cried as soon as he opened the door. She hurried past him. As she came into the light, he saw that she looked frightened. Her blunt haircut was disarrayed. The knees of her red corduroy trousers were soiled. "I've been attacked."

"Attacked?"

"Yes, attacked! On the way from Marie and Beatrix's."

"Come upstairs. I'll fix you a drink, or maybe you prefer some tea."

"Grappa is what I need."

She threw her faux fur jacket on the back of an armchair before collapsing into the cushions.

"Someone appeared out of nowhere and pushed me down. It was in a deserted *calle*. I became disoriented and wandered around until I found somewhere familiar. Thanks." She tossed down the grappa. "I need another."

"Did you see who it was?"

"It happened so fast. Someone in dark pants and a jacket. With a dark wool hat pulled down over the ears. It could have been a man or a woman. I got scraped, as you see."

She rubbed her knee.

"Here." He handed her the grappa. "It's good that you held on to your purse."

"There isn't much of value in it, not even my identity papers. I fell on top of it. It would have been hard to get me off. But it is something else that was taken. It is what I was bringing to show you."

Her slightly protruding eyes went to the manila envelope on the little table.

"An envelope like that one."

"What was in it?" he asked, ignoring her implicit question.

"Photographs. I wanted you to see them. I thought that they could have something to do with the death of the old lace maker."

"Why would you think that?"

"Oh, I do not know. I am living on Burano. We are friends. And there's this old lace maker. You don't think she died naturally, do you? We writers have imagination. After we spoke at Quadri's I thought about her and Barbara's visits to her son and the two women. And you are the Sherlock Holmes in residence. It is a simple conclusion."

Perhaps not as simple as she made out, Urbino thought to himself.

"What kind of photographs?" he asked.

"Photographs of men. Like on an identity card or a passport. Young faces. No more than thirty years old. There were photographs of four different young men. There were three copies of each one."

She watched him closely as she parceled out these pieces of information.

"Did you recognize any of them?"

"One." She took a sip of the grappa. "A young man I have seen Habib with. He has dark, dark skin and very blue eyes. Very handsome. All photographs of young men like him, but not of Habib."

Urbino hoped his face betrayed none of the nervousness he was feeling.

"Where did you find the envelope?"

"Where did you find mine? It is mine, is it not?"

"I came across it this morning among Habib's things in his studio."

"Habib had it? How?"

"That's what I'd like to know. I thought you'd be able to tell me."

"I misplaced it. It is what I have been looking for. Haven't you asked Habib?"

"I will tomorrow when I see him. He was arrested two days ago."

"Arrested? For what?"

Either she really didn't know or she was putting on a good show.

"On suspicion of murder. Giorgio, Barbara's boatman."

Frieda gave him an astonished look.

"Murdered? Horrible! I did not hear a word about it. I have been too busy to read the newspaper. Beatrix and Marie do not know either. They would have told me."

Urbino explained the situation.

"It must be some terrible mistake," she said. "The poor boy! He's too shy and gentle to hurt anyone, and I am sure you would never be sponsoring him if you had any doubts of his good character."

She looked at the manila envelope, then gulped down the rest of her grappa.

"No more, thank you," she said with a wave of her hand. "You must be very disturbed by my story, under the circumstances."

"Even without them I would be."

"Do not be angry. I am not a prophetess! It is just a story, and it is not completely original. No! It is one of my transformations. My reincarnations! Seeing you and Habib together pulled the idea from the back of my mind. It was stored there for the right moment. You understand, yes? It is a metamorphosis from *The Arabian Nights*. The book inspired our Barbara for her masquerade ball, and I have stolen from it. Yes! It is from there that I stole, and I—I made the theft my own. Ha!"

Her forehead was beaded with perspiration.

"At your party you said that you were writing something that I'd be interested in even more than a story about Burano. You were referring to this story."

"Yes."

"But I hadn't yet told you anything about how Habib and I met in Morocco."

"And don't we writers have imaginations? Do we always have to be told things in detail and with words? No, of course not!"

"That night I said that your stories made me realize how much you hate lies."

"And I said that you do not hate them."

"These days I do very much."

"I am not lying in any way. You are suspicious of me for some reason, yes? All those questions you asked me about the old lace maker. I told you the truth then, and now I am telling you the truth again!"

He stared at her for a few moments.

"You still haven't told me where you found the photographs."

"At Il Piccolo Nettuno. I went there in a desperation. I was looking everywhere. Nella said there was an envelope in the kitchen. I took it home. Inside, I found the photographs and not my story."

"You didn't notice before then?"

"I know it seems strange, but no. The envelope, it—it looked and felt the same. I went right home."

"Who else was at the restaurant besides Nella?"

"Salvatore, and some tourists."

"Did he see Nella give you the envelope?"

"I don't think so."

"Regina Bella wasn't there?"

"I told you it was only Nella and Salvatore. So many questions! Do not forget all the fairy tales about the danger of knowledge. Pandora's box, and Bluebeard's wife, and—and many others," she finished lamely, seeing that he wasn't amused.

"I'll risk putting myself in more danger with your help. Tell me something. When you and Habib went out to get Giorgio's help on the night of your party when I fell ill, you found a motorboat, but Giorgio was nowhere around. Think carefully. Was it Barbara's motorboat or not?"

"It looked like it, but there was the fog, and we were confused. All motorboats look more or less the same to me. But what does it signify if it was her boat or not? We found Giorgio, and he knew where the boat was! And so you were saved!"

She got up.

"I must go back to Beatrix and Marie. They do not like to stay up late."

He handed her the envelope.

"I'll walk you back. You might have been a random victim or you could have been attacked for the photographs themselves, but maybe it is the story someone wants. He—or she—now sees the mistake, and will not want to make a second one."

"Why would someone want my story?"

Urbino could give her no answer to this. Neither would he have been able to explain the collection of photographs.

On the way to the Fondamenta Nuove they walked through silent, empty streets. The night was damp and chilly. They tried to find the spot where Frieda said she had been attacked, but, in the end, she couldn't be certain.

"I don't know Venice as well as you do," she explained. "Everywhere looks the same now. It—it could have been any of the places we've looked at. Or none of them."

As they approached the building where the two women lived, she said, "You will ask Habib where he found my story. It is puzzling."

After he had seen that she got into the building safely, Urbino went to the water bus stop for Burano. He had to wait until shortly after midnight for the Burano boat to come in. The crew was the same one which had been working the night of the attack on Polidoro. No one resembling Frieda, Salvatore, or Regina had taken the boat that night.

Back at the Palazzo Uccello, he fixed himself one of Habib's *tisanes* to try to counteract all the alcohol he had consumed that day. He brought it to the library where, with Serena curled up on his lap, he skimmed through his English-language copy of *The Arabian Nights,* looking for the tale that Frieda said had inspired her own.

He couldn't find it.

He closed the book. His eye was caught by the seventeenth-century lace cover arranged over the chalice on a table near the ambry. He went over to examine it as closely as he had several years before when he had bought it from Polidoro, at a great profit to the man, as Rebecca had pointed out to him. It was an excellent example of Venetian *punto in aria,* which, according to one of the books he had been browsing through a few evenings before, was "the noblest and most Italian of all laces." He was sure that the pale, delicate hands of a nun had crafted this fine specimen of patience and elegance. Now it was in his much coarser, and certainly secular hands. He looked at the fineness of the thread, white against the white background, and imagined the long-dead nun bent over her work, straining to see, going a little blinder with each difficult stitch she pulled and drew, and clipped. And in the manner of *punto in aria,* doing it without any foundation, without any canvas or parchment or other material to guide her.

Urbino felt both inspired and discouraged by this exquisite creation, and put it back in its place.

An hour later he drifted off to sleep in the unusual silence of the house.

7

It was going to be one of the hardest things Urbino had ever done. He would soon see Habib.

He set out from the Palazzo Uccello the next morning in plenty of time to get to the prison on foot for his appointment at eleven. He carried a small paper bag. Inside were *tramezzini* Natalia had made for Habib that morning.

He took the Lista di Spagna to the Ponte Scalzi beside the train station, where he crossed to the other side of the Grand Canal.

Everything around him reminded him of Habib's circumstances. The residents going about their errands, the children and dogs running across the squares, the pigeons and gulls wheeling in the air—they all spoke a language of freedom.

A gondola came into view, with two reclining tourists covered in blankets. It glided past the copper dome of the Church of San Simeone Piccolo just as Urbino and Habib's had done on their first day together in Venice. Habib had cried out that it was their magic carpet from *The Arabian Nights*. Marvelous words they had seemed at the time. Now they were coldly ironic, even prophetic. In the weeks since that day Habib had been carried, inexorably, it seemed, to the confines of the prison—and all under Urbino's unseeing eye.

Urbino passed the Giardino Papadopoli, where Habib enjoyed sitting and having lunch with Rebecca when she lectured at the nearby Faculty of Architecture.

He crossed over the Ponte Tre Ponti, which Habib had painted one bright day soon after they arrived. Urbino had sat at a café in the working-class quarter, reading and watching him.

A few minutes' walk brought him to the Rio Terrà dei Pensieri. At the end of the street was the prison. He remembered with a pang how he had translated the name of the street for Habib's benefit on one of their walks.

"The buried river of thoughts," Urbino had said. "It's a romantic and melancholy name, isn't it?"

But today the street, which had once been a canal, had associations with only suffocation and immobility, darkness and death, for it led to the prison.

When he reached the prison walls a few minutes later, he walked around them to the entrance, guarded by the ubiquitous lions of St. Mark. Keeping their own kind of watch, but huddled to one side out of the wind, were several dispirited-looking women with baskets and shopping bags.

The building, once a monastery filled with silent devotions, had a palpable air of desperation and stood in the most dismal quarter of Venice. Across the oily canal squatted the gasworks, and beyond them stretched a double row of rusted railway tracks. Cranes lifted and carried indistinguishable objects within view of uniform rows of low tenements.

Taking a deep breath of the cold air with its faint odor of petrochemicals from the mainland, Urbino prepared to see Habib.

8

Habib jumped to his feet when Urbino came through the door of the small room. To Urbino's relief, he wasn't wearing handcuffs. A sallow young guard stood behind him.

"May God be thanked!"

His smile was only a ghost of its usual self.

He reseated himself when the guard made a movement in his direction.

"We are to be left alone at the request of Commissario Gemelli," Urbino said to another guard, a stocky man who had conducted him silently down the long, dark corridor. He spoke in as firm a voice as he could command.

"And by order of the warden," the guard added. "You have twenty minutes. If you need anything, just open the door. We will be outside."

He looked meaningfully at Habib before he accompanied his colleague out to the corridor and closed the door behind them.

The only furniture in the room was two mismatching wooden chairs and a folding table. A small, barred window pierced the wall far above their heads and emitted feeble rays of the winter sunlight. A sharp carbolic odor permeated the air.

"I am too glad to see you, *sidi*."

Urbino seated himself across from Habib, who was dressed in some of the clothes he had sent him yesterday. His face had a grayish pallor.

"What happened to your eye?"

Habib touched a bruise over his right eye.

"It—it is nothing grave."

"Did a policeman hit you? Or one of the prisoners?"

"I fell down a step. This is a very dark place. It is worse than the street in Fez where you were obliged to use your hands. Remember how we laughed?"

"That was a good day," Urbino agreed. He decided to drop the topic of the bruise. "This is for you." He indicated the paper bag. "Natalia made you some fresh *tramezzini* this morning with all your favorite fillings. She says hello."

"She is a kind lady. Please tell her thank you. How is Serena? Sometimes I dream that she is sewn to my lap as she likes to do. When I wake up, I feel sad."

"She's fine, but I can tell that she misses you. Rebecca sends her love."

Habib sneezed.

"It's cold and damp in here," Urbino said. He took off his scarf. "Here. Put this on. You should be wearing the heavy sweater I sent you."

He checked his watch. Nearly two minutes had already gone. Loud male voices rang on the other side of the door, followed by a woman's shrill weeping.

"Habib, we don't have much time. I must speak quickly and ask you some questions. I'd like to speak the way we usually do, but we have to use our time well. First tell me about the man from the Moroccan embassy who visited you today."

Habib frowned.

"He was angry, like I was a criminal. He said I was giving a bad word to Morocco. I told him I was innocent, but I do not think he believed me." He shook his head. "He wants to order a new lawyer but I said I want to keep the one you gave me. Signor Torino is nice, and I am sure he is very clever, if you have ordered him for me."

"Hired him," Urbino corrected automatically.

Habib gave a weak smile.

"I was happy to get all what you sent me." He sighed. "But

it also made me sad. You think I will be in this miserable place for a long time."

"You will be out soon. We will have a celebration at Barbara's ball. I promise."

"Do not promise. Perhaps the big party will come, and Habib will not be there. Then you will feel guilty. If I must stay here, it is my destiny. You cannot change it."

"You know I don't like that way of thinking. There are things that can be done, Habib," he went on in a softer tone. "When Giorgio's killer is found, you will be free."

"The police think I am the person! You know that is too true! Poor Giorgio! I do not know why someone would be bad to kill him."

"You must tell me everything, even if you think I will be angry. I promise I won't. I need to know why you went to Giorgio's apartment after you left me."

"To get my paintings for you. I said when I was angry that I would show something to you. Paintings of Burano that you like! Of the colorful doors you like so much, and the house with the strange patterns! They were my gift to you to try to thank you a little. Giorgio was saving them. You always like to poke around, and also Natalia. When Giorgio got his apartment, he said that I could hide them there."

"Why did he do that?"

"Because he liked me! He was good to me and to some of my friends."

Tears were shining in Habib's dark eyes.

"Like Jerome?"

"Yes. They did things together, the two of them."

"What things?"

"The things that I did with Giorgio for my part. To sit at a café and go for a walk, and sometimes to have a ride in the Contessa's boat when she wasn't there," he added with a slight air of defiance. "You will tell her?"

"No."

"You tell her many things."

"We're friends. She's yours as well. She says hello and promises she will do whatever she can to help you. She's already done a great deal you don't know about. I'm happy Giorgio was nice to you and your friends," Urbino said, bringing the conversation back to more pressing matters. "It's even more reason to find out who killed him. Tell me what happened when you got to his apartment."

"I got there very fast! I ran all the way. I knocked on the door. It was open. I—I went in." Habib covered his face with his hands. "Oh, *sidi*, it was terrible. Poor Giorgio was on the floor. There was blood on his head, and on his face, and it was all over the floor! I went down by him and touched him, but just a little! His—his clothes, they were all messed up and out of the right place. I got blood on my hands and my trousers. I ran out. Two men were at the door. I thought they had been the ones to hurt Giorgio. They stopped me. One of them telephoned the police. And then you saw the police take me to this place. Poor Habib! Are you angry with me, *sidi*?"

"Of course not." Urbino wished he had more time so that he could comfort him but he was obliged to continue with his questions. "Is there anything else you remember? Any loud voices from Giorgio's apartment when you were approaching it?"

"I have told you everything. I swear by God!"

"And the reason you didn't tell me that you went to Burano by yourself those times was because of the paintings?"

"Yes. I didn't want my good surprise to be spoiled and I didn't want to lie to you. You asked me too many questions."

Perhaps I should have asked even more, Urbino said to himself, or certainly different ones. He sensed that Habib was afraid of what he was going to ask him now, and what he would have to answer.

"Did you meet any of the people we know when you went there?"

"I did not meet anyone. I saw that evil old woman once, on the day before the German lady's party. She was speaking with the art man, the one who has a twisted body. He frightens me just the way that she did!"

"Marino Polidoro. He is in the hospital. He was attacked in his shop on the night you and Giorgio were moving into Giorgio's apartment. Was there any time then when the two of you weren't together?"

"Oh, no, *sidi*, Giorgio and I were together all the time, except when he went back into the Contessa's palace and I stayed to guard his things in the boat. You do not think I hurt that man?"

"No."

"And Giorgio did not hurt him either!"

Urbino found his loyalty to Giorgio both touching and exasperating.

During the past few minutes the odor of backed-up sewers had started to invade the room and overpower the carbolic smell. Habib took a handkerchief from his pocket and pressed it against his nose. The scent of the cologne Urbino had packed for him wafted across the table.

"The guards and the prisoners laugh at me when I use my handkerchief. Sometimes the smell is too much worse in my room."

This was one occasion when Urbino was grateful that the more appropriate word didn't come easily to Habib's lips.

"Were Polidoro and the old woman talking in a friendly way?"

"I don't know! I didn't want to look. She could have thrown the evil eye on me. Or maybe both of them could have done it! I am sorry to say it, but I am glad that she died. I would have been afraid to go to Burano all those days to do your paintings. It was very hard to go that time when I saw her with the art man, but I did it for you."

"I know she wasn't a good woman, Habib, but perhaps you will have a little sympathy for her when I tell you that I am sure she was murdered."

"Murdered, too? Like Giorgio? Oh, *sidi*, now I am sure I will never get out of this terrible place. The police will find out that

I was afraid of her, and then they will ask me all confusing questions about her, and—"

"Don't worry about that. But tell me why you were so nervous about staying in the restaurant the day we had lunch there. You said it was because it was dirty, but I think it was something else."

"I felt something bad about it! I got a cold feeling. The old woman, she was like a witch. Inside her there could have been an evil spirit. They like to live where there is a lot of food and water." He looked down. "Venice has a lot of water. I can hear it all night long. It keeps me awake."

Urbino knew that this wasn't the time to try to persuade Habib from any of his deep-seated superstitions. And, he thought, there had been something bad about Il Piccolo Nettuno, hadn't there? It was where Nina Crivelli had met her death, and the reason for her death might be directly connected with the place. It was possible that Habib, with some greater sensitivity, had perceived something that day that had been lost on Urbino.

"You saw no one else but Polidoro and the old woman?"

"I saw the young restaurant lady with the smart clothes. She was nice to me. It was one time when Giorgio brought me to Burano in the Contessa's boat. She was very friendly with Giorgio. One morning they were together at a café near the language school. Many people liked Giorgio!"

"But someone did not like him very much. Someone murdered him."

Habib held his head in his hands.

"Sometimes I get too confused with words. The police ask so many questions, and sometimes they can turn what is green into red. My head turns around."

"I hope you're telling them the truth, even if it's embarrassing."

He wasn't emphasizing this for the sake of whoever might be listening, but because he believed it to be an absolute necessity.

"They made me say things about you and me. They asked

me about Morocco. About how we met and other things." He
gave Urbino a nervous look. "About my family and my life
there. Oh, there are too many things they want to know!"

"Like about your brother who drowned? Why didn't you
ever tell me?"

Habib looked sad and defeated.

"I was embarrassed."

"Did you tell Giorgio?"

"Yes," he said in a low, frightened voice.

Anger and disappointment coursed through Urbino.

"Why did you tell him?" he said in a tone, which he hoped
held no reproach.

"Oh, I'm sorry! Believe me! It was easier to tell him. Forgive me."

"It's all right, Habib. But I need to know why it was easier."

Habib's brows drew together. He was silent for a few moments.

"It wasn't because I liked Giorgio more than you. I swear
to God! But—but he was always speaking about the sad problems of the poor immigrants. Like the Senegalese men who sell
the purses and belts in the Piazza. He didn't scorn them. I do
not mean that you scorn them. I know that you have a good
heart. You gave money to that woman by the Church of Health."
He sighed. "But—but maybe money cannot help poor Habib.
Oh, *sidi*, it is too difficult to explain!"

He threw Urbino a helpless look.

"Did Giorgio speak to Jerome in the same way?"

"He did! Jerome told me. So you see it wasn't just me."

Urbino took this in.

"Please understand. I was afraid that you wouldn't trust me
if you knew about how my brother broke the law. Lotfi and
I were brothers, but different brothers. He—he was braver
than me."

"You don't need to explain anymore. But Signor Torino and
I can help you only if you tell us important things like that,
especially once you've told them to the police. Important things,
and also things that you might not think are important," he

added. "For example, did you ever see a lot of photographs altogether, ones of Jerome and other young men?"

Habib's long, dark lashes flew up in alarm.

"Photographs of Jerome and other boys?" Habib repeated. "I don't understand."

"Did you?"

"No. But we have many photographs, Jerome and me. The school and the police need them for our dossiers. You know that."

"The photographs might have been in a large envelope like the one I found in your studio. The one that was pushed almost all the way under the divan."

Habib was silent.

"Where did you get that envelope?"

"From Giorgio."

"When?"

"The day before he—he died."

"Why did he give it to you?"

"He asked me to tell him what the pages inside say. They are written in German. I am sure you have read them all with no trouble. I could not understand more than the first sentence, even with your big dictionary. I was very bad to deceive poor Giorgio. I said that I know German well. I was too proud."

"Did he say where he got the envelope?"

"No. And he said for me not to tell anyone, but it doesn't matter now, and you have already found it and read it. What does it say?"

"It's just a story."

Urbino checked his watch. Their time was almost up. He reached out and patted Habib's hand. It was surprisingly cold.

"You must be strong. We both must. And remember that for every minute you're in this prison, I am too."

"Forgive me for saying this, *sidi*, but you do not look well."

"Perhaps not, but at least I do not have a bruise like yours."

He reached out and touched the purplish area over Habib's eye.

"Take care of yourself, *sidi*. We will be in worse trouble if you become sick again. You should not march over the city the way you do, especially not at night."

"Speaking of that, did you follow me one night when I was walking near the Church of the Salute?"

"Yes, on that night and on others. You could have fallen into a canal or tripped down the steps of a bridge." He reached into his pocket. He took out a prayer card of the Black Madonna from the Church of the Salute. "Here. Take it."

"No, Habib, you—"

"It is your religion, *sidi*. I want you to keep it until—until later."

"Thank you."

Urbino slipped it into his pocket and got up. A moment later the stocky guard opened the door. Beside him was the sallow young man.

"I'll come to see you again as soon as I can. If there's anything you want or any problem you have, no matter what it is, let Signor Torino know."

He paused at the door.

"The mother of your father's nephew!"

Urbino's voice resonated in the small, bare room.

Habib gave him a bright smile.

"My aunt!"

Let the police figure that one out, Urbino thought, as the guard conducted him back to the entrance.

9

The first thing Urbino did when he returned to the Palazzo Uccello was phone Torino and tell him about his meeting with Habib. The lawyer knew nothing about the death of Habib's brother, or the envelope that Habib had got from Giorgio. Urbino described Frieda's story, and then told him how the German woman had been mugged and had lost an almost identical envelope with photographs of young men, among whom had been Habib's friend Jerome.

"Has she reported the incident to the police?" Torino asked.

"I don't think so."

"I would neither encourage nor discourage her to do it. The existence of the photographs could be used against Habib." He paused. "I get the feeling that the Substitute Prosecutor is looking at this as a crime of passion. Jealousy on Habib's part, or some kind of rejection by Giorgio. I suspect the Questura knows something along those lines that we don't. Did Habib tell you anything else that could be of significance? He's been more forthcoming with you."

"Nothing he said about Giorgio even suggested that he had any negative feelings. As a matter of fact, he even defended Giorgio when he thought I was criticizing him. And I know Habib well. He wasn't pretending."

"I hope you impressed on him that he shouldn't hold anything back. This business of his brother's death makes me uneasy. I wonder why Gemelli told you."

"Trying to undermine my confidence in Habib."

"Habib isn't giving much help in that department by concealing information."

Before ringing off, Urbino told him about Regina Bella's apparent friendship with Giorgio and her rendezvous with him near the language school on at least one occasion.

Urbino threw on his cape and left the Palazzo Uccello.

Jerome lived somewhere in the Sant'Elena district at the far end of Venice, adjacent to the Giardini Pubblici where the Biennale modern-art show was held. Surely only a few inquiries there would lead him directly to the young man.

Urbino walked briskly through the cold, damp city toward the boat landing by Harry's Bar. A steady stream of thoughts coursed through his mind, but they brought him no enlightenment. There was still much he didn't know or, perhaps, was unable to see.

Within a relatively short time he turned into the Frezzeria, deserted of shoppers at this hour. Down one of the little streets on his right was the Colomba restaurant, where he and Habib had enjoyed a memorable meal a month earlier. It seemed like an eternity ago.

He dashed into Harry's Bar for a glass of wine. He was glad that he knew no one in the smoke-filled room but the bartender. He wasn't in any mood to socialize, and just stood at the bar for the few minutes it took him to drink the wine down.

He secluded himself in the stern of the *vaporetto* out of the wind, his cape wrapped around him, and watched the passing scene with almost unseeing eyes. Though it was called the *accelerata*, the boat moved at a pace that seemed slower than his own steps had been earlier. It eventually stopped at the Biennale exposition grounds.

When he got off the *vaporetto* in the Sant'Elena quarter, a young man in the Parco delle Rimembranze pointed him in the direction of Jerome's apartment. It was on the ground floor of a modern block of flats.

Jerome opened the door only after Urbino had knocked several times.

"Monsieur Urbino, it is you," he said in his French-accented English. He looked over Urbino's shoulder into the hallway. "You are alone?"

"Yes. May I come in?"

Jerome hesitated, then stood aside and let Urbino in. He closed the door behind them.

It was a small room with only two chairs and a lopsided wooden table. It smelled of mold. A one-burner portable stove stood on the floor surrounded by dirty dishes and cutlery.

"Habib needs your help, Jerome. Do you know what has happened to him?"

"He is in prison," came out in almost a whisper. His disconcertingly blue eyes were wide in alarm. "The students said it at school."

"The police think he killed Giorgio, the Contessa's boatman."

"I know. It is terrible!"

"How well did you know Giorgio?"

"Only a little! I said this to the police."

"When did you speak to the police?"

"They came to speak to me! It was yesterday. They were at the school. They brought the students and teachers into a room, one after the other. They asked many questions. But I said nothing bad about Habib. He is very nice."

"What did you say about Giorgio?"

"He was friendly and bought me coffee. That is all. *Je vous jure!*"

"Did you ever give Giorgio your photograph?"

"My photograph! What is it that you ask me?"

"You must tell the truth, Jerome."

"I am telling the truth."

Urbino stared at him until he looked away and moved to the door.

"Please! You must go. I want no problems. Tell Habib *bon courage.*"

I'm glad that Habib is holding up," the Contessa said to Urbino an hour later in her *salotto blu* after he had told her about his meeting with Habib. "You must do the same. Never more than now do you need tea and sympathy."

"What I really need is information. What did you learn on Burano?"

"Have something to eat first. You look frightful."

She poured out another cup of tea.

Urbino took a small sandwich from the plate. He was surprised to find how hungry he was. He took another and ate it quickly, then drank down his tea.

"That's a good boy. Now it's your turn to sit back and listen. You can tell me the rest of your adventures later."

The Contessa had gone to see Carolina Bruni.

"I endured a lot of bad singing. Fortunately, she still had enough of a voice to tell me more about Regina Bella than she told you. There's been talk about her carrying on with someone's husband. She's been caught talking with him alone. Carolina's friend smelled her perfume on him—or thinks she did. It may be nothing, but what sounds suspicious are those periodic trips to Milan. Shopping, she says, and she comes back with bags from the boutiques on Montenapoleone, but who knows? They could be stuffed with old newspapers."

"She does have a fashionable wardrobe."

"Not all that fashionable. She wears one expensive outfit to death every season like most Italians." The Contessa took a sip of tea. "I went to see Gabriela Stival again and managed to get around to the topic. She confirmed what Carolina said about the trips to Milan, but she was more doubtful about an affair. Gabriela lives only a few buildings away from Regina and has never seen anything suspicious, and it seems she's always looking out her window."

"Did she ever see Giorgio anywhere near her apartment?"

"Giorgio was handsome, but I wouldn't think he was her type in other ways. It could explain the cap in the kitchen, though. Do you think she killed Giorgio?" she asked after a few moments of musing. "And Nina as well?"

"It can't be discounted. Don't forget that she looked after Nina's heart pills."

"But what was she doing around the language school? Maybe that's a stupid question. Venice is a small place. There's no reason she shouldn't be there, although," she added dryly, "her kind of shops are nowhere nearby."

"The language school is somehow involved in all this business. Gemelli is bound to see it as something else against Habib."

"I don't know how to say this, so I'll just say it without any varnish. Doesn't it make you uneasy that Habib concealed his trips to Burano from you, and also his brother's death?"

"I understand why he did it."

"Well, you know him better than I do. He doesn't seem the type to hurt anyone intentionally, but he does have Mediterranean blood, remember, and it may be even stronger on the other shore. He's frightened. He may be telling you what you want to hear, and then off you run to construct a sand castle. Trust is a beautiful quality. I just don't want to see yours knocked down."

"Perhaps you should be more concerned about Habib's misplaced trust in me. I feel as if I've brought all of this down on his head."

"You're being absolutely ridiculous! And rather self-indulgent, if you'll excuse me for saying so." She stirred uneasily in the chair. "Perhaps, given the present state of affairs, it would be a good idea for all of us, Habib included, if I were to cancel the masquerade ball. It's only three weeks away. We could have a simple dinner and—"

"No!" he shouted. "You're going to have your ball and we're all going to be there! Excuse me, Barbara, but there are some other things you don't know yet. They've shaken me up quite a bit."

He went to the liquor cabinet.

"Please, *caro*. It would be best to stick to tea."

"I need something stronger." He poured himself a cognac. "It will steady my nerves."

"And cloud your mind! You need to think clearly!"

"Agreed. And one of the things I need to think clearly about is a manila envelope—or *two* manila envelopes," he emphasized.

He explained how Frieda had discovered the envelope of photographs.

"Photographs of young men! Habib?"

"It doesn't seem so. She says there was one of Jerome. I never saw any of them. Someone mugged her when she was on her way to see me, and snatched them from her."

"Well, at least we can say it wasn't Habib, although—oh, never mind."

"What were you going to say?"

"Forgive me for saying what you might not want to hear, but it's a service you need at the moment. Just because Habib is in prison doesn't mean that he couldn't be involved in the mugging. You said that Jerome's photograph was among them. Maybe Jerome, or someone else close to Habib, attacked Frieda. As a way of protecting himself and Habib."

Urbino considered this possibility for a few moments. He knew that, in other circumstances, he would have seized on it. Now, however, a part of his mind shut a door.

"I've just seen Jerome. The police interrogated him and the other students. He's frightened. It would be strange if he wasn't. And he's also hiding something about Giorgio, hiding it from the police and from me."

"And something about Habib as well?" the Contessa prompted.

"If he is, it could be something innocent."

"Or something not," she persisted.

He took a sip of cognac.

"There's another aspect to the envelope business," he began.

He told her, at first hesitantly, and then with borrowed courage from the alcohol, how he had found the other envelope with the German–English dictionary in Habib's studio. He plunged into an account of the story.

"It's an adaptation from *The Arabian Nights*," he said after a few moments of uncomfortable silence. "It doesn't seem as if you've been the only one inspired by it. Frieda calls it a transformation. I assumed it was one of her stories, even before she confirmed that it was. Somehow Giorgio ended up with it, and gave it to Habib to translate."

"According to Habib." The Contessa mitigated the words with a gentle pat on his sleeve. "He may have good reason to want to distance himself from the story."

"You mean that since he's concealed things from me, he may also have stolen. And from stealing to killing. Is that it?"

"Looking at it from another point of view," she said, refusing to be drawn in, "if Giorgio did give the story to Habib, it destroys your wild theory that he's Gino. We can assume that Gino would know German after spending twenty years in Germany."

"Unless he wanted to conceal the fact."

"But he made him promise not to tell anyone."

"So now you believe what Habib told me."

"We're trying to see this from all angles, *caro*. Or at least I am."

"In that case, how about this? Giorgio extracts a promise from Habib that he doesn't believe he can keep, or want him to keep. It would have been a way of protecting himself if he were Gino—or, at the least, of gaining time. He could have been using Habib as a pawn. Either alone or in concert with someone else.

Habib is a victim, you see, a victim of his own good nature, his own trust! Can't you see that?"

The Contessa shook her head slowly.

"Someone could be playing with your mind, *caro*. It's all too apparent how abominably easy that is these days."

11

After tossing and turning for several hours that night, Urbino finally fell asleep.

Nina Crivelli's face swam up at him. From deep in her throat came a cackle. A lace handkerchief frothed out of her mouth. She reached a gnarled hand to her face, tugged and pulled at the skin. It was a mask. Urbino's mother stared at him. She was kneeling in their garden in New Orleans, digging holes in the flower bed with a spoon. Urbino grabbed the spoon. Her gloves were covered with red soil. Golden flowers drifted from the sky. Brightness falls from the air, he said to her. He held out his white shirt to catch it. His mother couldn't breathe. The brightness scattered. Lace hung from the trees like Spanish moss. *Punto in aria, punto in aria*, Frieda repeated like a litany. Sad wives invented lace, she said. They copied the mermaids' seaweed hidden in their husbands' pockets like love letters. Photographs fluttered through the air, and settled in the flower bed. Urbino picked one up. It was a photograph of Habib. He dropped it and picked up another. There was a hole where Habib's face should have been.

Urbino woke up.

He felt hot and dizzy. He poured himself a glass of water from the pitcher on the table beside his bed. He lay still and listened to the sounds of the house around him. Since returning from Morocco, he had noticed new sounds, and wondered if they had always been there. He sometimes thought that they were the result of all the assault the building had undergone during the storm that had battered it right before he had left.

As he lay in bed, he remembered another night a few weeks ago when he had awakened, filled with premonition for the Ca' da Capo-Zendrini. He had gone out into the night and stood on the little bridge looking up at the Contessa's palace.

When he got up now, however, it wasn't to throw on his cape, but instead to put on his slippers, and walk from room to room.

The library where Habib had knocked aside the pile of books before storming out into the night and being arrested. The parlor where Beatrix had surprised him with the mask of the plague doctor. Habib's studio where Urbino had found the story of the prince and the jeweler's son that might hold a valuable clue to the murders of Giorgio and Nina—a clue to be ferreted out not so much in what the story said, but in how it had come into Giorgio's hands.

Serena was curled up on Habib's divan. He went over to stroke her. Together they listened to the silence and the sounds of the house.

E arly the next morning, groggy from too little sleep, Urbino took the *vaporetto* to Burano. As it slid slowly past the cemetery island on this damp, gray day, Urbino wondered what had become of Giorgio's body. Had a family member been contacted? Perhaps the elusive Signor Mazza, that is, if he wasn't dead himself? It was probable that the police had discovered relevant names and addresses among Giorgio's things, in addition to Habib's paintings of Burano.

Had anything else been found that might be incriminating for Habib? Among Giorgio's possessions, there was possibly even something that might help Urbino in his efforts to solve the two murders and clear Habib. He stood little chance, however, of knowing anything more than Gemelli wanted him to know for his own purposes.

Despite the unpromising weather the lace makers had set up their stalls on the street that stretched from the boat landing. At a café, Urbino tossed down an espresso, not giving in to the temptation to "correct" it with a portion of anisette. He headed for Salvatore's apartment.

The dilapidated building near the Church of San Martino contrasted in an almost sinister way with the many brightly painted houses on the island. Nina Crivelli's obituary notice had been removed from the entrance. But no one, not even her son, had washed away the blood-red scrawl of *Strega*!

Urbino climbed up the dark staircase to the second floor.

Tacked on the first door was a piece of cardboard with the faded name *Crivelli*.

He didn't have time to reach his hand toward the knocker when the door was opened quickly. Salvatore's bloodshot eyes stared at him out of an unshaven face. His body, dressed in a dark blue bathrobe, was tense.

"What do you want?"

"I need your help."

A wary look crept across the man's ravaged, handsome face.

"About what?"

"May I come in?"

Salvatore frowned and stood aside. Urbino went past him into a dark, sour-smelling room with a few scattered pieces of furniture. Salvatore closed the door and stood in front of it, with his arms crossed on his chest.

"It's about my friend Habib Laroussi. You know that he's being detained by the police in the murder of Giorgio, the Contessa's boatman?"

"What does that have to do with me?"

"You might know something that could help him."

"Why would I want to help a murderer?"

"I don't believe he murdered Giorgio."

"Of course you don't! Because you're as responsible as he is. You brought someone like that into the country. They all end up bringing trouble on the heads of us Italians. They should stay where they belong."

"I suppose you might say the same thing about me, being an American. But, nonetheless, I'm sure you wouldn't want an innocent person to be punished for what someone else did. Think of it this way, Signor Crivelli. Habib is someone's son. I know that you have a son who is about his age—or a little older, perhaps, more like Giorgio's age. Surely you have some sympathy."

A muscle started twitching at the corner of Salvatore's eye.

"He should have stayed with his own father instead of coming here with you! What do you expect of people like that who make a display of themselves praying in public, throwing down a rug or a scrap of paper wherever they want?"

"Catholics carry saints through the streets and bless themselves when they go past churches."

"That's different!"

"Yes, well, anyway, Signor Crivelli, although I see that you aren't positively disposed to Habib, I was wondering if you might remember something that could be of importance."

He paused for the effect, and then said, "It's about an envelope."

"An envelope?"

From the moment Salvatore had thrown open the door, Urbino had had an impression of alternating waves of fear and relief emanating from the man. He now furrowed his brow. The wary look returned to his face.

"Yes," Urbino said. "An envelope."

He described it, but not its contents.

"Did you notice one like it in the restaurant dining room, or perhaps in the kitchen, during the week before Giorgio's murder?"

"I don't know what you're talking about."

"What about photographs? Photographs of young men? Do you know anything about them?"

"Photographs of young men? I know nothing of such things, signore! You're not making any sense. If this is your way of helping your friend"—he came close to spitting out the words—"he will stay in prison where he belongs with all the rest of his breed. You must leave now. I have to get ready to go to the restaurant."

Urbino went down the *calle* to the little courtyard to the kitchen entrance of Il Piccolo Nettuno. Nella was inside, chopping vegetables.

"The German lady left the envelope, Signor Urbino," the little woman said. "I gave it back to her."

"Where did you find it?"

"On the floor when I wasn't cleaning up the restaurant. Now that Nina is gone, God rest her soul, I've been looking after that as well, but I told Regina she will have to find someone else. It's too much for me."

"Did Salvatore see it?"

"If he had, he would have given it to me. I look after the things people leave behind."

"Where did you put it?"

"Right there."

She indicated a counter next to the door into the courtyard. It was where Urbino had seen the white cap last week.

"Did Salvatore see it there?"

"All these questions about an envelope! What was inside? Money? Salvatore could have seen it as clear as day every time he came into the kitchen."

"And Signorina Bella?"

"The next morning she moved it from the counter to the shelf above the refrigerator. She puts things like that up there from time to time. Envelopes too. When the German lady asked for it, I couldn't find it on the counter. I thought I had misplaced it or that someone had picked it up when I wasn't around. Then I thought about the shelf."

"Did you look inside the envelope at any time?"

She stopped slicing a carrot to give him a critical squint.

"Do you think I don't mind my own business, Signor Urbino? I never put my nose or my eyes in matters that don't concern me."

"I'm sure you don't, Nella. It's just that I know you're concerned about whatever relates to your kitchen."

She continued to look at him for a few seconds longer, then, mollified, she finished slicing the carrot and started to attack an onion.

"I know that my cook Natalia doesn't like people coming in the kitchen and confusing things."

"Did I ever say that anyone confused things in here? Nothing like that has ever happened as long as I've been here, and it will be seven years in August."

Urbino let her go about her work for several minutes as he pretended an interest in the calendar on the wall.

Then, in as offhand a manner as he could bring off, he said, "When I was in the kitchen last week, I noticed a white cap on the same counter. I guess it was Giorgio's."

"Yes, poor man! They say that the African boy who lives with you did him harm, but I can't believe such a thing." She wiped tears from her eyes with the back of her arm. "You must be very disappointed in him, to say the least, for all the trouble he's brought down on your good head."

"He never harmed Giorgio, I assure you, Nella."

"Who knows these days? The bad seem good, and the good turn out bad. It gets more mixed up when it's a foreigner. We don't know their ways well enough to figure them out. And they can't understand ours."

"There's some truth in that," Urbino had to admit. "But to get back to Giorgio, did he come into the kitchen often?"

Once again she shot him a suspicious look, but kept up the rhythm of her chopping.

"When the Contessa came to Burano, I'd give him something to eat. He's come once or twice since Nina's death, it seems to me. Very quick into the kitchen and out of it. It was usually when I was busy with the cooking, but I didn't pay attention."

"Did he have much to say to Salvatore?"

"I never noticed. If he did, it wouldn't have been my business."

"Thank you, Nella. I hope I didn't put you behind in your preparations. Do you know if I might find Signorina Bella at home? Or perhaps I can stop by the restaurant a little later in the day?"

"You won't find her either here or there. She's gone off for a rest. To some clinic near Florence."

"When did she go?"

"Yesterday. And very suddenly. She didn't look very well. Circles under eyes and all white and pinched. I hope it does her some good, but she could have stayed in her own house and rested. I would have helped her. Why spend all that money?"

"Sometimes a change of scene is what a person needs."

"The best that poor folks like me can afford, signor, is a picnic on Torcello when the weather is good!"

After leaving the restaurant, Urbino wandered around the island. He went through the events on the night Nina Crivelli had died, replaying Frieda's party in his mind as best he could and trying to make some sense out of the tensions displayed. He also reviewed the departure of the guests after he had left with Habib.

And what about the figure he thought he had seen in the fog, the figure that had resembled some spectral form in the early days of cinema, all dark gray and indistinguishable as to sex or age? The figure had approached and then seemingly disappeared. Had the figure been someone he knew or some stranger returning home? Or had it all been conjured up out of his half-conscious state?

Urbino became so caught up in these thoughts that he collided with some fish traps on the edge of a deserted square. He saw that he wasn't far from the Casa Verde, and was soon standing in front of its door. The loud strains of the Volsungs' Battle Cry came through the unshuttered, but closed windows. He rang the bell in vain, and decided to leave Frieda to the rest of *Die Walküre*.

He was peculiarly reluctant to leave Burano. He felt as if he were overlooking something that could only be answered here.

He circled back to the main square and walked past Il Piccolo Nettuno. Salvatore was standing beside one of the tables, taking an order. Urbino didn't linger, but continued down the street. The sight of Da Romano Restaurant a short distance away gave him a pang. He hadn't had a chance to take Habib there since their first day on Burano. It seemed a long time ago.

Urbino's footsteps then carried him to the causeway that connected the island of lace with Mazzorbo. He went to the far end and looked back along its length. There was no one in sight. He felt chilled, and pulled his cape more tightly around him.

According to Habib's confused recollections of the crucial night, this was where he had lost his way in the fog. At the time, Urbino had been sitting on the overturned bucket, protected from the cold by Habib's burnoose. And Nina Crivelli had just been murdered, or had been about to be.

Urbino stood thinking for a few more minutes. He then recrossed the causeway and returned to the Casa Verde. It was now silent. There was no answer to his persistent rings.

14

As the *vaporetto* made the crossing back to Venice, Urbino's mind was filled with scattered pieces of information that kept shifting into different patterns like the colored fragments of glass in a kaleidoscope.

Each pattern possessed its own logic, and was seductively persuasive, until the next one fell into place, and seemed equally compelling. What they all had in common, however—other than that the same person had murdered Nina and Giorgio and that this person had also attacked Polidoro—was that Habib's role was an innocent one.

In the past his judgment had been good precisely because it had been detached. On one occasion, however, his fear of losing his special relationship with the Contessa had put him dangerously off the scent. Now he was being tested much more rigorously.

He had often been accused of being distant and cool. "You're above it all," an artist friend had once half-joked. "Sitting there in your palazzo and carrying on all these intellectual exercises. Your blue needs a bit of the red to warm and humanize it."

But not too much of it, a voice in his head warned him as the boat approached the landing on the Fondamenta Nuove.

15

Y ou've got a lovely view," Urbino said to Beatrix and Marie. He had come directly to their apartment from the *vaporetto*.

"A lovely view, yes, if you like a memento mori," the plainfaced Marie said. A small brimless hat with a tiny white feather perched on her head. Its violet color matched her trim little suit. "A sight to die for."

The cemetery island, with its brick wall, cypress trees, gate, and some of the higher tombstones, was visible in the near distance.

The two women occupied furnished rooms that looked out on the lagoon. Scattered liberally among all the mismatched, broken-down furniture and hanging from doorknobs, curtain rods, and pegs on the wall was a jumble of masks and hats. An entire wall of the adjacent bedroom was devoted to an assortment of masks, one of which looked eerily like Salvatore, except that it was painted a virulent shade of green. It hung next to the plague doctor that Beatrix had surprised Urbino with on her visit to the Palazzo Uccello.

"And there's a good chance we will do exactly that, my dear, unless we leave soon," Beatrix said. "Die, I mean. See Venice, and die. That is the saying, I think."

Her tall form was wrapped in a crimson dressing gown, giving her an even more regal look than usual.

"See Naples, and die," Urbino said from the window.

"At least it is warmer there. This apartment is always ice-cold."

She gave an exaggerated shiver.

Urbino took one more look out at the broad lagoon and then down at the boat station a short distance from their building.

"How's Habib?" Marie asked.

"Holding up fairly well, but you can imagine what it's like for him."

"I prefer not to," Beatrix said. "Oh, be careful!"

She snatched away a cream-colored felt hat from the cushions of the armchair as he was about to seat himself. She placed it on top of an empty vase.

"Everything will be straightened out soon," Marie said. "It is a big mistake."

"Of course," the Austrian woman put in quickly. "He'll be painting his impressions of Carnevale in a few weeks. He can do sketches of us all in our costumes for the Contessa Barbara's *ballo in maschera*!"

Urbino took a sip of the steaming coffee Marie had fixed.

"So many of us are affected by these sad and violent events," Marie said in her quiet voice. "You, and poor Habib all locked up. And Barbara. She brought Giorgio all the way from Naples to be murdered here in Venice.'

"Nonsense, my dear!" Beatrix shot out. "Barbara is not responsible. And it is Giorgio who is dead. Our sympathies must go for the dead and not just the living."

"The dead are past their troubles," Marie said firmly. "May Giorgio rest in peace, and his murderer be found, and punished severely." She looked up at Beatrix from beneath her hat. "We all will be happier then." She took a sip of coffee. "I feel sad for the young lady from the restaurant."

Urbino perceived a powerful will in the smaller woman that he hadn't noticed when he had first met them at Frieda's party, and also a simmering resentment.

"Do you mean Regina Bella?" he asked.

Beatrix, who was still standing up, gave another shiver, and put her coffee cup down. She hugged herself more closely as she walked around the room. Marie followed her movements as she answered Urbino's question.

"Yes. I saw her with Giorgio. From the window. They were down on the embankment. From the way she looked at him, I think she had feelings for him."

"You are too romantic," Beatrix said. "I have always said so."

Something sharp and cold glared from her blue eyes. She drew herself up to her full height.

"There are worse things to be. My father—he was an English teacher, monsieur—he was very romantic, more than my mother."

She had a look of satisfaction. Beatrix stiffened as if Marie had probed at some tender, private spot known only to them.

"Your imagination is sometimes silly, my little one."

"Laugh as much as you wish. She who laughs last, laughs the loudest."

She turned away from her companion, who was now standing beside a small table stacked precariously with books. On the top was a large, thick volume on Venetian china. Urbino had a copy of it in his library.

"In any case," Marie went on, "I saw the two of them down there not once, but twice. I would have drawn Beatrix's attention to it if she had been here, but she has been leaving me alone for hours."

"It is only because you do not want to come with me."

"We know what the truth is, Beatrix."

Despite Urbino's growing discomfort at being a witness to the apparent discord between the two women, he was noting it with particular attention.

"Speaking about romantic men like your father," Urbino said, "Wagner was blasting from the Casa Verde this morning. Frieda couldn't hear the bell."

"She will go deaf one of these days," Marie said.

"She is already a little deaf." Beatrix gave Urbino a sidelong glance that seemed to be crafty. "If not, she would have heard the man who was following her."

"Perhaps the man—or the woman—wasn't following her,

Beatrix dear. He—or she—could have been waiting and watching for her, like a big black spider," the milliner said. The white feather in her hat shivered in the draft.

"Your imagination is flying again, my—oh!" Beatrix cried out as she bumped against the small tale and sent the books tumbling to the floor.

She replaced the book on Venetian china on the table, with the others on top of it in a more secure pile.

"It's lucky that Frieda wasn't harmed," Urbino said. "It was dark and she was in a remote place. Muggings usually happen around San Marco, and during the tourist season. They're rather rare at this time of the year, and in this quarter."

"She was being followed by someone from this neighborhood," Beatrix said as she straightened up from her task and tightened her robe.

"Why do you say that?"

"All the neighbors see her come and go, go and come. And Marie and I, we are very obvious living here in this building with all Italians. In my opinion, Frieda caught the attention of someone. This person thought she carried a pile of money with her. Everyone must know the fortune we are paying to be frozen to death! They must think we have money to burn for the heat! If we have money, so must she. It is simple, yes?"

Beatrix's explanation, delivered with nervous energy, sounded more than a little elaborate to account for the attack on Frieda.

"Birds of a feather collect together," she added with a flourish.

"You mean *flock*," Marie corrected. "The man—or the woman—didn't take her money. She was bringing something to you, Monsieur Urbino."

"Something to show me."

"She was mysterious about it. I think it was one of her stories." Marie's eyes slid in Beatrix's direction. The Austrian woman was examining the clasp of her bracelet. "Writers are as thick as thieves," Marie went on when Urbino said nothing. She delivered this idiom with a self-satisfied smile on her round face.

"Writers are often quite the opposite."

He got up and returned to the window.

"Here's the number twelve from Burano pulling in. Isn't that Salvatore from Il Piccolo Nettuno? Yes, I believe it is."

Fortunately neither of the two women came to look over his shoulder. None of the disembarking passengers was Salvatore.

"You must be familiar with the people going back and forth to Burano. Does Salvatore keep to a regular schedule?"

Beatrix was staring at him as implacably as the green mask on the bedroom wall.

"Marie and I do not spend our time looking out the window." She started to collect the coffee cups and place them on a tray. "You will excuse us, please? We have to meet an old friend who is passing through town."

She gave Marie a look that seemed to dare her to disagree.

16

Early the next morning, while Urbino was still in bed, Torino telephoned him.

"I've been removed as Habib's *avvocato*."

"Removed?"

He came fully awake.

"I'm afraid so. The Moroccan embassy has appointed one of their own lawyers. I'm giving him a briefing this afternoon when he comes up from Rome."

"But what does this mean for Habib?"

"For one thing, it means that the Moroccans are considering this a very serious matter, as of course they should. It's even possible that it could be to Habib's benefit. A show of diplomatic force and all that."

"But he said he wasn't treated well by the official the other day."

"They might have one way of dealing with him, and another way of dealing with the Italian police. That's diplomacy. Their main concern is their own image and standing. To that extent they'll do everything they can for him. Don't worry about that. Of course, you realize how this directly affects you and Habib."

"How is that?"

"Your visit yesterday will be the first and the last one. You won't see him again until his trial—or until he's released, and that could be a long, long way off. The Moroccans are going to be very sensitive on the issue of your relationship with him. My professional advice is to keep a low profile, almost nonexistent. I'll try to find out how he's doing. I may even be able to get some messages through, but remember that we don't want to do anything that makes his situation worse, either in the prison or before the law."

"Of course not."

There was a longish pause. Torino cleared his throat.

"Habib asked me to give you a message. It doesn't matter, not now that you won't be able to see him anyway, but . . ." Torino trailed off.

"What is it?"

"Yesterday afternoon he told me that you shouldn't visit him anymore. I'm afraid he was firm about it."

"Did he say why?"

"No."

"There are some other things you should know," Torino rushed on. "They're not good. Corrado Scarpa called me late last night. It seems that Giorgio Fratino's sweater and trousers were disarrayed in a manner that might have been the result of a struggle—or something else. His trousers were pulled partway down. There were no signs of recent sexual contact of any kind, however."

"Habib said something about Giorgio's clothes. What was it?" Urbino searched his mind for the exact words. They seemed very important. "They were 'all messed up and—and out of the right place,' is what I think he said. I should have asked him to explain, but I didn't. You see, he wasn't trying to hide anything. He said that to you, didn't he?"

"Something like that, but I wish I had the opportunity to ask him some specific questions about it. I'll pass it on to his new lawyer. And now brace yourself for some worse news."

Urbino's heart sank even further.

"How worse can it get?"

"Judge for yourself. The Substitute Prosecutor has learned that Habib was arrested four years ago in Tangier and detained for two weeks. He attacked a Spaniard on the beach. Habib went into a rage when the Spaniard accused him of stealing his wal-

let. They had met each other in the medina. There seems to have
been some brief intimacy between them. Fortunately, the Spaniard dropped charges, and Habib seems to have had a friend
who pulled some strings for him from Rabat. He has no record,
and it's not clear how the Substitute Prosecutor found out, or
how he intends to use the information, but you can be sure he's
going to do his damned best."

"Habib does have a temper," Urbino said in a quiet voice,
"especially when someone confronts him. The more innocent he
is, the more violent he can become. It's his sense of honesty and
justice."

He had already told Torino all this, but he needed to say it
again.

"Well enough," Torino said, "but it means he can go from
being innocent to being guilty of something serious if he lets
himself go. I'll be as much help to the new lawyer as the Moroccans will let me. But don't get too down. I've saved some good
news for last. Marino Polidoro came out of his coma last night.
The police asked him a few questions but he's still very weak.
I've persuaded his nephew to let you see him briefly. Don't ask
me how I pulled it off. Just get over to the hospital before he
changes his mind. Ciao."

While having a hasty breakfast, Urbino tried to absorb what
Torino had told him. Habib seemed even farther away from him
now, and in even greater danger. The fact that he didn't want to
see him kept troubling Urbino, but he refused to consider it in
any way that put Habib in a bad light. Instead, he pushed it
into the already crowded room of unanswered questions.

Fortunately, there was something more pressing to give his
attention to. He telephoned the Contessa and arranged to meet
her at the Ca' da Capo-Zendrini in half an hour. They would go
to the hospital together to see Marino.

17

Marino Polidoro's deformed body was covered up to the chest with a crisp white sheet. Various tubes connected him to plastic bags on an infusion stand and to a mobile monitoring unit. His face was ashen beneath a head bandage.

His eyes, however, were lively as they moved back and forth between Urbino and the Contessa.

"He can't speak very loudly, and only a few words at a time," his nephew informed them.

Handsome and vigorous-looking, he couldn't have been more of a physical contrast to Polidoro, even in the best of health.

"Did you see who it was who broke into the shop and attacked you?" Urbino asked Polidoro.

Polidoro moved his head slightly from side to side on the pillow. His thin lips started to move. Urbino and the Contessa leaned closer.

He uttered a word, which was almost indistinguishable.

"*Naso*?" Urbino repeated. Nose, Urbino thought to himself. What could that mean?

Polidoro's eyes were closed. He nodded with an effort. Then he started to speak again. What Urbino thought he heard was *cozzi* or *pozzi*. Conflicts or wells. Which did Polidoro mean, and what was its significance?

"What did you say, Marino? *Cozzi* or *pozzi*?"

Urbino enunciated each word clearly.

Polidoro nodded again.

A nurse came into the room and checked the dials on the monitor, and looked at the plastic bags on the stand.

"That will have to be enough, Signor Macintyre," the nephew said. "Perhaps you can come in a few days when he has more of his strength."

"Just one more question, please."

Before the nephew could protest, Urbino said to Polidoro, "I know you visited Nina Crivelli on Burano. Did it have anything to do with Giorgio, the Contessa's boatman?"

Polidoro repeated one of the words he had said before, the one that had sounded like *naso* to Urbino. Now Urbino wasn't so sure.

Urbino and the Contessa had coffee in the café across from the hospital. The equestrian statue of Colleoni in the middle of the square, with its powerful image of a past age of forceful action, seemed to mock Urbino's confusion and hesitancy. It would have been an appropriate time to tell the Contessa what he had learned since they had last talked things over. He wasn't ready for that, however.

"I didn't hear any more clearly than you," the Contessa said.

She had been staring at him silently from time to time as soon as they had sat down. It was obvious that she knew he was keeping things to himself.

"But I have faith in you. You'll make some sense of what he said. You'll make some sense of it all."

What he caught in her voice was not so much a note of encouragement, however, but one of consolation.

18

U rbino turned his back on the scornful gaze of Colleoni and walked to the Piazza San Marco through the gray morning. The Contessa, sensing his need to be alone, had taken the boat back to the Ca' da Capo-Zendrini.

The chill air did nothing to clear his mind. It was still a confusing swirl. He stepped into the Basilica. The great church was empty, except for a scattering of tourists, one lone worshipper, and a man behind his easel. He seated himself in one of the wooden chairs.

The darkness and dampness of the church suited him, almost as much as it did on summer afternoons when he slipped inside to escape the hot light of the Piazza. He stared up at the vaults and into the various niches where the curved, mosaic figures against their golden background seemed to beckon and greet him familiarly. This morning they seemed a strange and impossible combination of the molten and the angular, the hollow-eyed and the observant, the faded and the brilliant. In all directions, his eye was being benevolently tricked.

He walked slowly over the uneven, undulating floor, both looking and not looking around at all the richness, both thinking and not thinking about all the things he had learned since the Contessa had found Nina Crivelli's body. He visited every corner of the church, and then began his circuit again.

He paused this time behind the young man at his easel. He had set it up outside the Baptistry. His painting was flat and dull, despite everything that he had to inspire him. Urbino was reminded of Habib's paintings that glowed with primitive life, although, perhaps wisely, Habib had never attempted to capture the Basilica.

Urbino checked his wristwatch. He had been in the Basilica for nearly an hour. It had seemed but a few minutes.

He went into Florian's and declined the invitation of some friends to join them at a table. He fortified himself with a glass of wine at the bar, and then went out into the gray day again.

He walked between the two columns of the Piazzetta and around the Ducal Palace to the Riva degli Schiavoni. The island of San Giorgio Maggiore, floating serenely and improbably in the Basin, was gradually left behind as he skirted the edge of the Castello quarter.

He went over, yet again, what he thought Polidoro had said. As he passed the Church of La Pietà where Vivaldi had written most of his work, his thoughts about noses became absurdly mixed up with Vivaldi's prominent one.

Surely, both he and the Contessa had misheard Polidoro. As he went down the Ponte del Sepolcro he asked himself over and over again what he could possibly have meant by referring to a nose.

Wrapped in reflections as impenetrable as the fog that was starting to come in from the Lido, he drifted past the Gothic Hotel Gabrielli Sandwirth where he and the Contessa sometimes came in summer to refresh themselves in the English rose garden. It wasn't until he had walked for ten more minutes that he realized his steps were taking him in a direction he hadn't been conscious of. He was going to Sant'Elena. He needed to talk with Jerome again.

19

This realization made him quicken his steps, but his only reward was to get no response after knocking on Jerome's door for several minutes. He called out Jerome's name. Either he wasn't there or he didn't want to talk to him. Urbino remembered how frightened he had been.

But Jerome would have to talk, Urbino said to himself as he went to the boat landing. He hoped he would find him at the language school, but if he didn't, he was determined to camp out in front of his apartment block, despite the weather, for as long as it took until the Senegalese either went in or came out.

Fortunately, Urbino didn't have to take this desperate measure. Jerome was in front of the school, darting nervous glances. He caught sight of Urbino. He looked as if he was about to bolt down the nearby *calle*. Urbino dragged him into the bar next to the school and pushed him into a chair, before seating himself across from him.

Jerome's face was drawn and ashen.

"I know you're afraid, Jerome. You'll continue to be afraid as long as you keep silent. And you'll feel guilty. Think of Habib. Hasn't he been a good friend to you?"

The young man put his head down.

"You have no choice but to tell the truth, to me and then the police!"

"The police!"

His head snapped up. Fear gleamed from his eyes.

"Yes. It's the only way to help yourself and Habib. The photographs, Jerome. You did give Giorgio photographs of yourself, didn't you?"

Something seemed to collapse in Jerome. He put his face in his hands. The waiter chose this moment to come over to their table. Urbino ordered a bottle of mineral water and waved him away.

"I'm right, aren't I, Jerome?"

"Yes," he said in a defeated tone.

"And some of the other students as well?"

He nodded.

"What about Habib?"

"I don't know. I don't think so."

"Giorgio promised you false identity papers and a passport."

"But I never got them! Never! So I am innocent of anything bad."

Urbino let this pass.

"Was a lot of money involved?"

"Too much. My brother sent it to me. He is a merchant in Dakar. But he did not know the reason! He will not be punished, will he?"

"Your brother did nothing wrong."

At this, Jerome stared at him, tears brimming in his blue eyes.

"But I have, yes. I will be punished."

"If you tell the police the truth, the punishment will be less severe. It might be forgotten about completely. But if you remain silent, you definitely will be punished."

"You will tell?"

"I have no choice. Habib is in prison. They think he murdered Giorgio!"

Jerome broke out into rapid French that Urbino couldn't follow. The waiter brought the mineral water and two glasses.

Urbino poured out a glassful for the both of them. Jerome gulped his down.

"The police will think that I killed Giorgio!"

"I'm sure they won't. Tell me, Jerome, was Giorgio the only person you were doing business with?"

"It was only to Giorgio that I gave the photographs and the money, but I saw him speaking sometimes with a lady. I think I saw him hand her a photograph of someone. She put it in her purse very fast."

"What did she look like?"

Jerome gave a fair enough description of Regina Bella.

"Come on. We're going to the police."

20

B ased on Jerome's testimony, and that of three other students, the police brought Regina Bella back from the clinic near Florence three days later. A thorough search of her apartment turned up incriminating documents that she had attempted to conceal, but not cleverly enough.

According to Corrado Scarpa, Bella confessed to having been involved in a lucrative traffic in false documents and passports, not only at Habib's language school, but two others in Venice and one in Milan. Financial difficulties had led her into the hands of a Milan-based group involved in smuggling and human trafficking. She had been put in contact with Giorgio, ostensibly during a vacation on Capri. Illness was forcing Ugo Mazza, who was a member of the group, to retire. Over the previous three years Giorgio had gained experience with transporting and collecting money from illegal immigrants, most of them from North Africa and Albania. An injury to his foot during one of these transactions was the mundane explanation for his limp, which so many women, including Bella, had found a touch romantic.

Bella had shown some ingenuity that hadn't gone unremarked by the group when she learned that Oriana was going to Capri. With Oriana's flirtatious manner and her eye for a handsome man, the rest had quickly fallen into place. Giorgio had been established at the Ca'da Capo-Zendrini, a position of trust and mobility that would make his and Regina's work all that easier.

Obviously enough, Habib had been particularly good prey. If they played their game well, they had hoped to benefit, through him, from Urbino's resources and perhaps those of the Contessa. To this ultimate end, Giorgio had calculatedly befriended the trusting Habib.

Bella also admitted that she had attacked Frieda in order to retrieve the photographs. When Giorgio had told her about the other envelope, which he had taken by mistake from the kitchen, she had realized what had happened.

One thing that she was adamant about, however, was that she had had nothing to do with Giorgio's murder. She had gone to the clinic because she had been emotionally exhausted in the days after his death and fearful for her own life. She knew that her relationship with him would eventually be exposed because they had grown careless.

They had found Giorgio's murderer, she said, and it was Habib. Perhaps someone had helped him. Giorgio had complained to her about Habib's impulsive behavior and his sudden, late-night visits to his apartment.

She claimed that no one associated with Il Piccolo Nettuno knew about her activities. Despite what Urbino had told Commissario Gemelli the previous week, the topic of Nina Crivelli hadn't been pursued.

In the opinion of the Questura and the Substitute Prosecutor, Habib became a stronger suspect, and he would continue to be detained. Along with what Bella had said against him, the revelation of the traffic in false documents did him absolutely no good, despite his denials.

And so Habib remained in prison.

21

S he's lying, *caro*," the Contessa said two evenings after Regina Bella's confession as she and Urbino sat in the *salotto blu*. "She killed Giorgio. It wasn't Habib."

"It's no good, Barbara. Your heart isn't in it."

Urbino had brought her up to date on everything he knew, including Habib's assault on the Spaniard and his desire not to have Urbino visit him in prison.

"My heart *is* in it. But my mind, my mind! When everything looks black, am I to tell myself it looks white? Are you?"

"I know the way things look. And I know that you're on my side, and that means you're on Habib's." He brushed his hand across her cheek as he got up to go to the liquor cabinet. "You're right. Bella is lying. She's lying about Habib and probably a lot of other things."

"Lying about not having killed Nina and then Giorgio to cover it up, or for some other reason!"

"I wish I could believe that, Barbara. It would make things easier. If only it were true! But I can't delude myself into believing something just because I want to."

She held his gaze until he looked away and poured himself more wine.

"But doesn't it make complete sense," she went on, "that Nina discovered what Regina and Giorgio were up to and was trying to get money from the both of them?"

"Yes," he agreed. "And also that Nina wanted to sell you

information against Giorgio. It fits in with everything she said to you, and with the way she became cautious and nervous when he walked into Santa Maria Formosa. She could have been taking the fullest advantage of what she knew."

"Which led her to her death," the Contessa said flatly. "That's what you should be arguing with Gemelli to get Habib out of prison."

"I'm well aware of that, but I just don't feel that it will come to anything. And then it will only be the worse for Habib. No, Barbara, I have a feeling, an intuition about this—"

"Feeling!" she cried out. "Haven't we had enough of feeling? Isn't it time to look at things in the cool light of reason? Isn't that what you've always done?"

"I know what you're thinking, that my feeling for Habib is blinding me, but something else is going on here. Regina didn't kill Giorgio or Nina. You're forgetting about the attack on Polidoro. How does that fit in? He appears to have been bludgeoned, just as Giorgio was. Whoever attacked Polidoro most probably also killed Giorgio."

"But Nina wasn't bludgeoned to death! You're making a big mistake."

"It won't do any harm to assume that I'm right. If Bella is the murderer, she's already locked up."

"If she isn't, then the murderer is free to strike again." The Contessa nodded. "Well, perhaps there's some method in your madness. The police aren't going to be any help. They aren't even considering that the two deaths are related, or that Nina was murdered. You have an advantage over them."

"Cold comfort."

They turned to speculations about what Polidoro had said, or what they thought he had. They soon reached a dead end.

Noses and *conflicts*—or *wells*—didn't add up to anything as far as they could see. Urbino theorized that Polidoro could have been referring in shorthand to fisticuffs with his assailant, whose nose he might have hit.

"It's a possibility, but it's like too many others," the Contessa said. "Unless we know exactly what he was saying, it's like the telephone game children play. By the time they get to the last child the word or sentence can mean the opposite of what it started out as."

As Urbino walked back to the Palazzo Uccello through the dark, deserted alleys, he tried once again to rearrange the various pieces in different combinations. Sometimes they grouped themselves around Salvatore, at other times Frieda, Beatrix, and Marie. He was stymied, yet at the same time he felt that if he had only one more piece, or if he were able to see one of the pieces he already had in the proper light or at the proper distance, he would have the answer he needed.

The Contessa's theory that Regina, or Giorgio, had murdered Nina, and then Regina had murdered Giorgio, was certainly plausible. But whether she did or she didn't, the police weren't asking her, or anyone else, it seemed, the right questions, the ones that could free Habib. Urbino intended to.

He would see Polidoro again in a few days when he regained more of his strength. It might be all he needed.

His steps took him behind the Palazzo Vendramin Calergi where Wagner had died on a cold February day like this one. The Palazzo was now the winter quarters of the Casino. The building's associations with Frieda's favorite composer invariably led him to think of her and her possible role in the violent and deadly events. Her German origins could be seen as a link between her and the Crivellis, since Evelina had not only looked German, according to Carolina Bruni, but also appeared to have run off to Germany.

He remembered, however, that Gabriella and Lidia had disputed whether it was actually Germany, or instead Switzerland, that Evelina had run off to. Beatrix Bauma was from Austria, which was close to both. She had seemed very nervous last week in her apartment, and even a little frightened of what Marie might tell him. At more than one point, the Austrian woman had stood silently, staring at him and at Marie as if—

His thoughts took an abrupt shift as an image flashed before his eyes. The mask of the plague doctor! With its long beak of a nose! Could Polidoro have been referring to the mask?

Urbino's initial excitement started to ebb as he asked himself why Polidoro would have referred to a detail of the mask instead of the mask itself. Of course, the man had been in a confused state of mind, and could barely speak.

Before going down the bridge over the Rio della Maddelena, Urbino paused to look at the little *campo* to his right. It was one of his favorite spots in the city. Even though the dark and the fog obscured most of the details, he re-created them in his mind's eye. The old houses. The tall chimney pots. The Renaissance wellhead. Habib had been looking forward to the spring to take advantage of the picturesque scene.

The sight of the wellhead sent his thoughts back to what Polidoro had whispered to them. If Urbino remembered correctly, there was a covered well in the courtyard behind Il Piccolo Nettuno. Could he possibly have been referring to that?

Anything and everything seemed a possibility at the moment, except, of course, that Habib was involved in any way but the most innocent and peripheral. If this were his blind spot, he would cling to it as if it were his most precious possession.

He went past Santa Fosca, then down the bridge where the Renaissance monk Paolo Sarpi had been stabbed. He was soon standing on the bridge that gave a view of the Palazzo Uccello, dark except for the two lamps by the entrance.

It was then that he had the sense that he was being followed. The feeling swept over him as it had that night in Dorsoduro. Then he had heard footsteps approaching, stopping, and retreating behind him. Habib had been following him then, he had said, fearful that he might come to harm. But Habib was in no position to be looking out for him now.

Tonight there were no footsteps. It was nothing more than an instinct, but he had learned to trust them. He looked behind him but saw and heard no one.

He crossed the short distance to the entrance of the Palazzo Uccello and let himself in, and locked the door behind him with relief, his heart pounding.

22

In the parlor, Urbino unlatched the window. The damp night air rushed in. The silence seemed suddenly and unnaturally profound.

He peered down into the *calle* where fog was starting to drift in from the nearby lagoon. A cat crouched by the bridge. Almost any of the dark shadows could have concealed a figure. Salvatore, Frieda, Beatrix, or Marie. The thought of the milliner lurking outside his house in one of her hats brought a smile to his lips, but then he thought, why not Marie? Hadn't he perceived a harder edge in the little woman recently? He couldn't discount her, any more than he could the others.

He stood staring out for a full five more minutes, but the scene became even emptier when the cat slipped into one of the shadows.

He put Britten's *Billy Budd* on the player to accompany his musings and sat on the sofa. He hoped that the opera would act as a kind of perverse exorcism of his deepest fears, but instead it reinforced them, as he should have realized it would.

The anguish of the fatherly Captain Vere, the openhearted nature of Billy, his violent confrontation of his accuser, and his punishment by death despite the absence of any murderous intention—they all rolled out with a frightening and familiar inevitability. He shut it off.

He stroked Serena as his mind wandered. Vague thoughts about fathers and sons, provoked by the opera, soon crystallized into specific ones about Salvatore and his lost son Gino. To have lost him in the way that he had, and to be searching for him, to be hoping that someday he would come back might be worse than knowing that he was gone forever, and perhaps even dead.

Were there indeed some things far worse than death? Than your own death or the one of someone you loved? He had no doubt that there were.

He had once speculated with the Contessa that Nina might have died because, after so many years, she had recognized Gino grown into Giorgio. Carolina Bruni had put it bluntly when she had said that if Evelina and Gino had ever returned, Nina would have dropped dead from the shock.

Although he no longer saw any reason to believe that Giorgio had been anyone but himself, he considered various possibilities of both true and mistaken identity involving Salvatore, his real or presumed son, and Giorgio.

They didn't lead anywhere as far as he could see, but something lingered in his mind like one of the wisps of fog outside. He would have to return to it at another time, when he had a few more pieces in his possession.

There were still holes in the fabric of his thinking. Were they the kind that made things fall apart or the kind that contributed to a meaningful design? He felt he was nearing the end, in one way or another, an end of either success or failure. He needed patience, but he also needed time, something he was afraid he didn't have, in order to give the necessary extra twists to the thread.

From his meditation on fathers and sons he passed on to mothers and sons—but not Evelina and Gino—but Nina Crivelli and Salvatore.

The death of a mother, Urbino thought. Does a child ever recover completely? He doubted it, if the ache he felt so many years after the death of his own was any good example. He still found it difficult to entertain even good memories. It filled him with guilt, because it made her seem all the more dead.

And what about Nina and Salvatore? Here was a mother not just dead, but both dead and murdered. If Habib's guilt, at any level, was something that he found impossible to face, Salvatore's villainy, though far from as personally tormenting, nonetheless violated a sentiment close to sacred to him.

The Contessa had touched on it several weeks ago when she had said that he often let his filial feeling get in the way of seeing things as they really were. She had been referring to his skepticism, at the time, about Nina Crivelli's deviousness.

She had been right. It had taken him perhaps more time than it should have to acknowledge the old woman's malevolence. Habib had registered it immediately.

And now there was the question of the son. He realized that he kept pushing away the idea that Salvatore, a son, could have killed his own mother, even such a mother as Nina Crivelli had been. Hatred and resentment could have festered over the years, only to erupt that particular night, with the proper trigger.

Even the best of sons of the best of mothers, a situation Urbino considered his own, could feel flashes of anger, even dislike, which were quickly and guiltily suppressed. But the feelings could surface all the more powerfully later, under any number of unpredictable and uncontrollable circumstances.

Is this what had happened to Salvatore? If it was, then surely the circumstances were in some way linked to the murdered Giorgio and, if his intuition was correct, with the attack on Polidoro in his shop.

Giorgio's clothes had been in disarray. His trousers had been pulled down, by Giorgio himself or someone else. Yet there had been no signs of any recent sexual contact of any kind.

What did it mean? Could this detail be related back to Salvatore? Or possibly to Gino? Although Urbino no longer believed that Giorgio had been Gino, he couldn't completely relinquish the idea, at least some ways of looking at it.

And so Urbino returned for a few moments to fathers and sons. He reviewed what he knew about Gino. He reconsidered Salvatore's breakdown after having lost him, his years of drinking, his meaningless life of waiting and looking, as he lived in the same house, day after day, with the cause of all his sorrows.

Urbino brought Frieda and Beatrix back into the picture,

both separately and together. He kept returning to Frieda's unsettling story, the mask of the plague doctor, and the German and Austrian nationality of the two women. He tried to work out family relationships involving Evelina Crivelli, Frieda, Beatrix, and even Giorgio, until it began to sound like the game he played with Habib about the son of someone's mother's niece.

He shook his head slowly. Once again, he was getting nowhere. Holes, but which kind were they?

Thoughts of the game with Habib reminded him of what the Contessa had said tonight about the game that children play. The telephone game. What came out at the end was a garbled version or even the opposite of what had been said at the beginning.

He repeated what he thought he had heard from Polidoro. *Naso*, nose. *Cozzi*, fights or conflicts. *Pozzi*, wells. He went back and forth through the alphabet, substituting different initial letters. Polidoro had been too weak to enunciate clearly. There were numerous possibilities, but they still made no sense.

He lifted the sleeping Serena and put her against the cushions of an armchair. He went to the library and took out a piece of paper. He wrote out the various combinations, as in yet another game.

After fifteen minutes of this, he stared at two juxtapositions: *vaso* and *cozzi*. Something clicked in his mind, and Beatrix Bauma's face seemed to leap out at him from the shadows of the room.

He positioned the ladder against the wall where he shelved his art books. He climbed the ladder and found the one he was looking for.

It was his copy of the book on Venetian china that Beatrix had accidentally knocked to the floor of her apartment.

He brought it to the refectory table, opened it, and ran his finger down a page of the index. His finger stopped when it came to *Cozzi Geminiano*. He then turned to the relevant pages where he read quickly through the description of the Venetian artisan's creations, many of which could be found in the

eighteenth-century museum of the Ca' Rezzonico on the Grand
Canal.

Vases were among them.

Urbino first called the Questura. The duty officer wouldn't
put him through to Gemelli's home number. After Urbino explained what might be at stake and where he was going, the
officer assured him, in indulgent tones, that two men would be
dispatched.

After ringing off, he dialed the Contessa's number.

"I'm coming over for the keys to Giorgio's apartment."

"It's past eleven! Can't it wait until tomorrow?"

"I need to find something out tonight. I'll be there in fifteen
minutes."

"Not just for the keys. For me too. I'm going with you."

23

Giorgio's ground-floor apartment was shuttered. The apartments above were vacant and dark.

The police hadn't yet arrived. Urbino pushed away the thought that they might not be coming at all. He realized that he wasn't acting in a prudent way, especially considering that the Contessa was with him. His desire to know was stronger than everything else at the moment.

He unlocked the grating and slid it back, then fumbled the key into the door and opened it. A musty odor exhaled from the apartment.

"Perhaps the police have taken it," the Contessa said.

Urbino had filled her in during their trip from the Ca' da Capo-Zendrini.

"They don't have the slightest idea of its importance. It's connected to Nina Crivelli, not Giorgio. Where's the light switch?"

"On the left."

"The police would have assumed it was one of your knick-knacks. All I told the duty officer was that there might be something here that could settle some questions about Giorgio's murder."

He pressed the button. A feeble light illuminated the room. Beyond it were a small kitchen and bathroom.

Urbino placed a stool against the door to keep it open and provide more light. They surveyed the small room.

"It's little more than a storeroom," the Contessa said apologetically. "I was reluctant to have Giorgio use it. Well, let's start looking, but as I told you, I didn't see anything like it when I was here with the police."

"Sometimes you can't see something unless you know you're looking for it."

"There's a fallacy somewhere in that philosophy."

"I'm surprised the police didn't ask you to go through everything to determine what was Giorgio's. But it seems they're being even more lax than usual with this case."

He looked through the open door out into the night. The alley was empty for as far as he could see into it. He turned his attention back to the room.

"It's a mess in here. Look at all these cardboard boxes. You'd think he would have thrown them out when he moved in. And the shoes!"

He pointed to a dozen pairs of brightly shined, stylish shoes, all lined up neatly.

He went over to a bookshelf. It held only a few books. Popular magazines, dirty cups, a large radio and cassette player, and a pile of cassettes took up most of the space. On the top shelf was Giorgio's white chauffeur's cap, protected in a transparent plastic bag. Hanging from the shelf, and also protected in plastic, was a uniform.

"I don't see it anywhere," the Contessa said. "Oh, what's this?"

She picked something up and brought it over to Urbino.

"It's a palette knife," he said, examining it. "It must be Habib's."

It was new and clean. He put it down on a small table and turned his attention to the sofa. Half a dozen cushions were all thrown together. He started to remove them. Beneath one of them he found a maroon necktie.

"The police probably thought you were crying wolf," the Contessa said. "Maybe it's just as well. We do look a sight scavenging through all this stuff."

Urbino's eye was caught by something against the wall,

shrouded with a frayed, faded blanket. He went over and re-moved the blanket. Beneath it were four paintings, oil on can-vas, thirty-by-twenty-five inches. Three of them were of bright-colored doors. The fourth was a kaleidoscope of different-colored geometrical shapes that Urbino immediately recognized as the designs painted on the building he had shown Habib their first day on Burano.

"Habib's paintings," he said in a low voice.

But in the silence and in the small room it was loud enough for the Contessa to hear.

She was kneeling beside a small wooden chest that stood to one side of the open door.

"I didn't see them when I was here."

She lifted the chest lid and started to look through it as Ur-bino went to a cluttered table.

"Nothing in here except moldy old maps and guidebooks," the Contessa said after a few minutes. "I think I'll look in the kitchen. Maybe it's among all the dishes and cups like the letter in that Edgar Allan Poe—"

"Here we go!"

Urbino held up a small, rose-colored vase.

"Is this one of your things?" he asked.

"I never saw it before in my life."

"You can be sure it's the one that Evelina forgot when she ran away." He turned it over. There was the anchor in red, the mark of the Cozzi factory. "Nina sold it to Polidoro and—watch out, Barbara!"

But it was too late for her to get out of the way. A figure came barreling from the darkness and through the door, its head down. As it went past the Contessa, it pushed her. She fell and struck her head against the chest.

It was Salvatore. Enraged, he pounced on Urbino. The vase flew through the air and broke into pieces against the wall. He grabbed Urbino by the throat. The smell of alcohol fumes as-saulted Urbino's face.

The inebriated Salvatore was at a disadvantage. His grip on Urbino's throat loosened enough for Urbino to pull his hands away. He threw him off balance. Salvatore fell backward over the sofa.

Urbino scrambled across the floor and grabbed one of Giorgio's shoes. Salvatore jumped to his feet and charged at Urbino.

With all his strength Urbino slammed the shoe against the side of Salvatore's head.

Salvatore dropped to the floor, unconscious.

Urbino rushed to the Contessa.

EPILOGUE
Woman of Venice

Blind! Blind! Blind!" the Contessa exclaimed, but not quite loud enough for the other patrons in the Chinese salon to hear.

If they had, they would have turned their eyes away in embarrassment, for they would have assumed she was speaking about herself. Her large sunglasses, worn inside her favored chamber at Caffè Florian as if it were suffused with summer sunshine on this February afternoon, were proof of her damaged vision, weren't they?

But Urbino knew better. The Contessa's exclamation was directed against him. In case he might have any doubt, she went on to clarify.

"You should have seen! You should have known! If you had, I wouldn't have this to deal with," she reprimanded with a mischievous air of self-mocking petulance.

With a hand temporarily free of a petit four, she made a vague motion toward her sunglasses and what they rather flamboyantly concealed. Urbino hadn't seen her black eye, but her descriptions and complaints had painted a vivid picture.

"Actually, Barbara, you look rather striking in those sunglasses," Urbino said, playing along with her. "I'm sure Oriana would be green with envy if she could see you." Oriana and Filippo were in Paris in the throes of yet another reconciliation.

"You've given yourself even more of a mystique."

The Contessa did have a special aura today. Her dress was in liquid tones of blue and green. From her neck cascaded a necklace of silver ovals that Urbino had brought her from Morocco. And her lips were touched with that faint, shimmering, airy pink that was the shade of Venice.

"Don't try to placate me."

He could tell she was pleased, however, from the characteristic way she ducked her head slightly and tried to suppress a smile.

"If the police had listened to me—"

"*Caro, caro!*" she interrupted. "If you had *made* them listen to you. Or better yet, if we hadn't gone to Giorgio's apartment at all."

"Who knows what might have happened then? Habib could still be in prison."

After Salvatore confessed to the murders of his mother and Giorgio, Habib had been released.

"All's well that ends well," the Contessa pronounced. "Except for a mutilation here and there."

She delicately massaged her temple with two well-manicured fingers.

"It's so wonderful to have a free mind after all this time!" She reached out for another petit four. It had pink frosting and was crowned with a hazelnut. "I don't know how I was able to eat through it all."

The Contessa had almost as many excuses for her appetite for petit fours as Florian's had petit fours to supply her with. In January, when Nina had lurked outside the Chinese salon, it had been worry. Today it was relief. Tomorrow it might be embarrassment and the day after joy. Never, however, would she admit that it was simply that she loved petit fours.

"If only my eye would clear up, I'd be completely content."

"Don't worry. It's already the time of masks. Look."

He directed her attention to the arcade where a figure in a yellow raincoat stood. On its face was a brightly colored

Harlequin mask. It was holding a stick used for stirring the character's preferred dish, polenta.

"I get no sympathy from you these days, and after all I've lavished on you."

The figure in the Harlequin mask remained stationary as it stared into the Chinese salon at the two friends. It raised the stick in an obscene gesture and strode off, throwing confetti through the air.

"These days most of my sympathy goes in a different direction," Urbino said, gazing out into the Piazza.

Pools of water had seeped up through the paving stones from the intense rains of the past few days. Raised planks provided dry passage over the deeper water in front of the Basilica.

"But I thought Habib was doing fine."

Habib was up in Asolo at the Contessa's summer villa. She had opened La Muta and provided just enough staff to have it run smoothly. She and Urbino had decided that what Habib needed was some fresh air away from Venice for awhile.

"He is." Urbino brought his eyes back to the Contessa. "I'll be going up there for a few days but we'll be back in good time for Carnevale. I'll do some work on *Women of Venice* and we'll start making plans for his mother and sister. No, it's not Habib I'm thinking of, but Salvatore. Despite everything, I feel sorry for him."

"*Il poverino.*"

Salvatore's story was indeed a sad one, which Urbino had been recounting to the Contessa on this gray afternoon. Much of it was pieced together from what he had learned from Corrado Scarpa, who had stopped by the Palazzo Uccello last night.

Salvatore had broken down after only an hour of interrogation. Urbino's original—but discarded—theory that Giorgio was Gino had become Salvatore's truth and obsession. It seemed to have been provoked by Giorgio's age, his good looks, and his limp that Salvatore was convinced was the vestige of Gino's childhood clubfoot. Giorgio's sudden and mysterious appearance on the scene and his apparent haunting of Burano had also probably played their key roles.

His fantasy of being reunited with his wife and his son took desperate hold of him. If Gino had returned, then so would Evelina. She might even have come back already. What stood in his way was not logic. It was the mother who had made his whole life a misery.

He was determined the past wouldn't repeat itself.

He had confronted Nina with the news that Gino had returned and soon Evelina would as well. It wasn't clear whether or not he told her that it was Giorgio he was talking about. Nina's reaction, however, had been what he expected. After all those years he knew her well.

Curses and warnings, and then the shortness of breath that made her grab for her lace handkerchief to push some pills into her mouth.

Except that Salvatore had removed them from the handkerchief earlier in the day.

He had watched her die, the mother who had loved him in her destructive way.

The position of the handkerchief by her mouth had not been the murderer's sign that the gossip and blackmailer was now silenced forever. Instead, she had pushed it there in her own desperation.

When Salvatore had been asked about the Contessa, he made it clear that both he and his mother resented her wealth and privilege. Urbino, it appeared, wasn't far behind the Contessa in having been a recipient of their bad feeling. However, Salvatore claimed to have no knowledge of his mother's attempts to get money from the Contessa or, for that matter, from anyone else.

A great deal still remained unexplained, which had provoked Urbino and the Contessa into frequent speculation during the past few days.

The authorities had obtained copies of Salvatore's medical records from the clinic in Naples where he had gone after Evelina ran away with Gino. He was undergoing psychiatric evaluation now. Urbino believed that in the end, however, Salvatore would be found fully responsible for his calculated deed to free himself.

"But still so many questions," the Contessa was now saying. "You were close to making some sense of it that day with your talk about Giorgio being Gino! What did I call it? A house of cards? But when did Giorgio know about Salvatore's wild idea? Was it before or after Nina's death? And what did he make of her death?"

"If we can believe Salvatore's confusion about the time sequence, he didn't tell Giorgio until more than a week after he killed her—or, to look at it from Giorgio's point of view, until after she died. There was no reason for Giorgio to suspect that Nina had died anything but a natural death, that is, not until Salvatore started to act more and more irrationally. Giorgio probably humored him at first. According to Regina Bella, Salvatore never gave any sign that there was any kind of familiarity between him and Giorgio. She said that they seemed to avoid each other. When he needed to, Giorgio would slip into the kitchen when Salvatore wasn't there. As for Giorgio, he never said anything to Regina about it all."

He paused to take a sip of his Campari soda before going on. The Contessa's hand was hovering over the three remaining cakes, as she tried to decide which would be the next to go the way of the others.

"Who knows? Maybe Giorgio smelled some money in the situation. It doesn't seem as if Giorgio denied being his son, not at first. It was only when Salvatore told him how far he had gone so that they could all be a family again that things started to really go wrong for Salvatore. Giorgio played something of a balancing act, or at least that's the way I make it out. If he denied that he was Gino, he knew he'd be in danger. But he seems to have started making the kind of noises that Salvatore interpreted as blackmail. Surely no son of his would be doing that to him, or would he? He needed to find out for sure."

"So Giorgio was tempted by the profit to be made out of what he knew. Like Nina."

"Except that she didn't die because of something she knew. Giorgio did."

"Was there any one thing that finally made the scales fall from your eyes?" the Contessa asked, showing a persistency in pursuing her earlier line of attack. It was a persistency she matched by selecting the little cake covered with pale yellow frosting.

"The condition of Giorgio's clothes when he was found. Of course, I never believed that it could be anything that Habib had done. But how to explain it? Then I remembered something about Gino. His appendicitis."

"And the scar from the operation afterward."

"If Giorgio didn't have a scar, then he wasn't Gino. And he didn't. And so he was murdered."

"And if Giorgio did have a scar? What then?"

"That would have been a different story, but only up to a point. It might have bought Giorgio more time, but he was doomed as soon as Salvatore revealed that he had murdered Nina."

"To murder one's own mother." The Contessa sighed and shook her head. "All that mother's milk."

"And the daily bread. Almost fifty years of it across the same table. How he must have hated it."

The Contessa's shoulders gave a quick movement that seemed like a voluntary shiver to rid herself of the vision conjured up. When she spoke, it was to pick up a less frightful thread.

"I'm still not completely clear on how the Geminiano Cozzi vase fits into it all."

"Salvatore put two and two together. When Evelina's vase went missing, he figured out that Nina had sold it to Polidoro. Habib saw Marino and Nina together on Burano. It's probable Salvatore did as well and knew what she was up to. Somehow Evelina had come by an exquisite little piece, something handed down through the years. Salvatore was determined to get it back. He broke into Polidoro's shop. Polidoro heard someone and came in. He just had time to notice that the Cozzi vase wasn't in its accustomed spot on the table, when someone hit him hard from behind. I saw the vase with some others on the same table when I was at the shop, but I didn't pay any attention to it. Not at the time. I hadn't even spoken with Carolina Bruni yet."

"And how did it end up in Giorgio's apartment?"

"Remember that Salvatore attacked Polidoro the night before he murdered Giorgio. Everything was falling apart for him. He went to Giorgio's, intent on settling once and for all the question of his identity. He showed him the vase, desperately hoping it would spark some recognition in him. Then there was the struggle about the scar. Salvatore must have been in a frenzy. He found the strength somehow, even against a younger man as fit as Giorgio and he smashed Giorgio's head with a brick. Salvatore left the vase behind but he took the brick and tossed it into the Cannaregio canal as he ran away. It will count against him, of course. He premeditated his mother's murder, and he made every attempt to cover up Giorgio's, even if he wasn't thinking rationally at other times. And he also was clearheaded enough not to take the *vaporetto* on the two occasions he had to do his dirty business in Venice. Like many Buranelli he has a boat with an outboard motor at his disposal."

The Contessa took this in.

"And don't forget," she said, "that he was all too willing to let Habib be punished for what he had done."

"I'm far from forgetting that. There was a good chance of his getting away with it. Let's face it, Barbara. Habib wasn't going to get much of a fair chance because of what he looks like and who he is. And especially not in times like these. Salvatore was trying to save his own neck. At least he had that excuse, but what about the others?"

The Contessa didn't respond right away. When she did, it was in a small, quiet voice.

"I hope you don't put me in that category."

His response might have come quicker than it did, and have taken a different form, at least from the Contessa's point of view.

"I never doubted that you had my own good in mind."

She regarded him for a few moments, or she seemed to do so. From this angle, the lenses of her glasses were an opaque, dark green, reminiscent of the Grand Canal in a certain light.

"Yes, I was worried about you. Very worried." She hesitated. "But I've never been so happy to be proven wrong."

Urbino looked at her sharply.

"I don't mean that I ever thought Habib could have killed Giorgio or Nina," she added. "It was just that I was afraid that—that he might have been involved in ways that could hurt you. If you were going to help him, to save him," she corrected, "you needed to keep some objectivity, some clear-sightedness. Call me a reluctant devil's advocate. Don't forget that I can be perverse and improbable, just like you!"

"Just like Venice, is more like it! After all these years, I'm still not used to it in either of you, and pray that I'll never be!" He gave her a soft look. "We've been through a lot. It's behind us now."

"But what's in front of Habib?"

"A bright future, if I have anything to do with it."

"May our jeweler's son thrive and flourish!" she exclaimed, referring to the character in Frieda Hensel's story. But a shadow crossed her face. "Some things won't be under your control, you know."

Urbino, even more than the Contessa, felt the brush of the dark wings of the story.

"I just had a good example of that, didn't I?" he said. "Whatever fate or *mekhtoub*, as Habib would call it, has in store, I intend to see that he's in the best position to cope with it or enjoy its fruits. Fate isn't always a bad thing, you know."

"How can I think otherwise? Our relationship has always been under a special star."

The two friends contemplated this for a few moments in silence.

"I have something to confess," the Contessa said. "It's about Habib."

"Indeed?"

"There's one thing in particular that's always made me nervous, since I first set eyes on him."

"What is it?"

"His looks. He's not drop-dead gorgeous, is he? Not like Giorgio. I saw it as a danger. Oh, don't misunderstand me. He's quite attractive. Those eyes, and that smile! But if he had been like the young Omar Sharif or Rudolph Valentino, I would have breathed a little easier. It would pass, I would have said. But you saw something else. You see something else. Despite what I've said, you weren't blinded at all."

"I find all that a bit confusing, but I'll take it as a compliment, for the both of us, for Habib and me."

"That's exactly how it was meant. I feel much better getting that off my conscience!" She rewarded herself by pouring out another cup of tea. "You know that you can count on me to help Habib, in whatever ways I can."

"You already are. Opening up La Muta and inviting his mother and sister to stay at the Ca' da Capo."

"That's nothing. I mean doing more than that."

"You'll have plenty of opportunities. Give Habib a month or two of dolce far niente. He needs it. Then we'll put our heads together, maybe with Marino Polidoro when he's recuperated, to see how we can best help him with his career. All he needs is exposure, and he'll soon be off. I'm confident about that. He has a special talent."

The Contessa nodded.

"Yes," she said, "we'll all look after the boy."

"And at least there's a positive side to this whole ordeal. The authorities are smoothing his way a bit. Things have been made easier for his mother and sister to visit him on such short notice. It's for the Questura's own good, of course."

There had been a spate of editorials and letters in *Il Gazzettino* criticizing the Questura. Although the Contessa had advised him against it, Urbino had sent an impassioned letter to the local newspaper himself, which had received a lot of attention when it had been published. It had spoken of racism and scapegoating, the right wing's encouragement of immigration fears, the problem in human trafficking, and the lack of a coherent or humane policy to deal with the country's growing number of immigrants and refugees.

"The Questura promises to issue the appropriate stamp and whatever else is necessary for the renewal of his residency permit. Gemelli's not showing too much resentment against me. Maybe he's saving it for another day. But I've had to fill out another declaration of responsibility, much more detailed this time. I'm hoping that once we can arrange a show for Habib, his situation will be even better."

"And he'll soon have his mother and sister with him for a while. How—"

The Contessa broke off, staring out into the arcade. Urbino followed her gaze.

Two tall figures, with a shorter one between them, were lined up by the window, looking in. One of the tall figures was none other than Richard Wagner or at least the mask was a very good semblance of the composer. The figure at the other end was the plague doctor with his large, cone-shaped beak. And in the middle, the small and squat form had the saucy face of Pulchinella, topped with a purple cloche decorated with red feathers.

"It's Frieda, Beatrix, and Marie!" the Contessa cried out. She waved. The three women returned the greeting and started to file off in the direction of the entrance. "We'll all have a great time at the ball!"

It was going to be the grand celebration she had originally planned—even grander, now that Habib was released and his mother and sister would be there.

"I've got the costumes all picked out for Habib's mother and sister," she enthused. "They can be altered to their proper sizes. Sultana and the first princess of the realm!"

"Splendid, but where does that leave you? Dressed up as a simple shepherdess like Marie Antoinette?"

"And we'll all eat cake at midnight! But why do you assume I'll be a woman, *caro*? It's Carnevale, after all! I might well surprise you yet! I might be a sultan, or a vizier, or a sorcerer, maybe even Sinbad or Aladdin!"

"Not Aladdin. That's Habib."

"All the more reason. We'll both wear masks, and you'll have to choose between us."

Frieda, Beatrix, and Marie were approaching, their masks still in place. Urbino and the Contessa had only a few more precious moments to be alone.

"No, no!" the Contessa said with a rich laugh when she saw the expression on his face. "To choose which of us is the more convincing! We women can play the man as well as you do yourselves. Maybe even better! You have no mysteries for us." She paused and reflected a moment. "Only the ones we let you believe you have! And so, *caro*, who will you be?"

"If you have to ask, it means that you don't know us men so well after all."

"My dear Urbino, the marvel of life is in its exceptions."

Once again, the Contessa had the last word.